THE WAKE OF
THE BERTRAND

C.J. PETIT

C.J. PETIT

TABLE OF CONTENTS

PROLOGUE

April 1, 1865
Sixteen Miles North of Omaha, Nebraska

The Missouri was running fast that day after a heavy winter of snow, and the waterlogged cottonwood trunk that had been buried in silt for six years had finally been freed from the bank north of the Desoto Bend. The rushing brown water had been tugging at the thick log since it had fallen into the river in Dakota Territory two years ago and now the swift current had it moving again as it pulled it into the main channel, its heavy end still dragging on the river bottom.

The only part of the massive cylinder of wood was the broken end that bobbed a few inches above the surface, hiding the deadly mass below. Even the trained eyes of a riverboat pilot might miss the threat if he wasn't observant or the shadows hid the obstacle.

Just a few miles downriver, *The Bertrand* was churning north, scheduled to arrive in Montana in just a few more days, but would find its death much sooner.

———

Charles Burleigh smiled at his wife and said, "It's a beautiful spring morning, my dear. Soon all your fears will be proven to be for naught."

"I'm sorry, dear. I wish I could conquer my fear, but ever since the *Erasmus*, it has grown to an overwhelming size," Abigail replied.

"I know, sweetheart. That was a horrible nightmare for you. But this is a riverboat, not an ocean-going ship. The water isn't very deep, and the shore is very near."

"I know that, Charles. As unreasonable as they are, my worries are ever present. I will feel much better when we reach Yankton and shall never set foot on a boat or ship ever again. When we leave Yankton to return to civilization in a few years, it will be by rail."

"I should think that is more than likely soon. The Union Pacific is getting ready to build to the west and they say the Northern Pacific will be going through Yankton just a couple of years thereafter."

"I think I'll need to return to the cabin soon, Charles. Just seeing that water causes me some measure of distress."

He patted his wife on the shoulder and said, "Just a few more days, Abigail, and we'll be in Yankton and soon be settled into our new home."

Abigail glanced back across the main deck to the cabins and asked, "Have you seen Edmund or Emily?"

"Not since breakfast."

"Well, maybe it's just newlywed fever," she said as she laughed, despite her uneasiness over the voyage.

James Bristol, their butler and guard, stood silently next to Charles Burleigh as the couple conversed and, like all butlers, acted as if he hadn't heard a word, but had listened intently.

The Bertrand was making acceptable headway up the Missouri since leaving its docks in St. Louis two weeks before. It was a solid sternwheeler, one hundred and sixty feet long and thirty-two feet abeam and was fairly new, having been built in Wheeling, West Virginia only the year before. It was carrying cargo and passengers bound for Fort Benton, Montana Territory, but Charles Burleigh and his party would be disembarking in Yankton, the capital of the Dakota Territories. *The Bertrand* seemed the most logical and comfortable method of arriving there on time, not to mention the safest. They also were carrying quite a bit of luggage, as they were planning to remain there for some time. Or at least, in the mind of Abigail Burleigh, until the railroad arrived in Yankton.

The steamboat was making about eight knots against the swift current and the captain was on the bridge with two crewmembers standing on both sides of the bow looking for changes in the river. The pilot was guiding the boat through the ever-changing waters of the Missouri as they approached the Desoto Bend.

The pilot was one of the highest paid men in the west as it took a great amount of skill and knowledge to guide the riverboats through the twists and curves of the great waterways of the United States that were the economic life blood of the country. They'd still be critical after the railroads began to expand across the untamed West and it helped that the Missouri River not only wound its way into those lands but emptied into the Mississippi at St. Louis. It made for one big lane of commerce all the way to the Gulf of Mexico and the Atlantic Ocean.

Emily and Edmund strolled across the upper deck toward Charles and Abigail.

Abigail heard them approach, turned and said, "Ah. There you are. We were just talking about you."

"Good morning, Mother," Emily said as she gave her mother a kiss.

"How are you doing, Emily? Still adjusting to the married life, I imagine?" she asked with a smile.

Emily glanced at her new husband and said, "Edmund wasn't feeling well again this morning. I think the smoke from the steam engine is upsetting his stomach."

Abigail turned to her son-in-law and asked, "Are you quite well now, Edmund?"

Edmund smiled weakly, before he replied, "Perhaps a trifle under the weather still, but I'll manage."

Abigail didn't mention her own aversion to water and the havoc it was playing on her stomach.

Emily strode to the front railing and closed her eyes. It was a brisk morning and the breeze was coming from the northwest when the boat turned in that direction as it was guided into Desoto Bend.

Closing her eyes let her dream and the breeze made her feel free and alone. She imagined herself on horseback, feeling the wind in her face as the horse thundered over a grassy field that stretched as far as the eye could see.

She had been married to Edmund in St. Louis three months before they embarked on the journey to Dakota Territory and had been excited more by the trip than the engagement and marriage. But Edmund was of good family and had prospects, or so she had been told by her parents. *What more could any young woman ask for? What more could she ask for?*

As she leaned with her hands on the rails with her eyes closed while Edmund talked to her parents beside her, she knew what she could ask for, but knew she'd never have it.

She finally sighed, then opened her eyes as the riverboat completed its turn into the wide-curving Desoto Bend and the two couples, with the ever-present James Bristol, turned to go back to their cabins. They hadn't walked thirty feet when there was a shout by the crewmember on the port side of the bow followed almost immediately by a loud, extended crunching noise from that same side.

The Bertrand shuddered as the powerful steam engine continued to turn the paddles and move the boat into whatever it had struck, then it began to veer toward the port shore. Almost immediately, the bow began to drop into the water's surface.

"Charles! I believe the ship has struck something!" cried Abigail in panic as she scanned the river.

Charles watched as more crewmembers raced to the port bow to evaluate the damage and loudly replied, "I'm not sure how serious it is, but we must prepare for the worst. Let's return to the cabins and gather as much as we can."

"We'll do the same, Mother," shouted Emily as she turned and raced back along the deck with Edmund trailing.

James Bristol hurried behind the Burleighs as they quickly stepped to their cabins.

The captain had run from the bridge to assess the damage to his vessel as other passengers began swarming the deck to see what had happened.

When they reached their cabins, both couples began packing their travel bags. There was one travel trunk in Bristol's cabin for their use enroute to Yankton, but the rest of their things were in the cargo hold below deck.

THE WAKE OF THE BERTRAND

Captain Bixby had returned from his inspection and his prognosis wasn't good. *The Bertrand* was sinking quickly and would never see Montana. He returned to the pilot house and spun the wheel to the port side to beach his sinking vessel on the riverbank. The bow was low as the Bertrand's port side slid onto the muddy shelf while the swift current was already pushing the waters of the Missouri River over the deck, taking some of the deck cargo down the river. Many of the thirty-two passengers were already diving into the river and swimming ashore, but they were all men while the women passengers all waited in their heavy skirts.

Charles turned to Abigail and Emily and said, "I don't think there is any need for panic. The bow is close enough to the shore to permit us to simply walk off the boat before it succumbs to the river."

Abigail was as white as a sheet. *How can she be caught in two shipwrecks in just two years?* The last time, when *The Erasmus* had gone down, it was in the Gulf of Mexico during a gale and the terror it had implanted into her soul made even this relatively benign sinking, if there is such a thing, turn her almost catatonic in fear.

Charles understood her intense distress and put his arm around his wife's shoulders.

"Abigail, we'll be all right. Don't worry," he said in a calming voice, but he could feel her shaking.

The captain was already preparing to get the remaining passengers off *The Bertrand*. After he had his sternwheeler beached firmly on the Nebraska shore, he had the crew bring the boarding ramp from the stern of the boat to the bow and soon had a firm pathway off the main deck.

Once the gangplank was secured, the passengers began to leave the vessel and form a large group onshore.

Edmund was the first to get off the boat, before Charles and Emily practically towed Abigail across the narrow walkway that crossed the shallow water from the sinking riverboat. James Bristol brought up the end of the group as he carried their two travel bags. He'd have to return to get his own bag.

Captain Bixby sent one crewmember to the nearby village of Desoto for help and had the rest of the crew start bringing ashore what they could salvage using the forward cranes.

They managed to unload the ship's stove and victuals from the stores to feed the passengers as well as the passengers' personal effects that were not in the hold, including the Burleighs' trunk.

Two hours after *The Bertrand* struck the waterlogged cottonwood, Charles and Abigail Burleigh, Edmund and Emily Falstaff and James Bristol were together as the trunk was brought to them.

"Thank God for that, Charles," Abigail said as she took a seat on their trunk.

The captain told everyone that the *General Grant*, another sternwheeler owned by the company, would be by in a couple of days to take them to their destinations, and they would be housed in Desoto at the company's expense.

There was debate among some of the passengers about continuing their journey at all, and an even more heated argument between Charles and Abigail Burleigh about their mode of transportation to their destination.

"I am not getting on another one of those floating deathtraps again!" Abigail said firmly, "If you wish to proceed on the next one, then you and Edmund can take James and go. Emily and I will stay in Omaha City until you can find acceptable overland conveyance."

"But Abigail, you must be reasonable. It is only a few more days to Yankton. Surely you can just close your eyes for that long."

"I will not, Charles, and that is final. The captain is arranging for coaches to bring passengers to Omaha City. We will take the trunk and go there, with or without you."

Charles knew he had lost the argument before it had even begun. He loved his wife and knew that she was usually a soft, sweet-hearted woman, but also knew before they even married, that once she had her mind set, it wasn't going to change.

Getting overland passage to Yankton might prove difficult, but he wasn't about to let Abigail stay in Omaha without him. He wasn't going to risk any danger to her, and it would only take a few more days to reach Yankton anyway. It was a small price to pay to make her happy.

"Alright, dear. We'll return to Omaha, get a room, and I'll make arrangements for a coach to Yankton."

"Thank you, Charles. I don't mean to be so stubborn, it's just that terrible but illogical fear that grips me."

"I know, dear," he said as he hugged his wife.

There was a small group of men that were enroute to the gold fields of Montana who were displeased at having their plans postponed at the very least, and made their displeasure known to the captain. The heated argument was threatening to come to blows as some of the riverboat crew approached with belaying pins to protect the captain.

James Bristol heard the commotion and fingered the Cooper Pocket pistol in his jacket pocket. He knew he was at a significant disadvantage when it came to firepower as each of those men was armed with a more powerful pistol than his Cooper, and there were six of them.

Charles Burleigh didn't carry a pistol and James doubted if Edmund Falstaff even knew which end of a pistol was the business end. He didn't have a high opinion of Mister Edmund Falstaff, but he had a very high opinion of his wife, Emily.

A few hours later, the crewmember returned with two coaches. It took a while, but soon, all the passengers were boarded somewhere in Desoto, Nebraska for the night. Over the next day, salvage began on *The Bertrand* while the Burleighs, Falstaffs, and James Bristol rode in carriages to Omaha.

They stayed at the Herndon House in Omaha, and it was at the Herndon that the task that Charles Burleigh had considered difficult, that of finding overland passage through Sioux lands to Yankton, was solved almost immediately. He was asking at the desk where he could find someone willing to provide guide and protection services for his party to Yankton when he met Claude Bernard, a long-time guide.

Claude told Charles that he and his partner, Louis Martin, had made the trip eight times without any problem and gave him a list of supplies and other things that he would need for the journey. They agreed on a price, and the problem was solved.

Claude left to find his partner while Charles walked to their room to give Abigail the good news. He then went to the adjoining room to tell Emily and her husband about the arrangements. Emily seemed excited with the news, which surprised Charles, but his son-in-law was much less enthusiastic. He hadn't been pleased with the riverboat trip, and this was much worse.

Ove the next week, Charles and Abigail roamed Omaha City purchasing the items on the list provided by Claude. They hadn't seen him since that meeting at the hotel, and Charles began to wonder if something was wrong. But just as he grew concerned, Claude stopped by the hotel, introduced him to his partner, Louis, then reviewed the list, made a few additions, then they agreed to a starting date and time. Claude and Louis would meet them at the hotel's livery.

Ten days after arriving in Omaha, the Burleighs and the Falstaffs departed the city on a recently purchased wagon.

Edmund Falstaff was riding alongside on his new gelding, as was James Bristol. The two hired guides rode out front.

Aside from James Bristol's pocket pistol, the guides were the only ones armed. Charles was told it would take them a week to make the one-hundred-and-sixty-mile journey, and Charles reassured Abigail, not mentioning that the *General Grant* had docked in Yankton a week earlier and was probably in Montana Territory by now.

CHAPTER 1

Kyle MacKenzie was absently scratching the back of his left hand as he said, "It's beginning to sound like I'm not going to have a quiet trip, Captain."

"You should stick around, Kyle. Take a short vacation before you head up there."

"I don't think the colonel would be happy about it if I did."

Captain Richards laughed before he said, "No, I suppose not. You know, Kyle, I think you really like doing what you do."

"Parts of it, I like. I don't really like running into a passel of Lakota too much, but it's part of my job."

"Well, better you than me, MacKenzie. When are you leaving?"

"Tomorrow morning. You know, Captain, I was just getting used to good news from the East after Lee surrendered, but then some crazy Confederate assassinates Mister Lincoln thinking it would somehow turn a loss into a victory."

"I agree, Kyle. The whole idea that killing the President would have even the slightest impact on the war is idiotic. That insane assassin just murdered the best friend the South ever had and didn't know it."

"Well, I'd better get moving."

"Got everything you need?"

"Yes, sir."

They shook hands and Kyle headed for the door. It was going to be a long ride to Fort Sully in the Dakota Territory, but he estimated he could get there in a week or so, as long as the Sioux didn't object too strongly. They usually didn't care too much about a lone white man, but at a distance he might be mistaken for a warrior from another, unwelcome tribe. He would also be traveling with a lot of firepower that might be worth a few warriors' lives. His best option was always the same, see them first and then avoid them if possible.

———

Three days later, Kyle was leading his packhorse northwesterly and knew they were there behind him. They'd been following him almost since he left Fort Omaha, but he really didn't care all that much as long as he knew where they were and didn't run into any more hunting parties.

There were only six of them and they were more curious than anything else. They may have been thinking about how nice it would be to have his guns and ammunition, but Kyle knew they were in no position to take them from him. Right now, they were probably just wondering what he was doing and where he was going. They were Santee Sioux and were at the very edge of their tribal territory now so they probably would return to their camp soon.

He'd left Fort Abercrombie on April 4th and had been on the trail since then. He was originally thinking of riding straight through to Fort Sully but decided at the last minute to go to Omaha City to make a deposit to his account there and then load up on the supplies he couldn't get in the trading posts or the forts along the way.

So, he had made the run down the Red River and then the Missouri to Omaha. After he had made his deposit, he resupplied at Fort Omaha, made more purchases in the city, and started his journey. Fort Sully was in a bind with the Sioux and had specifically asked for Kyle. He knew why they'd asked for him, too.

The new commander at Fort Sully, Lt. Col Harry Carpenter had known him at Fort Abercrombie. He had recently taken over Sully and was unhappy with its location and situation. The location was already being remedied before he arrived, but the situation with the Lakota seemed to be getting worse. It would be a long ride, over three hundred miles altogether, but nothing that Kyle hadn't done before.

He had requisitioned everything he thought he'd need and headed out, not expecting anything drastic for a while. Then he had seen something odd his first day on the trail. For the last two days he had been following wagon tracks; wagon tracks where they had no right to be. It was escorted by four outriders, and he had identified one of the riders by his horse's hoofprints, but he had only been curious about the unusual route at first.

Then he came upon their first campsite and he was really surprised to see the small footprints of two women. *What in tarnation would they be doing heading northwest into Lakota Sioux territory?* He couldn't figure this out at all. Nothing made any sense in the makeup of the party, its location, or its destination. He hadn't spotted any recent kills, so they weren't hunting, and some of the discarded food tins really had him wondering. Those items weren't normal fare for anyone traveling in the Plains. The mystery of the wagon made him pick up his pace, but it was going in the same general direction he needed to go anyway.

The reason that the direction of the wagon tracks was so odd was that the nearest settlements of any size were either behind him or north or south. There just wasn't anything where they were headed.

The only destination that he imagined for the wagon party wasn't a good one. Their wayward path was probably under the guidance of Claude and probably Louis, who appeared to be guiding the party. With those two, it was more than likely that the folks they were guiding would become victims more than clients.

He knew he was gaining on the wagon and its riders and picked up his pace even more to close the gap more quickly. He suspected that if Claude and Louis hadn't executed their plan yet, it would be soon. He hoped he could get there in time to stop what they were planning but doubted if he would. He didn't understand why they were taking so long. They were already a few days out and even at the slow speed of the wagon, they were well away from any witnesses.

———

Charles Burleigh had realized that he had made a horrible decision. He knew they weren't heading north toward Yankton and should have suspected something was amiss when the guides had assured him there was no reason for them to be armed.

Claude Bernard and Louis Martin had accepted the job for a hundred dollars each, half of which was paid when they agreed and the other half when they arrived in Yankton. Now Charles didn't believe they would ever arrive in Yankton. They had departed Omaha City four days earlier and had probably traveled over a hundred miles. Yet since they had departed the city, their direction had been more westerly than north.

Edmund Fallstaff was even more miserable than when he'd stepped onto that riverboat deck in St. Louis. He never should have married Emily Burleigh. Right now, there would be spring balls and parties, but his parents had wanted him to marry into money to help with the family finances. The family name was honored in St. Louis, but their bank account couldn't support the lifestyle much longer. The boat trip had been bad enough, but this! He had heard the whispers about going in the wrong direction but thought more about the incredible discomfort of sleeping in a tent and in a sleeping bag, of all things! He thought he had sacrificed enough just by sleeping in that horrid cabin on the riverboat. Surely, it couldn't get any worse.

Emily and Abigail were just afraid. They had seen how the two guides had been watching them, even if the men hadn't noticed. They had mentioned it to Charles when he had told them about the misdirection, but he said there was little they could do. He had asked Claude about the direction and Claude had told him that they had to swing wide to avoid a hostile Indian tribe. That had sounded plausible for two days, but not four. Charles tried to reassure the women, but he was certain that neither really believed him any longer.

Claude and Louis had only one problem, and that was James Bristol. it had been the butler and bodyguard that had been the reason for the delay in their plans. They were leery of him at first but were surprised when he had approached them on the second day and asked to be cut in on the plan. For the past two days, they had been in negotiations and now they were close to an arrangement.

———

Kyle was close to the wagon now as his Sioux friends had returned to their camp yesterday. He didn't know if they'd be back with more warriors or just leave him alone but was reasonably sure that they would remain in their own lands.

He was well into Lakota Sioux territory now and neither group was particularly happy with the whites or each other.

The packhorse carried the supplies he needed to get to Fort Sully with enough firepower and ammunition to get him there and quite a bit further.

He was armed with a Spencer carbine, a Henry repeater, and a Sharps rifle for long guns and two Colt New army pistols for close in work. He was different from other army scouts in that he carried a bow and two quivers of arrows as well.

He had marked the arrows with his own brand, so if he used it against the Sioux or most other tribes on the Plains, they'd know who had done the killing. He was also armed with a massive ten-inch Bowie knife with a custom handle covered in shark skin. He had bought the knife at Fort Kearny in 1861, and no one seemed to know how a knife with a shark skin covering had made to the middle of the country. It had cost him twelve dollars, an outrageous price for a knife, but he never regretted it. Even when his hand was wet with either sweat or blood, he'd been able to maintain a good grip.

He guessed he was just a couple of hours behind the wagon and they'd probably be stopping to make camp soon. At each of their campsites, he learned more about the party and was even more amazed they were still alive. He as sure now that it was Claude and Louis, which made it likely that the rest of the party wouldn't be alive much longer. He had also noticed one more interesting facet of the group when he had found that one member of the well-shoed group had spent private time with Claude and Louis on more than one occasion.

He knew the two men who were guiding the party and didn't like either of them. Kyle knew them when they had trapped with his father and had crossed paths with them more recently as guides and even once when Kyle was scouting in the Dakota

Territory. Both were of French origin, but Claude was the traditional French-Canadian trapper whereas Louis was much darker, his mullato makeup from his Louisiana roots. They were simply not good men and would take advantage of anyone, white or Indian. When they had been guides in Montana Territory, some of their clients had disappeared from unspecified accidents, but only the other guides and scouts really understood or seemed to care about their murderous habits.

He knew Claude was there because of the unusual gait to his horse and was surprised that Claude still rode that gelding. He'd been riding him for almost ten years now while Kyle had gone through three horses since then. Claude rarely was seen without Louis and Kyle was confident that this party was going to meet with an unspecified accident soon. He was almost shocked that it hadn't happened yet and was curious about why it hadn't happened. He was so close now though, that he thought he'd have a good chance to deny them that opportunity.

———

"We'll camp there tonight," said Claude, pointing to a copse of cottonwoods.

"Isn't it early?" asked Charles, "We've still got an hour of daylight."

"Good water here," replied Claude.

"Alright," said Charles half-heartedly as he turned the wagon to the spot indicated, not seeing still or moving water anywhere nearby.

James Bristol made eye contact with Claude and nodded slightly. It would be soon now, and he was ready. The butler's only concern was if he could be fast enough to kill both of the guides before they tried to shoot him in the back.

Charles brought the wagon to a halt and set the handbrake as the four men dismounted from their horses.

Once on the ground, Edmund stretched his back and rubbed his buttocks. He wasn't used to spending so much time in the saddle.

James Bristol walked over and offered his hand to assist Emily down from the wagon, but she just stepped down on her own. She had noticed him looking at her much differently than he would have dared before they left Omaha. Charles climbed down and walked to the other side to help Abigail from the driver's seat.

When they were all afoot, Claude, Louis and James stepped to the trees, ostensibly to set up camp.

Charles was uncomfortable as he watched the three men walk away. James had become more distant these past days and spent more time talking to Claude than he did to the family. Something was not right, and he believed that it was his fault.

The two guides and James were still talking as they went through the motions of setting up the camp while Charles and Emily watched them warily.

Edmund was leaning on the wagon with his head down as Abigail brushed off her dress. No one noticed the buckskin-clad rider approaching a quarter of a mile from the southeast, not even the three conspirators as they were so intent in their discussions.

Kyle had been watching them carefully as he walked his horse quietly and immediately saw the split in the group. He also couldn't help but notice that five of them were dressed as if they were waiting for a carriage in St. Louis and not in the middle of the prairie. He spotted Claude and Louis right away and wondered who was talking with them. Whoever it was, he was the man who must be in cahoots with Claude and Louis. He was dressed like the other four city folk but a more plainly.

Kyle figured he might be a manservant or a guard of some kind, which meant that he might be armed. Suddenly, the reason for the delay in the execution of Claude's plan became obvious. They had to convince the city folks' man to join them, or maybe it was the other way around. It really didn't matter how they got together, but Kyle was convinced that he'd thrown in his lot with the two notorious guides.

He pulled both hammer loops free and decided to make himself known as he was within a couple of hundred yards and had the advantage of having his Henry repeater in its nearby scabbard. He picked up the pace a bit to a slow trot, making a lot more noise.

All seven heads turned in his direction almost immediately.

"Is it an Indian?" asked James Bristol when he spotted the buckskin-clad rider.

"No, I know who that is. It's the Green-Eyed Devil, himself," spat Claude in disgust.

Louis glared at Kyle as he rode into their camp. *Why the hell did he have to show up just when they were ready to make their move?* He suspected that Kyle had been tracking them for days.

"Hello, the camp!" shouted Kyle as he slowed the horse.

Charles didn't know who the man was, but he couldn't be much worse than the men he had hired and could tell by the guides' faces that they weren't happy the stranger had arrived, either. He may be a stranger, but he seemed to be heavily armed and maybe he could pull them out of the dangerous situation in which they'd found themselves. *But he looked so young!* Charles thought he wasn't even old enough to shave, yet here he was out in the middle of nowhere all by his lonesome.

Kyle was fifty feet away when he stopped and saw Claude and Louis walking toward him and waited to see if they even thought about pulling their pistols. He knew they were probably well aware that his own pistols weren't restrained by their hammer loops, so he had an advantage; that and his reputation.

James walked ten feet behind the guides, put his hand into his jacket pocket, cocked the hammer of his Cooper pistol and watched for his opportunity to shoot the intruder.

Kyle grinned at the two guides and said, "Hello, Claude and Louis. What are you two doing out here with these folks dressed like it's a Sunday in St. Louis?"

"Just guidin' them to where they wanna go, Kyle. What about you?" replied Claude.

"Just passing through on my way to Fort Sully. It seems that they have some problems and want me to scout for them."

"Well, you go ahead on through then. We're settin' up early."

"I can see that. Where are these folks going, anyway? There's nothing northwest at all, at least not for white folks."

"We had to swing wide around some hostiles."

"Now, that's really interesting, Claude. I was followed by a small band of Santee Sioux for a while, but they didn't bother me. Which hostiles are you talking about?"

Claude had a serious problem. His excuse for going in the wrong direction would be easily dismissed by anyone who knew the area, and Kyle knew the area better than anyone.

"Just actin' on what information we got at Fort Omaha."

"Claude, you're not making any sense again. I left Fort Omaha three days ago and they hadn't heard of any serious problems on the eastern end of Nebraska in a while. In fact, it looks like you're guiding these folks directly into hostile territory. The Lakota are in a bit of a state right now."

Claude knew it was true, but he and Louis had figured on taking the Burleigh party a day or two away from the city before killing them all. James Bristol had put a delay on that plan, but now the modified plan was ready to begin, and he needed to get rid of MacKenzie.

"I musta heard wrong then."

"Well, whatever. If you don't mind, I'll just set up my own camp right nearby. I won't be a bother and I'm sure you'd like the added firepower for more protection against those hostile tribes that seem to cause you so much worry."

Louis finally spoke, adding an even more unlikely reason when he said, "I don't think the women would want to have a stranger so close, Kyle. I think you should move on."

Charles and the two women were watching the almost civilized confrontation intently, and none of them expected Kyle to live much longer when the civilized part of the confrontation evaporated.

Kyle had enough banter and quickly pulled and cocked both pistols, aiming one at each man.

"Drop your pistols, Claude. Yours, too, Louis," then he looked at James and shouted, "You! Right behind them, take that pistol you have in your jacket and lower the hammer before you drop it to the ground."

James Bristol was stunned. *How could he have known he had a pistol?* He lowered the hammer and pulled the pistol from of his pocket and dropped it to the ground, the muzzle ramming into the Nebraska dirt before it toppled over.

Claude and Louis each unbuckled their gunbelts and let their rigs fall to the ground as they glared at Kyle.

Once the three men were gun-free, Kyle said, "Now, I want you three to step over to the side there, about fifty feet away while I talk to the other folks."

The other folks were shocked at the sudden escalation from what sounded like normal conversation to armed intervention, but Emily and Abigail felt a flush of relief. Charles was more astounded that the young man had not only survived but had gotten the upper hand on the two older guides.

The three men moved away to the point indicated by Kyle as he kept them under his pistols then walked the horse closer to the other city folk.

"Who's in charge over here?" he asked without looking away from the three men.

"I hired them. It's my party," answered Charles.

"Where are you folks headed?"

"Yankton."

"Yankton? Well, there's a surprise. You're over two hundred miles from Yankton right now. You were sixty miles closer when you were in Omaha City. It looks like those three were planning on leaving you and your party under the prairie. I need one of you to go over there and pick up those pistols."

Charles replied, "What about James? Shouldn't I give him back his pistol? I can understand why the other two shouldn't be armed, but James is our butler and guard, not one of them."

"Just pick up the pistols and then we'll talk."

Charles nodded, then walked to the two gunbelts, picked them off the ground, then snatched James' smaller pistol before he returned to stand near Kyle's horse.

"What do I do with them?"

"Just put them in the wagon's footwell for now."

"Alright."

He carried the pistols to the wagon and dumped them into the foot well like an armful of rocks, making Kyle cringe.

Kyle released the hammer of his left-hand Colt, holstered the pistol then, as he kept the other pistol on the three men, dismounted and said, "Now, let's find out exactly what is going on."

He stepped over to the three men who glared at him as the others followed behind him. When he was fifteen feet in front of them, he stopped and asked, "Claude, are you going to tell me what your plans are now, or do I have to find out the hard way?"

"MacKenzie, you're gonna pay for this!" Claude snarled.

"Well, I guess I know what your plans were. How'd you convince the butler to help? What was the price?"

Claude stared at Kyle as he replied, "He wanted the young woman, at least to use her for a while. You can have him if you let us go."

"Now that's interesting," he said, then looked at James and asked, "What's your full name, James?"

James replied in an expected servile monotone, "James Bristol. He's lying. I never agreed to any such thing. I was playing for time to make a defensive stand."

Kyle smiled as he said, "I might believe you if you had done anything earlier. You had days to take them out. I guess they never slept during that time. I noticed that you were getting friendly with Claude and Louis a couple of days ago. Even a few minutes ago, you had those two with their backs to you and a loaded pistol in your pocket. If you had wanted to make a defensive stand, you could have just disarmed them yourself when I was talking to them."

"I wasn't sure if you weren't just as dangerous."

"You could have figured that out quickly by the direction of the conversation. Besides, even if I was a threat, you would have had the drop on all three of us. I'm not buying what you're selling, Mister Bristol. Claude may be a worthless bastard, but he's telling the truth. My only question is what am I going to do about it. You boys have really made a mess out of things, including my trip to Fort Sully. The first thing I've got to do is get you all nicely bound, so I can put this pistol down. It's getting kind of heavy and I don't want to shoot one of you accidentally."

"Mister…, what is your name, anyway?" Kyle asked Charles.

"Burleigh, Charles Burleigh."

Kyle didn't turn his eyes away, but his eyebrows arched as he asked, "Burleigh? Not as in Walter Burleigh, the Indian Agent in Yankton?"

"He's my cousin and now a U.S. Representative. I'm to take over his staff in Yankton."

"Are you a government man?"

"No, not at all. I own the Little Shipping Company in St. Louis and only took the position to help my cousin."

"Well, don't go and tell any of the Sioux your family name. It's not very popular among the Dakota tribes. Mister Burleigh, I need you to tie those men up with some leather strings I have in my saddlebags. The one on the right flank of my horse."

Charles shook his head and said, "I'm sorry, I won't tie them up. They've committed no crime. We can just send them away."

Kyle really wanted to look into Mister Burleigh's eyes to see if he was really this stupid or was just trying to be civilized but couldn't afford to give Claude or Louis the chance to lunge at him.

"Alright then, I'll just holster my pistol and leave you with them. You can apologize to the women after I'm gone, unless they kill you first."

"I'll do it," Emily said quickly, knowing what awaited her if Kyle left and surprised that her father had refused to bind the men.

Edmund couldn't believe what he just heard. *His quiet demure wife offering to bind those dirty, despicable men's wrists?*

Emily walked quickly toward Kyle's horse, flipped open the covering leather flap to the saddlebag, took out a handful of leather strings and walked to each man.

Kyle kept his pistol trained on each man as Emily walked behind them and tied their wrists securely, adding extra tightness to James Bristol's wrists hoping that they'd soon be useless.

Once she finished with their wrists, Kyle said, "Okay boys, each of you will take a seat while the lady ties your ankles."

After sitting, they sat glaring at Kyle as Emily went from man to man, quickly wrapping his ankles in leather cord.

Emily was only concerned that one might try to kick her as she wrapped the pigging strings around their boots, but expected that if one tried, he wouldn't live very long. She was already impressed with the young man in the buckskin suit.

Once they were all secure and Emily had trotted back to the wagon to join her mother, Kyle put his pistol in its holster, but left the hammer loop off. He walked up to Claude, pushed him onto his back, opened his jacket, then slid Claude's eight-inch knife from his sheath and tossed it aside. He did the same to Louis before he decided to pat down the butler. He didn't suspect that James had a knife but checked anyway, not finding any more weapons. He sat each man up again before picking up the two knives and walking back to the staring Burleigh party. Each of them wore a very different expression.

Charles had a mixed look of admiration, curiosity and a hint of worry. The older woman, he was sure was his wife, looked at him with a combination of disdain and relief, while the younger man, probably the young woman's husband, just glared at him as if he was a savage Indian or maybe only a snake. The young woman though, whom he was sure was the older couple's daughter, was almost smiling at him with gratitude. She seemed to understand that she was safe now and that Kyle wasn't about to hurt her or her family.

After he'd made his almost instant evaluations of the four family members, Kyle said, "Now, let's iron out this mess somewhat. Mister Burleigh, I need ask why in God's name you were going overland to Yankton instead of using the steamboats? Second, why did you hire this pair once you decided to go overland? Claude and Louis don't have the best reputation in the territory."

Charles felt somewhat embarrassed to answer the question because he knew he'd made the mistake, but replied, "Our boat, *The Bertrand* sank just a few hours out of Omaha City. My wife didn't want to get on another one, so we decided to use a wagon. We were in the hotel in Omaha City and I was asking about a way to get to Yankton and Mister Bernard was in the lobby, overheard my request, and agreed to guide us to Yankton. It took me over a week to get all the things together after the riverboat sank."

"Well, to be honest, you chose just about the worst way to get to Yankton. You're lucky to get twenty miles a day with that heavy wagon. Forty isn't difficult on horseback but impossible driving that wagon with all sorts of obstacles in your path."

"Well, we had the trunk to consider."

Kyle shook his head in disbelief and began to wonder if it was simply ignorance or if Claude had somehow pushed him to make so many mistakes.

"You could ship it on a steamer, then buy six horses, including a packhorse and move faster. It would also cost a lot less. Who's your traveling companion? I'm guessing that he's your son-in-law?"

"How would you know that?" Charles asked in surprise.

"The young lady is obviously your daughter, and he bears no family resemblance. So, he's your son-in-law?"

"Yes, his name is Edmund Falstaff. How will we get to Yankton now?"

"I'd recommend you return to Omaha and take the next steamboat, but if not, I could get you there. I don't mind making the side trip to guide you there, but the other question is what to do with those three. I don't want to have to drag them along, and I don't suppose you want me to shoot them either. The only suggestion I have is to turn them loose when we're ready to leave tomorrow. I'll leave them with enough ammunition, food and water to get back to Omaha City."

"But what about James? He's been with the family for years."

"James was going to assault your daughter, Mister Burleigh. If you don't believe Claude, then I'll let you know that I had already figured out that he was conspiring with Claude and Louis before I reached you, and I'm pretty sure that he's the only reason that you're all still alive. He was probably negotiating a better deal. If you want to forgive him for that and let him come along, that's fine. I just won't give him his little pistol back."

"No!" exclaimed Emily, "I don't want him to come with us."

Kyle wasn't surprised at her reaction but did notice that her mother didn't seem to have the same response, which did.

Her father turned to her and said, "Emily? Surely you don't mean that. James hasn't done anything."

31

"You haven't been paying attention, Father. He's been making eyes at me more and more the past three days. It was as if he was telling me that he'd have his way with me soon."

Kyle looked back at Charles and waited, surely the man couldn't keep denying the reality of their situation. Obviously, their butler had been with them for a long time or Charles wouldn't have been so resistant to understanding the threat that James now posed.

Charles finally nodded and said, "Alright. You can send him back with the others."

"Okay. Now, this isn't exactly a great location for a camp, but it'll do. I'll need to get water for the horses, though. The nearest water is a stream about a quarter mile east of here. We could move the whole camp, but it's easier to just leave it here rather than reload your wagon."

"Mister MacKenzie? Is that right?" Charles asked.

"Kyle MacKenzie."

"You seem a bit young to be riding out here alone," said Charles.

"Old enough," Kyle replied as he led his horses away to a spot about fifty yards from the wagon to a grassy area, then began unsaddling his animals.

After the horses were unsaddled or unharnessed, Kyle led them all to the stream to water. As he walked away from the campsite, he thought about the near tragedy that had just been avoided. Even though the family was still alive, keeping them that way might be difficult. The events that had led them to the empty Nebraska plains had him completely flummoxed.

Everything that they'd done had been one mistake after another. He couldn't fathom how anyone could be tricked so easily. Mister Burleigh, despite his apparently trusting nature, seemed to be an intelligent man of good character, yet he'd given into his wife's demand to avoid traveling on a riverboat, then hired Claude and Louis without even asking about them while they were in Omaha. Then even though he had a large wagon, and not even a covered wagon, he hadn't brought any extra guns on the journey. *Who in his right mind wouldn't have packed at least a couple of shotguns?*

By the time the horses were all satisfied, he still had no answers as he led them to the grassy area where he'd left his saddle and pack saddle, then tied them to a long hitch rope to let them graze.

He was already running through the trail to Yankton from their current location as he returned to the camp as the sun was going down and Kyle saw everyone just standing around not doing anything. *Were they all expecting him to take care of them like a cook or a maid?*

It bothered him that they seemed to think of him as a servant but thought that maybe they really didn't know what to do, so he approached the Burleigh party.

"Do any of you have any clothes that would work out here? Mister Burleigh, you and Mister Falstaff are wearing high collars with ties, and spats on your shoes. The ladies are wearing petticoats and corsets and have their hair up with pins and are wearing hats that are easily seen. You need to have much more freedom of movement and try to blend in better with the background. The dark trousers and jackets are fine, but then you have bright white shirts underneath. It's like wearing targets on your chests. Don't you have any flannel shirts?"

"No, we thought we'd be in Yankton by now."

"Well, you might want to at least lose the high collars, ties and spats. All they'll do out here is get dirty."

Again, it was Emily who surprised everyone by asking, "Where can we get changed?"

Kyle said, "I'll set up your tent. It's too large anyway, by the way."

"How do you know?" asked Charles.

"I saw your campsites. I was surprised at first because I thought you'd at least have a covered wagon. But examining your campsites was how I knew you had two women with you, knew you were being led by Claude and figured that you'd have a problem. Claude's horse is easy to spot because it leaves an unusual track."

"Are there any Indians nearby?" asked Edmund.

"There are always Indians nearby. The question is how close they are and what their intentions are. Most of them just want to live their lives like everyone else, but they're being pushed now, and they're angry."

"It sounds like you like the Indians," Edmund said, making it sound like an insult.

"Some of them I like, and some I don't. It depends on the Indian."

Edmund didn't respond, but just turned and walked away.

Kyle watched him leave and suspected that of the four, the son-in-law would be the biggest problem. He then stepped to the wagon and pulled out the large canvas tent. After it fell to the ground, he dragged it to the best spot, and then took almost twenty minutes to set it up. He'd never seen one so large before and almost giggled when he realized that it even had a floor.

Once the tent was finished, he dug a fire pit, but didn't have enough rocks nearby to build a wall around it, but there was plenty of firewood, which was a rarity on the Great Plains in Dakota Territory. There the best fuel was the plentiful buffalo chips left by the great herds of bison. The chips burned hot, but fast, so a lot of it was necessary to keep a fire going for a long time. It made those brutal winters even harder on folks and as he worked on the fire, he recalled many of them when he'd lived under those conditions.

He would occasionally glance over at the three bound men, and by the time the fire was blazing, they had all slipped onto their sides and were asleep. It was just as well.

Emily had gone into the tent with her mother as soon as Kyle had finished and wanted to talk to her alone.

"Mother, what do you think of all this?" she asked as she began to peel off the petticoats.

"Emily, I'm still nervous. What if this Kyle MacKenzie turns out to be as bad as the others?"

Emily looked at her mother and said, "I don't think so, Mother. He has a way about him."

"He does have that. I'm shocked about James, though. Are you certain?"

"Absolutely, Mother. When Claude told Kyle about what James wanted out of their arrangement, I wasn't the least bit surprised."

"Kyle? Aren't you getting a bit familiar? Don't forget you're a married woman, Emily."

"I'll never forget that, Mother," she replied as she began to work on the corset.

Each woman had to help the other get out of the restrictive garment but ten minutes later, the whale bone fitted corsets were on the tent floor.

"I feel naked, Emily. This feels so indecent," her mother said as she dressed without the corset.

"I like it, Mother. I hated that thing. I could barely breathe."

"Yes, I suppose there is that benefit. I'll feel better with the camisole at least."

"I'll wear one for the added heat, but at least I won't have to worry about inspiring Edmund."

Her shocked mother exclaimed, "Emily! Stop saying things like that! It's un-Christian!"

"Mother, I am what I am, and while you may not want to admit it, I am not about to change, and I intend to enjoy my freedom before we get to Yankton. After that, it'll be back to the corset, but not because I want to wear it."

"Emily, I don't know what I'm going to do with you."

"Just what you always have, Mother. You'll waggle your finger at me and then give me a hug."

Abigail laughed and smiled at her daughter. Emily had a way about her.

As Kyle watched, Charles removed his collar, tie and spats, but Edmund had preferred to keep his on. He was used to them and no self-respecting gentleman would be seen without them.

"Who did the cooking, Mister Burleigh?" Kyle asked.

"Claude and Louis did."

"Can't your wife cook?"

"She hasn't in years. We had a cook back in St. Louis."

"Alright. I'll handle the cooking, but don't expect any gourmet meals."

Kyle put a large pot on the fire, cut up some smoked beef and bacon, then after they had cooked down somewhat, he added four cans of beans, then some onions and peppers. He added some salt then just let it simmer while he returned to the creek and filled the coffee pot. When he returned, he noticed that both women were freed from their unnecessary frilly things and approved of the change. Emily with her hair down was nothing short of spectacular in his opinion, but he avoided spending too much time in admiration as her husband was nearby and probably watching him in distaste.

He put the coffee pot on the fire along with the pot, stirred his mix, then stood and took out some cups, plates and spoons. He was mildly surprised they didn't have china and silverware, or perhaps some fine crystal…monsieur. He smiled to himself as he envisioned the civilized place settings.

He let them serve themselves, if they knew how. He just took a plate, filled it with some of his bubbling stew and then poured himself a cup of coffee before he stepped away from the camp.

He walked away from the camp to his saddles, sat on the ground and ate his dinner alone in silence. He watched as the Burleighs began to dish out their own dinner, but still glanced at the three now awake men and wondered if he should feed them. He was leaning toward letting them go hungry for what they were planning on doing, but then thought that Charles would object anyway, and it would be better if he fed them.

After he finished, he took his plate over to the pot and removed it from the dying fire, then scooped out more stew and picked up his canteen near his saddle before he walked over to Claude and sat him upright.

"Open up, Claude. I'm going to give you some food. If you don't want to eat it, just keep your mouth closed."

Claude opened his mouth and Kyle began to shovel in the stew. Then when he had finished, Kyle gave him some water. He made two more trips to the pot before all the prisoners were fed. Kyle wondered if they were silent because of anger or shame. He figured they'd break their self-imposed silence when one had to go pee.

He took his plate down to the stream and washed it before returning to the wagon and made a quick inventory of their supplies. When he finished, he estimated that they would be short of food in three more days. He had enough to supplement it for four or five more, but he'd have to do some hunting on the way.

It was getting dark, so Kyle extinguished the fire and took the empty pot to the stream and washed it, then returned it to the wagon. He didn't mind doing what other's considered woman's work when he was alone, but he was a bit annoyed that no one had even offered to help. This whole man servant demand was in stark contrast to his normal way of life.

He didn't know that Emily had said that she was going to help but was stopped by her mother who thought it was inappropriate on several levels, especially as she was no longer corseted.

Charles approached Kyle after he had finished and asked, "Mister MacKenzie, do we have enough food to get to Yankton? I only bought enough for a week."

"No, you don't, Mister Burleigh. I have more on my packhorse, but that'll still leave us a few days short. I'll do some hunting when I can and get some native foods as well."

"Mister MacKenzie, if you don't mind my asking, how is it that you speak so well? Most men that I've meet out in the west speak rather crudely."

"It's not crude, Mister Burleigh, it's efficient. They drop a lot of useless letters and combine words. I never picked it up because Father Lapierre wouldn't let me."

"You were taught by a priest?"

"Father Lapierre was a Jesuit and ran the school where I grew up. He wouldn't tolerate improper use of the language. He was quite a disciplinarian."

"How long were you in school?"

"Until I was twelve. Then I was expected to go with my father."

"What did your father do?"

"He was a trapper before I was born but saw that trapping as a way of life was dying, so he began to serve as a guide for hunting parties. So, I was a guide until I was eighteen."

"Then you began to scout for the army?"

"No, I rode for the Pony Express for all nineteen months of its existence."

Charles was surprised and asked, "Aren't you a bit large to be a Pony Express rider?"

"Not back then. The weight limit was a hundred and twenty-five pounds, and I was close enough that they let me ride. By the time the Express went out of business in '61, I was well over their weight limit, but it didn't matter by then. After that I started scouting for the army."

"You said that my family name wasn't well-liked by the Sioux. Why is that?"

"The Santee Sioux and the Yanktonai Sioux have had less than a pleasant experience with your cousin. They've petitioned the Federal government to have him replaced but had no luck, which shouldn't have surprised them. I don't believe that the government in Washington have ever sided with them on one of their petitions."

"I hadn't heard that."

"I'm not surprised. Mister Burleigh, do you know how to shoot a gun?"

"No, I've never had cause."

"Can I imagine your son-in-law hasn't either?"

"No, I'm sure that he has not."

"There's nothing I can do about it now. We'll just have to hope we don't run into any Lakota in a bad mood between here and Yankton."

"Why do you have a bow and arrows? When I first saw them, I thought you might have been an Indian."

"I have them because they're quiet. If I'm hunting and don't want the local population to know I'm there, I use the bow. If they already know I'm there, I'll use a rifle, take what I need and let them have the rest. I use it for other situations as well."

Charles just nodded, not having the slightest desire to know what those 'other situations' were.

"Well, I'm going to get ready for sleep," Charles said.

"Go ahead, I imagine the boys will be asking for some relief here shortly. Oh, and Mister Burleigh, you might want to pass along some news I heard just before I left Omaha City."

"What is that?"

"President Lincoln was assassinated on the 14th."

That stunned Charles, as it had stunned most Americans, even Southerners.

"Who? What? How?" he mumbled.

"Some Southern sympathizer named John Wilkes Booth killed him. It was a plot to kill others, too, including the Vice President, Secretaries Stanton and Knox. They're hunting for him now. They already rounded up some of his accomplices. The president was shot while he was watching a play."

"I'll pass that information along. It's so sad. He survived the whole war just to be taken by some lunatic."

The news had shaken Charles, so he just turned and walked back to the wagon to retrieve his and Abigail's sleeping bag. He told everyone in the tent about the president's death when he entered and they all had the same reaction as he had, even Edmund.

Kyle headed for his panniers and pulled out a blanket and tossed it over his saddle. He'd stand guard for a few hours before turning in.

In the tent, Charles had just straightened out the double bedroll before Edmund walked out to the wagon, pulled the second double bedroll out and carried it into the tent. He flattened it out next to the first bedroll, then turned to Charles.

"Charles, what did that man tell you. Is he going to get us to Yankton?"

"He says he will, but it will take some time. We're over two hundred miles away and he estimated another ten or eleven days of travel before we arrive."

"That can't be right! We've already traveled over fifty miles. We should have no more than a hundred miles to go. He's lying. He's planning on something, I'm sure."

"I don't think so, Edmund. He seems to be a very capable young man."

"He's probably five years younger than I am and has had no education. He's nothing more than an ignorant backwoodsman."

"I wouldn't categorize him so quickly, Edmund."

"Well, I have. Telling us to remove our collars and ties, and to suggest that our wives go around flaunting themselves because he thinks that they shouldn't wear corsets or petticoats. Who does he think he is?"

"The only man who can get us to Yankton, Edmund."

Emily and Abigail had been listening to the two with different perspectives. Abigail tended to agree with Edmund, still feeling uncomfortable walking around uncontained while Emily thought her husband was just being obstinate and missing the reason for Mister MacKenzie's recommendations. Besides, she wasn't the least uncomfortable.

Kyle had to assist the three bound men to empty their bladders during the next hour and none were very happy about it, making various threats or running strings of obscenities and invectives as they were being helped. Kyle washed his hands afterward, knowing he'd have to do it again in the morning.

He finally leaned back against his saddle and pulled his blanket around him as he almost hugged his Henry rifle and eventually drifted off to sleep.

CHAPTER 2

Kyle was the first non-restrained person to wake in the morning and quickly trotted to the stream and took care of his morning needs before having to hustle back and take care of his prisoners. But instead of helping them, he simply walked to the wagon and pulled off the five percussion caps in each of their pistols, noticing that James Bristol had no empty cylinders, maybe because the Cooper only had five cylinders, and he didn't want to leave one empty. He set the pistols on the ground near their horses, then he walked to where they left their rifles. Both were Burnside carbines, so he yanked off the percussion caps as well, then went through Claude and Louis' saddlebags and pulled out their ammunition pouches.

He pulled out some food and put it in a bag, then dumped only ten of the small percussion caps into the bag before he walked to the three men.

"Claude, your pistols are over there. I'm going to cut you all loose now. If any of you give me a fight, I'll kill you as sure as I'm talking to you. You can go and saddle your horses and leave and can take your knives with you, too. You have enough food and water to make it back to Omaha City if you set a good pace. You can even have the money that Mister Burleigh gave you. I'm not a thief. If he wants it back, that's his business. You saddle your horses, take the food with you and head southeast. You and Louis both know the way. Besides, those wagon tracks are easy to follow. You got off lucky this time. Don't press your luck and come back. If you do, you'll die. It's that simple."

None of them replied, so Kyle began cutting their wrists and then their ankles. As soon as he finished, each man tried to stand, fell, then after a few seconds were able to get to their feet and stumble around a while until things began to work again. After a few minutes, they all just walked five feet and emptied their bladders.

Kyle had his own pistols untethered in their holsters as he watched Claude and Louis retrieve their knives before the three men picked up their revolvers.

Claude flipped his open and asked, "Where are the caps?"

"In the bag with the food. I only left you ten percussion caps, though, so don't go wasting any trying to drygulch me. Now saddle those horses and get the hell out of here!"

They continued grumbling and cursing as they saddled the three horses, James Bristol suddenly not much different from the other two as his polished veneer vanished. He was just another thug now.

Claude's parting comment as they turned their horses away from the camp was the expected, "We'll get you for this, MacKenzie!"

As they all rode off at a decent pace, Kyle didn't expect them to go more than ten miles before deciding to find a route around them to set up an ambush. He decided to start a fire and get breakfast going before the Burleigh party hit the trail. He wanted them moving within an hour.

He started the fire and found a frying pan but had to jog to the stream for water. He had the coffee pot in position soon afterwards, sliced up some bacon and set out a dozen eggs. There were only seven left after that.

He began harnessing the wagon, taking breaks to run back and flip the bacon. It was difficult, but he had set aside nine strips of bacon by the time the horses were in their harness. He finished the bacon before someone from the tent walked out and he wasn't in the least surprised that it was Emily. Her hair was disheveled and flowing in long brown locks across her chest as she saw him and smiled, stunning Kyle for a few seconds.

After the delay, Kyle couldn't help but smile back before she quickly ran out of the tent and trotted into some bushes. A couple of minutes later, she came out more sedately and wandered over to where Kyle was preparing to put the eggs into the bubbling bacon grease.

"I can do that," she said.

"I was beginning to think that no one in your party could do anything."

"That's because my parents, especially my mother, thought it would be inappropriate."

"But you don't?" he asked.

"No, I don't. It needs to be done. Why is it inappropriate?"

Kyle handed her the eggs and sat on his haunches as he said, "I let the three of them go this morning, but don't think they'll go far and surely not back to Omaha City. They'll probably ride for a few hours and then try to cut us off."

"Why?"

"Greed, mostly. That and their injured pride."

"You're an unusual man, Mister MacKenzie," she commented as she broke some eggs and plopped them into the frypan.

"Aye. I'll admit to that."

She smiled and said, "Your Scottish roots are slipping out."

"It happens sometimes. My father was very proud of those roots."

"Was your mother a Scot, too?"

"No, my mother was Lakota Sioux."

Emily was startled, but asked, "What was her name?"

"Sa Hanhepi Wi. It means Red Moon."

"Where are your parents now?"

"They're living on a ranch in the western part of Dakota Territory."

"You don't talk like someone who's spent his life in the wilderness."

"Your father said the same thing, and I guess it does seem a bit incongruous with how I dress. I was taught by a Jesuit priest who didn't let us slip into heathen ways."

Emily laughed lightly, and replied, "I was taught by the nuns at St. Francis of Assisi school in St. Louis. They were a frightening group of women."

Emily continued to cook while she talked, taking the eggs out of the pan and putting them on a plate held by Kyle, who added two strips of bacon.

Kyle just listened to her voice and found it somewhat astonishing that she seemed so different from her parents or her husband. She wasn't reserved or stilted like the others. She talked, smiled, and even cooked like a normal human being.

The tent opened, Edmund stepped out, and spotted Emily cooking next to that MacKenzie creature in her corset-less dress. He was embarrassed and angry as he marched toward the fire.

"Emily! Get back here this instant!" he exclaimed.

Emily glanced at Kyle and said, "Uh-oh. I need to go."

"Tell them that breakfast is ready, and I want to be moving within forty minutes."

"Alright," she said, then smiled once more before putting on a more serious face and turning back toward the tent.

She walked to Edmund who began explaining to her that she was never to shame him again by doing such a thing. She didn't know if he meant the cooking or talking to Kyle MacKenzie, but just nodded and walked into the tent.

Kyle noted the overbearing, superior attitude of her husband and marked the contrast between him and his wife. *How did such an interesting woman get married to such a shallow man?* Maybe he was rich, but even that didn't seem to make much sense, especially not after talking to Emily for a few minutes. Her father owned a shipping company, so that couldn't be it. *Why would the owner of a shipping company leave St. Louis to go to Yankton to help his cousin anyway?* He guessed it was a family thing. If his parents had asked him to drop everything and come to their ranch, he'd do it. He wouldn't be happy about it, but he'd go.

Emily's father left the tent as she entered, then Charles and Edmund ran off to the bushes to relieve themselves.

Edmund wanted to use the opportunity to tell Charles what Emily had done…at length.

Inside the tent, her mother was putting on her corset and told Emily to do the same. Emily knew she would lose the battle and followed her mother's orders, but quickly regretted it. At least she didn't have to wear those damned petticoats. They made her legs itch and gave the bugs more places to hide.

Kyle just continued cooking the eggs and when he was finished, he took the last plate and poured himself a cup of coffee, then walked to the horses and ate his breakfast. He was leaning against one of the cottonwoods when Emily and Abigail left the tent, then walked to the fire and poured themselves some coffee, filled their plates, and began to eat. He noticed that both women had donned their corsets again, which he thought was odd because Emily had already dressed without it.

Kyle wondered when Mrs. Burleigh had answered the call of nature because he hadn't seen her leave the tent earlier. Maybe she didn't have to anymore because it was inappropriate, he thought as he suppressed an inappropriate, but necessary snicker.

Kyle walked over to the women with his empty plate and said, "Mrs. Burleigh, if it makes you feel any better about your decision not to take the *General Grant* or another boat, the Grant's pilot and crew were attacked by Santee Sioux and three were killed. The next boat behind the Grant sank just two miles south of where your boat went down. So, it wasn't totally irrational."

Abigail was surprised at his level of knowledge of such things and asked, "How did you know all that?"

"I was briefed at Fort Omaha just before I left. I always like to know the news of the day, especially if it involves the Sioux."

"Well, thank you, Mister MacKenzie. I'll tell my husband," she said with a smile.

"It never hurts to be able to say, 'I told you so'," he said as he smiled back.

Abigail's opinion of Kyle MacKenzie suddenly made a dramatic upswing.

He smiled to himself as he walked to the stream to clean his dishes. He wasn't going to clean theirs anymore. As he stepped along, he almost bumped into Edmund as he and Charles came out from behind the bushes and Edmund was so intensely talking that he failed to notice Kyle. Kyle just waltzed around him and continued to the stream.

As he knelt by the stream cleaning the plate and cup, Kyle assumed that the two men had spent so long behind the bushes so the son-in-law could bend Mister Burleigh's ear about the savage Kyle MacKenzie spending time with his wife.

But even as he understood it could be a problem over the next few days, his bigger concern was where Claude, Louis and that butler would set up to shoot him.

———

Twenty minutes later, he had his horse and the packhorse saddled before taking down the tent. He wasn't about to saddle Edmund's horse though. He rolled up the tent and packed it on the wagon before tying his packhorse to the wagon with a trail rope.

He mounted, then saw that Edmund had finally figured out that he had to saddle his own animal now and suppressed a grin. Kyle guessed that James Bristol had been responsible for that mundane task in the past and now Edmund would have to get his hands dirty.

"Too bad," Kyle thought, "I'm not your butler."

And after this morning, he wasn't going to be their cook, either. It wasn't even disdain for having to serve them, it was the very rational understanding that he'd have to protect them from the three men who would probably try to ambush them soon and the Lakota who were probably already watching them.

He walked his horse to the wagon and said, "Mister Burleigh, I'm going to set as short a path as possible for the wagon. It won't always be a straight line though. As the crow flies, Yankton is about a hundred and eighty miles from here. If we're lucky, we can do it in two hundred and ten miles. I'll generally be out front to make sure the path is clear, but I'll scan our backtrail as well, especially for Claude, Louis and James Bristol. I expect they'll try to make an attack sometime this afternoon."

"But you sent them to Omaha City? Why would they come back?"

"Why did they plan on doing what they did in the first place?" he replied, then turned his horse and rode east-northeast at a walk.

Charles snapped the reins and the wagon began to move as he mulled over what Kyle had told him. Unlike Edmund, he understood that driving for four days going west or northwest had added distance to Yankton, not subtracted it. So far, everything that the young man had told him was accurate and he began to realize what Emily and Abigail already knew. Kyle MacKenzie knew what he was doing and could be trusted.

Edmund had just finished saddling his horse and stepped into the saddle, cursing the name of Kyle MacKenzie as he did. He had to ride at a fast trot to catch up to the wagon and already noticed that the savage was riding away from them and hoped he kept going.

It was good traveling weather as they set out and Kyle knew that Claude and Louis would be back, but the question was where? The good news was that the trees were few and far between in this area, so sneaking up on them would be difficult.

The only way they could manage it would be to ride ahead, find a bushwhack location like a gully or creek bed deep enough to hide a horse and just wait. It'd be hard to pull off because they wouldn't know where Kyle might lead the Burleighs, but it was their only real option, at least for the next day. Once they left the plains just a few miles to the east, it would be a different story.

Back in the wagon they rode along in silence. Charles was still thinking about the horrible mistake in judgement he had made. He had almost gotten Abigail and Emily killed and he owed Kyle MacKenzie.

Abigail was wondering if she had made a mistake about the corsets. It was already getting warm, and she was beginning to itch and wished she had followed Kyle's advice. She needed a bath but knew that she was unlikely to have an opportunity until they reached Yankton.

Emily was looking at far off Kyle MacKenzie and had very different thoughts as the wagon rolled and rocked over the uneven ground. Everything was so wrong. She felt as if she didn't belong in the wagon at all, but on a horse with the wind in her face and the sun at her back. She wanted to be free of the restrictions placed on her by her parents, her husband and society.

It was as if life was just a giant corset, strangling her. She wanted to do what she wanted, not what everyone told her to do. But now she was married to that nitwit riding beside the wagon. She glanced over at him riding his horse with his back straight in his dark clothes and black bowler hat. To many women, he would be the epitome of a modern man, refined and well-mannered.

But to her, the essence of a real man was riding a half mile ahead with no hat, wearing buckskin clothes and a casual almost effortless motion on his horse. He seemed so pleasant and had a wonderful sense of humor. But it was too late for such girlish musings or fantasies. She was cast into the life she was living. They'd get to Yankton and she'd be right back into the balls and dances that her husband craved. They'd hire a maid, if one was available, and probably a cook and a manservant. It may not be St. Louis, but it was what passed for civilization in Dakota Territory.

Edmund was still disturbed by Emily's behavior. *What had gotten into her?* When he had first met her, she was a quiet, proper young woman. She had just turned twenty-one and was at the right age for marriage, at least in proper society. Out here, girls wed in their teens and he found it positively animalistic.

They had set a date for the wedding after a short courtship, and then came the summons from her father's cousin. He had argued to just leave Emily with him after the wedding, but Emily had stated her objections and her parents had wanted her with them, leaving him no real options. His future was tied to that of Charles Burleigh. *But now this! They were being led across the wilderness by a perfect stranger and his wife was beginning to act like a damned Indian squaw!*

———

Claude, Louis and James rode fifteen miles before Claude stopped for a break at a stream. After they rode away from the Burleigh campsite, they'd been talking almost non-stop about what Kyle had done to them but now, as they stood beside their horses, their long time spent complaining, suddenly shifted to a more concrete plan for action to change their luck.

"Louis, this isn't right. We gotta go and get that bastard!"

"I know, Claude, I was thinking the same thing. I say we just cut north and pick up his trail before he enters the hill country. Then we can run him down easy."

James was surprised and said loudly, "What are you two talking about? You saw all the guns he has. He'd shoot us all!"

Claude replied, "Nah! He can't shoot us all, not even one if we play it right. We ride around him and wait for him when he reaches the hill country, maybe tomorrow or the day after. Once he's in there, we spot him from the hill, and we pick him off. Once he's gone, we take care of the rest without a problem."

James thought about it for a few seconds and realized that it should work. Claude and Louis sure seemed to know how to handle their guns. He'd only been involved in short-range shootouts before he became the Burleighs guard and butler.

Before that, he'd been a strongarm for a gang leader named Sir Thomas Wilford in Chicago. His real name was James Woodley and his job had mostly involved protecting the man and Sir Thomas, who was no closer to being a knight than James was to being a frog, but had insisted that his guards appear to be gentlemanly. It didn't mean that he had to be less ruthless, as he had killed two men, but only one with his pistol.

When his boss had run afoul of a less genteel gang leader, James had decided it might be better to abandon the city altogether and took the boat to St. Louis where he found employment at the Burleighs almost by chance. He'd been with them for three years now and was close to leaving anyway when he thought the St. Louis police may have gotten wind of his true identity, and when the opportunity to leave town suddenly arrived, it was almost a godsend. But the more removed he became from civilization, he found that his skills were becoming more limited.

He'd realized the intentions of the two guides before they left Omaha City and thought he'd be the one to return with the money he knew that Charles Burleigh had with him.

Now there was a chance to get it after all. He would have to depend on the outdoor skills of the two others before he did, though. He figured he could always find his way back like that kid told them, follow the wagon trail. His real concern now was the Indians.

His own plans settled, James was almost grinning as he said, "Alright, I'll come with you."

Louis turned to him and said, "Who says we want you to come with us? If it wasn't for you, we would have taken care of them before that green-eyed bastard got close."

"But now, we get his stuff, too," said James, "and I know where Burleigh keeps everything, too."

Louis looked over at Claude and asked, "What do you think?"

"I say bring him along. He's one more target for MacKenzie," he said as he laughed, knowing that he was deadly serious.

"Alright, but we gotta move fast now. Let's get riding," said Louis.

They mounted their horses and changed to a northeast direction. James was satisfied that his argument had worked, not realizing that he was about to be turned into cannon fodder. He still believed that the other two would be so intent on killing MacKenzie and then taking the two women, that he'd still have his chance at killing each of them.

———

Kyle had reached a stream that had banks that were too steep for the wagon to cross at that location, so he began riding north along the bank looking for a suitable ford and after two miles, found one that was barely workable.

He'd probably have to handle the wagon, as it was still steep enough to cause problems for someone unaccustomed to driving a team, and he was sure that none of them qualified as a teamster. He knew it would be difficult even for him to get the wagon across the wide creek, but first he'd have to test the creek bed to make sure it could support the wagon wheels. If it wasn't, they'd have to unload some of the cargo and bring it across piecemeal, which would waste a lot of time.

He walked his horse down the bank, into the water and slowly crossed the twenty-foot-wide creek, then watched the depth on his horse's legs until it passed just to his knees, then it began to drop again and soon they reached the opposite bank, and clambered up the other side. It wasn't as bad as he had expected, the ground was pretty firm, and the water wasn't too deep.

He wheeled his horse back and went back into the stream, let his horse drink, then walked him out of the creek, up the western bank, then headed for the wagon at a medium trot.

"Why did he do that?" Charles asked rhetorically as he watched Kyle riding towards them.

When he was close to the wagon, Kyle said, "We're going to head north a bit. I found a reasonable ford for the stream up ahead. Do you think you can handle the wagon going down the bank and back up the other side?"

"I don't know. I'll try."

Kyle smiled and said, "Good man," before he wheeled his horse around again and followed his own prints back to the ford.

Charles was surprised that Kyle's short praise when he'd called him a good man made him feel proud of himself and was determined to drive the wagon across the ford.

"Charles, do you think you should? It might be difficult," asked Abigail.

"Abigail, I can do this," he replied confidently as he flicked the reins.

Emily noticed the firm answer and was pleased that her father seemed to be ready to take charge as he had done for years in St. Louis. Ever since they'd left Omaha City, she wondered why he had been less than his usual assertive self. She suspected it was because he was uncomfortable with their surroundings and felt out of place, just as her mother was. But now, her father was her father again and she was glad that he was.

Edmund watched Kyle riding away and thought his request bordered on being nothing short of silly. Anyone could drive a wagon across a stream. *How hard could it be?*

Twenty minutes later, they arrived at the ford and suddenly, Charles wasn't so sure about his ability to get the wagon across. It looked mighty steep to him.

Kyle rode up next to the wagon and said, "Now, after the horses go over the bank, apply the hand brake so you don't slide into them. They'll want to stop and drink, but you need to keep them going. When they're in the water give them a crack of the whip to let them know you're in charge and then release the brake when they start moving again. They should pull you straight out. Don't let them stop, or it'll be hard getting the wagon out without using the other horses. I'm going to untie the packhorse before you do, though."

Kyle rode behind the wagon, leaned over, untied the packhorse, then attached the trail rope to his horse before leading him down the bank of the ford and then crossing the stream before climbing back up the other side. He wheeled his horse around, looked across the stream at Edmund and shouted, "You need to come across before the wagon, Mister Falstaff, or you can wait until the wagon is over on this side."

Edmund didn't need anyone to tell him what to do, especially not this ignorant backwoodsman. He'd prove him wrong just for the satisfaction, so he waited until Charles started the wagon over the bank. As the horses walked down, Charles pulled the handbrake into its locked position, and the wagon skidded down the slippery bank as Edmund began to ride down at the same time, just four feet to the right of the wagon.

The draft horses pulling the wagon wanted water, so they began to stop and dip their heads. Charles had the whip in his hand was preparing to crack it when Edmund's horse slid into the wagon, sending Abigail into the water on the other side.

Charles watched his wife flailing arms as she splashed into the creek, then immediately dropped the whip and jumped into the water next to her to keep Abigail from being crushed under the rear wheels which were still sliding. He grabbed her and her then yanked her backwards away from the wheels into the ice-cold water.

The horses stopped and began to drink as Edmund regained control of his horse, walked him across the creek quickly and climbed up the other bank.

Kyle muttered a curse as he dismounted, then raced down the bank into the water to help Charles pull Abigail out of the water, her dress adding a lot of weight.

Charles was trying to get her into the wagon, but Kyle knew it wasn't possible with her soaked clothing, so he shouted, "Mister Burleigh, just pull your wife up the other side of the creek."

Then he looked at Emily who had been watching the scene just feet away and said loudly, "Mrs. Falstaff, I'm going to need you out of the wagon. Do you mind getting wet or would you rather have your husband carry you across?"

Emily looked at her husband still in his saddle on the other side of the creek, then wordlessly hopped down into the water, shocked by the cold, and began walking to the other side. It was only a couple of feet deep, but it soaked her dress and her shoes were full of mud as she struggled to the bank.

Once she was safely on the opposite bank, before she emptied her shoes, she turned and helped her father pull her mother from the water, then took her mother's left arm while her father took her right and helped her up the east embankment to dry ground.

Once he was sure that they were out of the way, Kyle walked to the front of the wagon and began to talk to the horses as if he expected an answer.

But he wasn't speaking English. Emily was listening, and like most sophisticated men and women in St. Louis, she spoke French as well as English, but what Kyle MacKenzie was speaking wasn't close to either.

When Kyle finished talking, he clapped his hands loudly before the horses' noses, then shouted at the horses in the same tongue before he grabbed the lead horse's collar and pulled.

The horses began to move and soon were fighting to pull the wagon up the bank and then suddenly, their hooves gained purchase on the dry, flat ground and jerked the wagon quickly forward.

Kyle ran alongside and yanked the brake, bringing them to a halt.

Without saying a word to Edmund, Kyle reattached the packhorse to the back of the wagon and climbed aboard his horse.

He stopped next to the Burleighs and asked, "Are you all right, Mister and Mrs. Burleigh?"

"Are you all right, Abigail?" Charles asked as he turned to his wife.

"Yes, Charles. Just wet and muddy. I need a bath badly."

Kyle turned to Emily next and asked, "And you, Mrs. Falstaff, are you all right?"

She smiled up at him and replied, "Just like my mother, I'm wet, muddy and in dire need of a nice bath."

He nodded as he smiled back at her and then turned back to the east-northeast as the Burleighs all emptied their shoes, wrung out their clothes, and finally boarded the wagon.

Charles helped Abigail back into the wagon and crossed around to the other side to climb in himself. Emily climbed up into the seat as her father released the brake and the wagon began rolling again.

Edmund just rode alongside, having learned nothing from the episode except that Mister MacKenzie had irritated him even further.

By the time the wagon was moving again, Kyle was already a good half a mile ahead and searching for any potential threats.

Kyle had said nothing about the incident because he was so angry with Edmund and this whole setup. He'd had city folk show up asking to be guided for a hunt before, but they usually went over the top the other way and arrived looking like Davey Crockett.

These people had no idea how even the little things can be deadly. If that idiot Falstaff had slipped a little earlier, he would have been dead. He knew why he hadn't listened to him and had obviously chosen to do exactly what he had told him not to do ,because of his gentleman's pride. It was the same thing that would drive Claude and Louis to try to kill him rather than stay alive and return to Omaha. He thought that Mister Burleigh was making some improvement, but he doubted if Mister Falstaff ever would. Kyle knew he had to be careful or Falstaff would get them all killed.

––––––

The three men had covered a decent distance, but their horses were tired and thirsty. It had been a warmer day than they had expected, and they needed to stop earlier than they would have preferred.

They finally stopped and set up camp near a stream. It was the same stream that the Burleigh party had crossed just a couple of hours earlier, but they were twelve miles south of the ford that Kyle had found.

When they finally opened the food bag that Kyle had given them, they found that Kyle had unloaded the foods that he thought weren't suitable for their journey.

"*Oysters? He gave us oysters?*" screamed Claude.

"Don't worry, Claude. They're really pretty good," said James as he began to open a can.

"Who travels with oysters?" asked Louis, but he took a can and opened it as well.

———

Kyle was aware of the ladies' dilemma about needing a bath and began to look for a campsite with a good water supply. They were nearing the hill country and there was no water problem. If anything, the water problem was that there was too much of it, so he soon found a nice, clear pond nearby with a creek running out of it. It must be a spring-fed pond, which meant that the water would be clear, but even colder than that creek they had just provided them with an involuntary bath.

He headed back to the wagon, then pulled up alongside.

"Mister Burleigh, I found a good campsite just ahead. Mrs. Burleigh and Mrs. Falstaff, you'll be pleased to know that it has a nice spring-fed pond nearby. It's ideal for bathing, if you don't mind the water temperature. You can set up the schedule."

He wheeled his horse back around and rode to the campsite as Abigail asked in disbelief, "Did he mean that? I'm expected to bathe in a pond?"

"Mother, I don't know about you, but I'm taking a bath!" exclaimed a smiling Emily.

Abigail asked, "Don't you think it would be scandalous to be outside without clothes?"

"No, Mother. There is no one around but Mister MacKenzie, your husband and mine. I'm sure father and Mister MacKenzie will be perfect gentlemen. Of course, my husband has never had a desire to see me naked anyway."

"Emily! Stop that! You shouldn't say such things," her mother replied, in utter shock as her father stared ahead and pretended not to hear anything.

"It's true, Mother. He doesn't even want me naked when he needs me to perform my wifely duties. Decorum, you understand."

Her mother was stunned by her daughter's risqué talk. It was bad enough to be talking about being naked in the bath, but to talk about being naked in the bedroom was much, much worse. She decided to drop the subject instantly.

Charles, stuck in the middle, was almost as shocked as his wife, but for a different reason. *Edmund didn't like to have his wife naked in bed?* He'd have to ask Abigail about it later when they were back in a bed…naked. Decorum in the bedroom wasn't something that he and Abigail practiced and had been somewhat surprised that she acted as if she was offended. Even now that she was a socialite, all that civilized nonsense was thrown out the window in their bedroom.

They pulled the wagon to the spot Kyle had pointed out as they saw him begin to unsaddle his horse.

Five minutes later, as Edmund was taking the saddle off his horse, even Charles noticed how he would cast angry glances at Kyle.

When he was finished, Kyle walked to the wagon, untied the packhorse and led him to his saddle and began unloading him. After he had the horses stripped, he unharnessed the two wagon horses and led all four to the creek that was winding away from the pond and let them water. Once they were settled in a grassy area, he walked to the panniers and pulled out clean buckskins and underpants as well as a towel and bar of soap.

He approached Charles and said, "While you come up with a schedule for you and the ladies to bathe, if you intend to use the pond, I'm going to take a bath myself. I should be out in twenty minutes."

He then turned and headed for the pond, leaving Charles to scramble to get Abigail and Emily's attention. He walked swiftly to them and turned them away from the pond.

"Abigail, Emily, I need you to come to the wagon and have a seat. Mister MacKenzie is availing himself of the pond for a bath. He said he'd be back in twenty minutes. If either of you wish to bathe, he said we should set up a schedule. I believe that I will take a bath myself. Edmund, are you bathing?"

"I'm not sure yet."

"Abigail? Emily?"

"I'm definitely taking a bath," said Emily.

"Then I think I shall also," replied Abigail.

"Alright. As soon as Mister MacKenzie returns you both can take a bath. I'll inform Mister MacKenzie, and I'm sure he'll be a gentleman about the matter."

"I'm sure he will," said Emily, which attracted a scathing look from her husband.

Before going into the pond, Kyle made a quick scan of the area, looking for any indications of human presence and finding none. He quickly stripped off his buckskins and grabbed his bar of soap before he dove into the clear, chilly water and felt the shivers strike him before he popped to the surface and began to scrub. He was just a boy when he found it was much better to hit the water fast than just tiptoe into the cold water.

As he scrubbed, he felt better as his skin began to feel almost raw. He finally washed his hair before he plunged back under the water, surfaced again and tossed the soap onto his dirty buckskins. He took five more minutes just exulting in the brisk water until he finally stepped out and dried off quickly. He was dressed five minutes later and then used the same soap to wash his sweat-stained buckskins. He got them reasonably clean and then wrung them damp before he ran his fingers through his long dark hair and walked back to the camp feeling invigorated.

When he arrived, he found Charles and said, "The water is chilly, but very satisfying."

"I'll pass the word along to my wife and daughter. Um, Mister MacKenzie, about that..."

"Mister Burleigh, I'll be setting up the tent and will have my back to them the entire time. This is their private time just as my bath was mine."

"Thank you, Mister MacKenzie. It is a delicate matter."

"No, it's not really, Mister Burleigh. Society just makes it that way," he said as he smiled then walked to some bushes, spread his newly-cleaned buckskins over them to dry and then began to set up the tent.

As he did, Abigail and Emily were just entering the water, but Abigail was expecting cool, not cold. She was thinking of changing her mind when Emily dove in, throwing up a wave that soaked her mother. Her condition made getting wet no longer a decision and she plunged in as well. After a minute, she felt like a young girl again when warm baths were a rarity. She began to enjoy swimming again and diving under the water as all of the memories of her time as a young girl flooded back into her mind and she contrasted the simple happiness with the ordered life that she was following now. It was as big a shock as first entering the icy water.

Emily had never known a cold bath before but exulted in the sensation. Just like many of the other things that had happened since Kyle MacKenzie had arrived, she felt alive and free.

Kyle heard them splashing around and smiled when he heard giggles and laughter mixed in with the sounds of bathing. Maybe the icy water would wash away more than just the mud from the river crossing. Maybe Mrs. Burleigh would begin to loosen up a bit, too. He didn't realize that his simple comment about being able to say, 'I told you so', had already begun the process.

Both women were squeaky clean and were getting dressed when Emily noticed her mother had bypassed the corset, then turned to Emily and suggested she do the same. Emily had planned to do just that anyway, as the blasted thing was getting smelly and she didn't want to wash it or start splashing lilac water on the damned thing to hide the odor.

Clean skin and clean clothes made all the difference as mother and daughter walked out holding hands and laughing as they approached Charles.

"The bath is all yours, gentleman," Abigail said as she smiled at her husband.

Charles noticed the lack of the corset and smiled, liking the change in Abigail. She seemed more natural and younger, too, just as he remembered her when he'd first met her.

Edmund noticed the change in wardrobe as well and was going to chastise Emily when Charles walked up to him and announced that he was going to take a bath now and asked if he would join him.

Edmund was going to decline, but thought he needed to wash anyway. So, he and Charles retrieved some clean clothes from their travel bags and headed for the water.

Charles stripped and dove in quickly, the bar of soap in his hand as Edmund looked around furtively and bent down, feeling the water. It was icy! He squatted near the water's edge and began lathering his hands then washed his hands and face. His beard needed trimming, but he wasn't about to get his hair wet, not with that water. He decided that he'd change in the tent, so he scooped up his clean clothes and stalked off toward the campsite.

Kyle was busy making the fire pit, had noticed that Charles was still in the water and Edmund was still dressed, but wasn't surprised a bit.

The first full day of travel was behind them, and he estimated they had covered thirty miles today. That was very good because sometime tomorrow, they'd hit the hill country.

Emily walked over with Abigail and they both sat nearby while he set up the fire.

"I'm glad to see you both enjoyed the bath," Kyle said as he smiled, but kept his focus on the firepit.

"I was just happy to get out of that damned corset. Who invented those things, anyway?" Emily asked.

Kyle broke a dried branch and tossed it into the fire pit as he replied, "I believe it was Jeremiah Corset of New Jersey."

"Really?" Emily asked, astonished that he would know such a trivial thing.

"Well, he's better known for his nickname, 'Choker' Corset. He died just four years ago."

Emily then realized he wasn't serious and expectantly asked, "And how did he die?"

"His wife was so angry for inventing the thing, she forced him to wear one, and his forty-eight-inch waist, once squeezed into the corset, caused his head to explode."

The imagery caused Emily and Abigail to break down in laughter.

Just as they regained the control, Kyle added, "Of course, his head was the second thing that exploded. The first was much lower, messier and smellier."

Abigail and Emily had to hold onto each other to keep from falling over.

It took two minutes for them to stop before Kyle finished the story by saying, "It was so bad that they had to condemn the house, too. The newspapers of the day reported the story as 'The Exploding Corset Catastrophe of Camden'."

They finally both gave up and let it go. What was astonishing was that Kyle had kept a straight face while delivering the story, which he had constructed on the fly.

They were both still sniffing when Charles returned with a big grin on his face.

"That was invigorating, Mister MacKenzie. And what was going on out here?"

"I was telling the ladies the story of the famous Camden catastrophe, but it was overblown," he replied as he built the fire.

The women started laughing again and Charles looked at Kyle, who just shrugged his shoulders and looked as if he had no idea what they found so hilarious.

Emily and Abigail eventually stood and walked to the wagon and began going through the bags of food while Kyle set the cooking grate in place and took the coffeepot to fill it in the stream. He returned to find the two women putting a pot on the grate and smiled at them as he placed the coffeepot on the side of the grate.

"We'll take care of dinner, Mister MacKenzie," said Abigail, still wearing a grin.

"I'm sure it'll be a significant improvement, ma'am," said Kyle.

Both women smiled back, hoping he'd throw another line in, but Kyle had to hold back because he saw Edmund approaching.

Edmund walked closer wearing close to a grimace and was aghast to see his wife cooking, then waited for Charles to say something, but when he didn't, he decided to hold his own chastisement until he could talk to his wife in private. *No corset, a bath in public, and now cooking! What was going on with his wife? And all that laughter!* No doubt it was instigated by that MacKenzie, probably telling some unseemly story. What added to his seething anger was now even his mother-in-law seems to have accepted that uneducated buffoon as an equal.

Kyle was going to leave the two couples to their private time when Charles began to talk to him.

"Mister MacKenzie, you told me you rode for the Pony Express. How did that work?"

Kyle was glad to talk about something not involving the family, so he replied, "It was pretty simple, really. It must have been hard to set up, though. They built these small stations every ten miles from St. Joseph, Missouri to Sacramento, California, then put a half-dozen horses at each station and manned and supplied them to keep the horses ready to run.

"At St. Joseph or Sacramento, or anyplace in between, the mail was placed in a special set of pouches that slipped onto the saddle, and the rider would sit on it to keep it in place. The rider pushed the horse as hard as he could for ten miles, dropped off the horse, grabbed the pouch and tossed it onto the new horse, mounted then took off again. The changeover took less than a thirty seconds. Each rider would have a water bag and a pistol with him but nothing else. We'd ride seven or eight stations then turn the pouch over to the next rider, have something to eat and rest until a rider came back with the mail heading the other way."

Charles was fascinated as he asked, "Did you ever go more than eight stops?"

"The most I had to do was fifteen, but that wasn't unusual. The record was over three hundred and eighty miles in forty hours by Pony Bob Haslam."

"That's impossible!" said Edmund.

"Tell that to Pony Bob," Kyle replied as he grinned.

"Did you have any problems?" Charles asked.

"I had to run from some Paiutes a couple of times, but the company didn't want us to stop and shoot it out with any of them because it wasted time and they wanted us to ride hard and fast. They didn't want to lose the mail, either."

"Why did Claude call you the green-eyed devil?" asked Abigail.

Kyle turned to her and replied, "That's what the Lakota Sioux call me, and it spread to the other tribes."

She then asked, "You're so young, how could you have gotten such a reputation?"

"I've been out here for quite a few years and began scouting for the army when I was nineteen. I was an aggressive scout and did a lot more than just reconnaissance work. If I could prevent the Sioux scouts from getting close, I would. Most of the times, I used my bow to stop them. I have specially marked arrows, so they'll know who did it.

"It's not as if I'm bragging, it's just another weapon. A lot of the tribes get worried when they know that I'm around and I play on that fear to keep the peace. Too many times though, it's our cavalry that breaks that peace and once that happens, all bets are off.

"It's one of the reasons I'm heading for Fort Sully. The commander of Fort Abercrombie when I was there is now in charge of Fort Sully. He thinks I'll be able to spook the Lakota that are harassing the troops out there."

"Mister MacKenzie, why do you seem to have a vendetta against the Sioux. Didn't you tell me that your mother was Sioux?" asked Emily.

Before he could answer, Edmund interrupted with, "*Your mother was an Indian?* So, you're a half-breed!"

The Burleighs were shocked at his accusatory tone and statement and expected Kyle to pull his pistol and put a .45 right through Edmund's eyes, so they were more surprised by Kyle's mild response.

"It's a silly term, don't you think, Mister Falstaff? What is a half-breed? Half of a full-breed?"

"You know what it is. It's a mix of the races. Your father was white, and your mother was an Indian."

Kyle nodded then said, "Ah! Misogyny. You're a misogynist."

"I am. I believe that God created the races to be separate or he wouldn't have created them."

"So, you're a firm believer in the Bible?"

"I am."

"Then you must believe that we are all descended from Adam and Eve, the first parents."

"I do."

"So, after that, when did they become different breeds? When did God start loving one race over another? Did you know that among the Indian tribes, each considers its tribe to be the best, and the one that was blessed by their gods? Many tribal names translate to simply, 'The People'. It's the same thing with the Europeans. The French think they're special, and so do the Germans and everyone else. You're of German heritage, are you not?"

"I am, and I'm proud of it."

"Why?"

"What do you mean, why?"

"What did you do to make yourself of German heritage? I'm not proud of my Scot or Sioux heritage. I honor my father and my mother, not their bloodlines. Someone who was very wise once told me, 'be neither proud nor ashamed of what you are, only of what you do'."

"But your mother was a savage!"

Kyle suddenly had to control his anger at the man's ignorance but kept a calm voice as he replied, "A savage, Mister Falstaff? A savage, you say? You have never met my mother and I hope that you never will. How can you be so ignorant as to make such a statement?

"My mother is easily the most beautiful woman I have ever seen. She's very intelligent, speaks four languages fluently and is a genuinely wonderful person. It was she, in her wisdom, who told me about not taking pride in what we are. No, Mister Falstaff, my mother is as distant from a savage as any human being I've ever met."

Edmund sneered as he asked, "I suppose you wouldn't mind marrying one, either. You'd marry an Indian, wouldn't you?"

Kyle stared at Edmund and needed all of his restraint from even replying, then finally realized that there was no point in arguing with the pompous 'gentleman', let his anger dissipate, then just stood, turned and walked away.

Edmund felt a measure of satisfaction, knowing that he'd wounded the arrogant, over-stepping half-breed and leaned back with a slight smile.

Charles and Abigail were stunned into silence by Edmund's rudeness, but it was Emily who suddenly launched into him as Kyle continued to walk away.

Her eyes were blazing as she exclaimed, "You hypocrite! *How dare you say those things?* I know where you used to go on Saturday nights. I never said anything about it to anyone, but would you like me to tell you now, in front of my parents?"

Edmund didn't think she had known and was momentarily stunned before he pointed his finger at her and shouted, "You will not say a word, Emily! That was all before we married, anyway. This discussion is over!"

Emily knew that the Saturday night visits had most assuredly not ended when they were married, but let it go for the moment, and just as Kyle had realized, she knew that whatever she said would have no effect on Edmund.

Dinner was almost forgotten in the hostility, but soon they returned to eating in silence.

Kyle had walked to the edge of the campsite, where the horses were standing, undisturbed by the commotion. As he rested his right arm on his gelding, he let out a long breath. He thought he could shut Edmund up with logic that he'd learned from Father Lapierre, or the wisdom from his mother, but neither had any impact whatsoever. He loved his mother intensely and it had hurt when that ignorant bastard dared to call her a savage. He had never met her and even then, he doubted if he would recognize just how special she was. She was so gentle, so perfect that he felt blessed to be her son.

He had always avoided any childish pranks just to keep her happy, and knew his father did the same. His mother was the most extraordinary person he had ever known. She had one unusual feature that had made her something of a freak in her village. She was born with vivid green eyes that made many of the others fear her magic. Despite her beauty, or actually because of it and the eyes, no warriors would declare for her.

When Kirk MacKenzie, with his blue eyes, had arrived at the village in 1838 to trade, he was awestruck by Red Moon. Her parents readily accepted him as a suitable suitor for their daughter who they had worried about growing to be a forgotten woman. After the marriage, Kirk MacKenzie and Red Moon moved to Kirk's cabin, where Kyle was born a year and a half later. When he first opened his eyes, both parents smiled as they looked at his own vivid green eyes. The same eyes that now marked him as The Green-Eyed Devil.

Kyle finally reached over, patted his horse, then turned and walked back to the campfire.

When he was close, he took a seat and as if the conversation had never strayed into argument and asked, "So, Mister Burleigh, what did you do in St. Louis?"

Charles was taken aback by the normal question and hesitated for a few seconds before replying, "Oh. I own a shipping firm. It was actually Abigail's father's, but it's ours now. Before that, I was a commodities broker."

Kyle smiled and asked, "Now you have me. What is a commodities broker?"

Charles was almost surprised that he didn't know as he replied, "You know, I'm not so sure myself."

Kyle laughed and so did Charles.

Abigail and Emily were both relieved to have the tension relieved, although Emily knew she'd catch hell for even admitting that she knew about Edmund's Saturday nights.

But for now, she'd just cook and enjoy some freedom time as she watched Kyle. *What an amazing young man!*

"Mister MacKenzie, I noticed when we were going through the food, that the oysters were missing," said Abigail.

"I told Claude I would give him food for a few days, but I didn't say there would be a variety."

"You gave them nothing but the oysters?" asked a smiling Emily.

"No, I gave them some hard tack, too. Just to add some variety and to protect their horses after the shellfish had an adverse reaction," he replied as he grinned.

Charles said, "Well, I'm sure they appreciate it."

"I'm not expecting any thank you notes."

Kyle thought he'd try to include the sulking Edmund in the conversation and asked, "Mister Falstaff, what do you do for a living?"

"What do you mean by that?" he snapped.

"You know, how do you spend your time?"

"I am a gentleman, sir."

So much for trying to calm the waters, Kyle thought, so he changed the subject yet again.

"Tomorrow, we'll probably reach the hills by midmorning, and I'm guessing that's where we'll run into Claude, Louis and Mister Bristol. I don't believe they'll do anything to your party, Mister Burleigh because I'm the only threat. So, if you see me disappear for a while, don't worry, just continue following my tracks."

"What if they kill you? We'd be riding right into a trap," Edmund said quickly.

"Mister Falstaff, if they kill me, and that is highly unlikely, you've got no chance anyway. I need to do what I do best. Mister Burleigh, there is one other thing we could do if you really wanted to get to Yankton sooner and even avoid those three, but it's not something I'd recommend. I'm just letting you know about it."

"Alright, go ahead."

"If we headed due north, we could reach the Missouri River in two days. Once there, it would take a day to convert the wagon into a barge, then only take another day to get to Yankton with the current being as fast as it is."

"Why isn't it something you would recommend?"

"Because I'd have to stay behind. The wagon couldn't support the weight of the horses. It could support your party and your supplies, but no more. I'd cut some logs to attach to the sides of the wagons to add stability, then make some poles, so you could guide it downriver. There still would be hazards, but I'm confident that you could make it in one day."

Charles thought about it for a few seconds then said, "No, I think we'll stay with our original plan. Well, maybe not our original plan, but the current plan. It does sound rather scary, though."

"It would be, but I just wanted to give you the option now before we get into the hills."

"Thank you, but I believe we should continue."

Dinner was ready, and Kyle admitted it was much better than the stew he made on the first night. When he finished eating, he still washed his plate, but left the others to clean their own plates. He was sure that Edmund would have his wife wash his.

When he was squatted at the pond, he heard Mister Falstaff talking to his wife in French behind the tent and he wasn't pleased with her.

Edmund had seen Kyle at the water but disregarded him for the moment. He'd be able to berate that rebellious wife of his without the buckskinned buffoon understanding a word.

Kyle noted that the Falstaffs were far enough away from the Burleighs, so they wouldn't be overheard, but Mister Falstaff was lecturing his wife in French so Kyle couldn't understand him. *Did he not hear Kyle say that he had been taught by Father Lapierre?* Besides, most of the trappers were French, and most of the others had at least a smattering of French. Kyle had much more than a smattering, so Kyle just listened as Edmund spoke quietly, but with restrained anger to his wife.

Edmund glared at Emily and said in French, "Don't you ever bring up my private life again!"

Emily met his glare with one of her own as she snapped, "You dared to insult Mister MacKenzie for having a Sioux mother and yet you go galivanting down to the colored whore house every Saturday night. You are nothing more than a hypocrite of the highest order!"

"Say another word and you will regret it. I am your husband and I own you, Mrs. Falstaff."

"No one owns me, Mister Falstaff!" were Emily's final words as she turned and stalked into the tent.

As she disappeared behind the wide flap, Emily knew that she had angered Edmund, but he couldn't strike her with her parents nearby. She also had a strong suspicion that Mister MacKenzie would take a more direct approach than her parents if Edmund decided to use physical means to drive his point home.

As she plopped onto the sleeping bag, she wondered how Edmund would punish her for her defiance. He'd never really gotten to know her that well in St. Louis, and even after they'd married, she'd never had to stand up to him before, mainly because he was either out at his club, with his parents, or visiting the fancy whorehouse.

Kyle stood from his extended dishwashing and as he was returning to the wagon, he reviewed what he'd heard. The fight between Edmund and Emily disturbed him, and even though he already despised Edmund Falstaff, the situation would only be exacerbated if he spent too much time in the camp.

He needed to calm everything down and stop the infighting. He didn't know how he could diffuse this whole situation except by keeping as much distance as possible and not joining them for meals, starting tomorrow. Right now, he just needed to get back and get ready for guard duty. He didn't think Louis and Claude were that far away.

———

Louis, Claude and James were getting hungry already. They had divvied up the oysters and hard tack at lunch and had eaten everything by dinner. It didn't amount to a filling meal and they were all testy.

Claude snarled, "We had better catch up to them soon, Louis. My stomach is already growling."

"We'll catch them tomorrow. They can't drive that wagon very fast. I think we catch up with them before noon."

"Can't we hunt for some meat?" asked James.

"If we don't catch up to them by tomorrow afternoon, we'll do that. But right now, we can get by on mushrooms and wild onions. Perhaps I will trap a rabbit for breakfast."

The next hour was spent setting out snare traps for rabbits. Claude and Louis knew the odds weren't good, but it kept their minds off their empty stomachs.

———

While Edmund had been berating Emily, Abigail and Charles had been out of earshot intentionally, understanding the growing rift between their daughter and her husband.

Abigail said, "Charles, this is getting too tense. Can't you talk to Edmund and have him restrain his opinions? I thought Mister MacKenzie behaved admirably in light of the insults that Edmund had thrown at him, but even a saint will lose control if it continues. I don't think Edmund has a prayer against Mister

MacKenzie, and even if he did somehow manage to win, it would mean the loss of all of our lives."

"I'll talk to him, Abigail. I must control my own temper as well. Why didn't we see this side of him before we consented to the marriage?"

"We were blinded, Charles. He was a sophisticated, handsome young man that appeared to have prospects. But when he gave his answer to Mister MacKenzie's question about what he did by saying, 'I am a gentleman', it was painfully obvious that he has no future at all. We didn't do right by our daughter, Charles."

"I am very aware of that, Abigail, but there's nothing we can do about it. Go to the tent and send him out and I'll speak with him."

"Thank you, dear."

"Oh, and Abigail, I do like your new fashion. You appear very enticing," he said as he smiled.

Abigail Burleigh, a forty-four-year-old woman with twenty-three years of marriage to the man who made the comment, blushed. But she still smiled and walked to the tent with a gentle sway to her hips to the approving eyes of her smiling husband. Despite the dangerous location and situation, Abigail was beginning to enjoy herself.

A minute later a still moody Edmund Falstaff exited the tent and walked over to Charles.

"Charles, you wished to see me?"

"Yes, Edmund, this business with Mister MacKenzie has become quite unacceptable. You must withhold your views and limit your conversation with him to the mundane. He is critical to our safety."

"He is nothing more than a savage himself. Look at him over there, Charles. He could pass for an Indian."

Charles' jaws tightened as he said, "Nonetheless, you must think of the welfare of the group. You will restrain yourself in the future. Do I make myself clear?"

"You do, but I refuse to be lectured to by that pompous outdoorsman."

"You only were lectured when you insulted the man."

"How can one insult someone who dresses in animal hide?" he asked as he sneered.

"Edmund, keep this up and you will be the death of us all."

"I will make it simple. I will not address him at all."

"That will be acceptable, Edmund."

"Very well," he replied tersely, then turned, glancing once at Kyle before he entered the tent.

Kyle had seen them in conversation and didn't doubt that he was the subject, but it didn't matter. Tomorrow, he would effectively cut himself off from the group as much as possible, and he was just getting fond of Mister and Mrs. Burleigh, too. And as fond as he was about the Burleighs, he was much fonder of Mrs. Falstaff. He was getting too fond of Mrs. Falstaff and that was probably more dangerous than those three bastards who were going to try and kill them all soon.

His growing infatuation with her had to stop right now because all it would lead is to a lot more trouble for everyone, especially Emily.

CHAPTER 3

Kyle was up earlier than usual then quickly washed and shaved. He didn't have to shave that often, maybe three or four times a week because of his Sioux heritage. He was the only clean-shaven male in the group, as both Charles and Edmund sported fashionable full beards.

He saddled his horses and harnessed the wagon's animals before he removed some hard tack and jerky from one of his panniers and put them in his saddlebags. He headed to the bushes, picked up his dry buckskins from their leafy supports and folded them before returning them to his saddlebags. He was squatting as he built the fire when he heard a female voice.

"Leaving early, Mister MacKenzie?"

Kyle didn't turn as he had heard Emily Falstaff leaving the tent and using the private area.

"Good morning, Mrs. Falstaff. I thought I'd better get out ahead and make sure we don't have any visitors."

"Mister MacKenzie, I want to apologize for my husband's abhorrent behavior last night. What he said was rude and thoughtless."

"Mrs. Falstaff, it is kind of you to apologize, but unnecessary. You didn't speak the words. You chided your husband for them, and it is he who should apologize, but I don't think an apology is forthcoming. Do you?"

"No."

"I'm going to reduce the chance of another episode by maintaining my distance from the group. Just advise your father to follow me. I'll show myself every so often so that will be possible."

Emily sighed and said, "Mister MacKenzie, why were you so hurt when Edmund made the comment about you seeking a wife among the Indians? He had insulted you grievously about your mother, but you seemed to be able to deflect what must have been an enormous amount of anger, but not at the suggestion of marriage with an Indian woman. Why?"

He turned and looked at her, debating about how to answer, but decided quickly that he wanted her to know, just didn't know why.

"Mrs. Falstaff, his comment affected me so badly because I was married to a Cheyenne woman. Her name was Hesta 'se Vo 'e, which means Snow Cloud. She wasn't as pretty as my mother or you, but she was such a sweet, good woman and I loved her dearly. I met her as my father had met my mother when we went to their village to trade. Even though my mother was Lakota Sioux, I was allowed to wed Snow Cloud because we loved each other.

"We lived in her family's lodge for three months and I told her that I would go to earn money for our own home. She was very happy that we would live together in our own lodge, so I went out to guide for some white hunters and was gone for three months. When I returned, I found the village had been raided by the Lakota and my wife had been among those killed. She was carrying our child when she died.

"I joined the Pony Express after that to gain some measure of independence and solitude. It was a very lonely existence if one chose it to be so, and I did. After that, I started scouting for the army to seek vengeance against the Lakota and to maintain my independence and isolation. But as much as I desire revenge against the Lakota, I will not harm their women or children as they have. I only take my revenge against their warriors."

Emily was heartbroken by the tale and asked quietly, "Will this need for revenge ever be satisfied?"

"Perhaps, but I'm not sure. The passion has lessened over the years as the memory of Hesta 'se Vo 'e fades. It is a sad thing, our memory. I can't see her face as clearly as I did before, but I wish I could. Not because it would rekindle my desire for revenge, but just to be able to see it again."

"I have never suffered that kind of loss, Mister MacKenzie," she whispered.

"I wouldn't wish it on you, Mrs. Falstaff. It is a terrible, lonely thing."

"Have you no one now?"

"I still have my father and mother, and we are very close, but I don't see them often. They understand that I must follow my own path. One day, I'll return to their home and stay, but with the hostility between the Americans and the plains tribes increasing almost daily, that may be a while. I'm not sure they wish to stay where they are either."

"Do you think it's wrong? The settlers, I mean, pushing the Indians off their lands?"

Kyle shrugged and said, "It's the way of the world, Mrs. Falstaff. The land my wife's people lived on used to belong to the Shoshone until the Cheyenne took it from them. The Sioux have pushed many other tribes off their lands. How can they complain when they are pushed off their lands by a bigger, more powerful tribe?

"There are many admirable things about their way of living, Mrs. Falstaff, but it isn't what matters. It is the rush of civilization that will prevail. Father Lapierre had it right when he pointed out that the Indians' biggest weaknesses were in their division and their Stone Age culture. They never worked hard metal like iron. They have no industry, and they're still separate, warring nations. If at least they were to unite, they could make a more reasonable stand, but with the War Between the States coming to an end, I don't think it will matter. They will lose."

"I wish you wouldn't stay away, Mister MacKenzie."

"I don't have a choice, Mrs. Falstaff. Your husband isn't going to change. Sooner or later, he would go too far. I have no intention of making you a widow."

Emily suddenly realized that she didn't care one bit if she was a widow. Edmund had never been very attentive, even as a newlywed. His aloofness and stiff demeanor had carried over into their private lives, but his true character had been exposed in the past few days, and Emily had been repulsed by it.

Now, she would have to live with it for the rest of her life, and she was only twenty-one. She was twenty-one and talking to a handsome young man who touched her soul with his words and character. A young man who would leave her life in ten days and, just as his Snow Cloud, would leave her memory after a few years. That thought made her intensely sad and Kyle noticed the change.

"I apologize, Mrs. Falstaff. I shouldn't have told you the story."

Emily shook her head and said, "No, it wasn't what you said, Mister MacKenzie. It was another thought."

"Well, I'm going to mount up and start ahead."

"No breakfast, Mister MacKenzie?"

"I've got some jerky and hard tack with me. When you need more food, by the way, it's in the left two panniers on my packhorse," he replied.

Emily nodded and watched as Kyle stood and mounted his horse, but didn't think he'd even wave, but Kyle turned and looked down at her and smiled.

"Thank you for letting me talk to you, Mrs. Falstaff."

"No, Mister MacKenzie, thank you for letting me share your memories," she said as she smiled back before he nudged his horse and rode east.

Emily had felt her heart quicken when he had smiled at her and it was getting to be a frequent reaction whenever he talked to her, too. She sighed and returned to the firepit before Edmund awakened.

———

There were no rabbits in their snares and that meant no breakfast. The three men were riding before the sun was fully above the horizon, their empty stomachs adding impetus to their greed as they rode to fill the need for both.

———

After Kyle had gone, Emily began to cook breakfast and her mother joined her after a few minutes.

"Where is Mister MacKenzie?" she asked as she looked around.

"He's already out front. He said he would look for any possible trouble out there, but his real reason was he didn't want to run afoul of Edmund again."

Abigail's eyed widened as she asked, "He's afraid of Edmund? Surely not."

"No, I should have said that more clearly. He said he didn't wish to make me a widow if Edmund continued to confront him."

Abigail paused before saying, "That was very considerate, Emily."

"Mother, I asked him why he was so upset by Edmund's comment about seeking a wife among the Indians and he told me."

"What did he say?"

Emily told her mother about everything Kyle had told her and had a difficult time narrating the story as she fought back her tears.

When she finished, Abigail said, "He's had a remarkable life already, our Mister MacKenzie."

"Yes, Mother, he has," she replied and was almost ready to tell her mother about her dread of spending the rest of her life with Edmund when the two men approached the fire.

"Where is Mister MacKenzie?" asked Charles.

"He's already out front looking for possible enemies," replied Emily.

"Didn't he have breakfast?"

"No, Father. He said he had some jerky and hard tack and it was sufficient."

"Oh. Well, then I suppose we'll have to take the tent down ourselves," said Charles, "But after breakfast."

———

Kyle had ranged two miles ahead and had found no recent sign of Sioux presence or of the three white men. He swung in a wide arc before turning in the direction of the wagon. He had also seen the hills another six or seven miles away. For the rest of their journey once they arrived in the hill country, the trail would be snakelike, turning one way and then the next. There were at least two places where they would have to climb and go over a pass. They were nothing like the passes out west through the Rocky Mountains, of course, but they were still obstacles.

It was about an hour after he'd left the campsite when he rode to where he could see the wagon more clearly, then sat on his horse and waited. When Charles waved to let him know they were ready to roll, he waved back and turned eastward.

He had been able to see four miles behind the wagon and no one was coming, so that meant that Claude, Louis and the wayward butler would be trying to cut them off.

He kept riding until he reached the first of the hills, then stopped, took his army-issued field glasses out of his saddlebags and just ground hitched his horse to let him graze as he stalked up the hill.

When he was near the top, he bent at the waist and then crawled to the highest point. After reaching the summit, he slowed then scanned with his eyes to get a more panoramic view. He wasn't sure, but he thought he might have seen a dust cloud in the distance to the southwest. It was a good eight miles away.

He stared in that direction for a minute before pulling up the field glasses, saw the dust cloud more clearly now and soon identified three riders, all white men. They were riding north-northwest, right at him and debated about staying there, but they were a good hour and a half away, and he needed to stay where he could get back to the wagon quickly. Right now, he needed to warn the Burleighs.

He slid down the hill, trotted to his horse, mounted, then set off at a medium trot toward the wagon. It took him ten minutes before he pulled up on the side of the wagon away from Edmund.

He looked at Charles and said, "Mister Burleigh, our friends are riding north-northwest about seven miles south of here. I saw them from the first hill. I expect that they'll head for that hill and set up their ambush there. Their rifles are only effective out to maybe two hundred yards. My Sharps has a much greater range than that, but I'd only get one shot before they'd leave and find another ambush site."

"What should we do?"

"Keep going, but at a slower pace. I'm going to get back near the hill and set up. If you see my horse, then slow down to a crawl, as I'll be close."

Kyle didn't wait for a response before he wheeled his horse back to the northeast and set off.

"We surely aren't going to keep getting closer to those murderers, are we?" asked Edmund.

"You heard the man, Edmund," replied Charles as he flicked the reins and the horses began moving.

Emily glanced at her husband and wondered if Edmund was a coward in addition to his many other failings.

Kyle rode toward the first hill but didn't want to pass the hill because it would put the three men between him and the wagon. He wanted to be within five hundred yards of the crest of the hill and hidden from view but wasn't going to be a simple thing to find an optimal location.

He looked both north and south as he rode, and he almost missed it about two hundred yards to the north. It wasn't the best of locations, but it was acceptable. It was a grassy hollow running north for just a hundred yards, but it was about six hundred yards from the hilltop. He'd never made a shot at that distance before, but he knew the Sharps was capable of the range.

He stepped down and led his horse into the hollow. It was a bit flatter than he had hoped to find and his horse would be visible from the hill. It couldn't be helped, so he hitched the horse to a small bush, pulled the Sharps out of its scabbard and loaded it with a cartridge and then placed the percussion cap in place. He put a second cartridge and percussion cap in his right pocket in case he was able to get a second shot, which was highly unlikely, then sat in the tall grass and waited.

The wagon was still two miles behind Kyle and moving at its slower pace.

Claude, Louis and James had seen the hill just as Kyle had settled into his waiting position.

"Let's get up that hill and see if we can spot them. They'll be coming from the southwest," said Claude.

They set their horses to a fast trot, and if they'd looked just before reaching the hill, they could have spotted the wagon to the west, but they didn't realize that it was that close, so they missed the opportunity to spoil Kyle's trap.

By the time they'd reached the start of the hill's southern edge, the wagon was no longer visible.

A mile away, Kyle could hear them approaching from the south and wondered if they would ride around the front of the hill, exposing themselves to his fire. He quickly stood and trotted back to his horse and pulled the Henry repeater from its scabbard before jogging back to his previous position and took his seat next to the Sharps. Now if they came around the front, he'd be able to take them all.

But they didn't come around the west side of the hill, but rode around the east side, away from the wagon.

Kyle had spotted them before they disappeared behind the hill a half a mile away and estimated it would take them another twenty minutes to climb the hill and look for the wagon, so he just waited in the bright Nebraska sun. The bugs were active and annoying, but he had learned long ago how to ignore their presence even if they were biting, and they were already busy nibbling on his skin. He simply sat and waited like the sniper he was about to become.

The three men had hitched their horses, then Claude and Louis had taken their Burnside carbines, six rounds of ammunition for each rifle along with the few percussion caps, and all three began the climb to the top.

Kyle guessed it was almost time, so he cocked the hammer to the Sharps and adjusted the ladder sight. He held it loosely in his hands waiting for the proper moment. If anyone popped up on that hill, he would be shot with no niceties and no warnings. They had already been warned but had returned to kill.

Because he wasn't carrying a heavy rifle, James Bristol was ahead of the other two. He was almost at the top and was anxious. He wanted to see if the wagon was there, and Claude or Louis had intentionally neglected to tell him to stay low. They were going to let James Bristol act as their caged canary to warn them of any danger. If Kyle MacKenzie was somewhere nearby, they'd find out soon enough.

James Bristol reached the crest, popped on top and saw the wagon in the distance immediately.

He stood, pointed to the southwest and turned his head, shouting, "There they are!"

His head was turned, so he didn't see the bloom of smoke from Kyle's rifle. By the time he heard the boom of the big gun, it was too late. The .52 caliber bullet smashed into the right side of his chest and only stopped after it had punched through ribs, his right lung, and then lodged in his heart. He dropped like a sack of flour to the top of the hill, with only a small pool of blood to mark his passing. His heart had stopped pumping before he hit the ground.

Even though they had almost been expecting it, both Claude and Louis were stunned by the swiftness of the shot. *MacKenzie was out there already!*

They both slid, stumbled and ran rapidly down the hill.

Kyle was already running to his horse to continue the pursuit, knowing that there were only two of them now, but they were the more dangerous pair.

The Burleigh party had all heard Kyle's shot and Charles immediately stopped the wagon. They all witnessed their ex-butler's demise at the hill's summit.

Kyle was racing his horse around the northern side of the hill, hoping to catch Claude and Louis before they could reach their horses.

They had run down the hill quickly and jumped on their horses and lit out to the southeast, away from the wagon and Kyle. They were heading for the next hill to see if they could either get an advantage on the other side or get away.

Kyle rounded to the east side of the hill, saw them a half a mile ahead and slowed down immediately, realizing there was no point in chasing them now. He needed to go back and ensure the wagon was safe and he'd worry about them later.

He rode to Bristol's horse, took his reins, then led him away from the hill and headed west to the wagon. He'd let the butler stay where he was. The critters would find him soon enough.

Claude and Louis rode their horses harder than they needed to but didn't know that Kyle had already started back. They swung around the hill and rode for four miles before slowing down and looking at their backtrail and finding it empty.

"He's not comin'!" shouted Louis.

"He must have figured we'd ambush him or something."

"We are, aren't we?"

"We have to. Now the Sioux will know we're here, too. We got to act fast."

They stopped and let their horses rest while they figured out how to get Kyle MacKenzie.

———

Kyle approached the still unmoving wagon and spoke to Charles.

"Mister Burleigh, this is Mister Bristol's horse. I'll tie him off on the back of the wagon. They were setting up their ambush on the top of that first hill you can see in the distance. The other two made a break to the southeast. I'm sure they're already setting up a new ambush, just not from the top of a hill again."

"What will you do?"

"I'm going to head back and see if I can figure out what they're planning on doing next. I'll go out tonight if I have to."

Edmund couldn't resist himself and shouted, "You shot that man without warning!"

Kyle glanced at Edmund and said, "He'd been warned."

He turned his horse northeast and set off at a trot, uneasy about Claude and Louis. They weren't amateurs in this game. Sneaking up on them would be difficult at best, but Kyle knew he'd have to rely on instinct and a bit of guessing about their tactics, and it had better be a good one.

The wagon was moving forward again. No one had said anything to Edmund, but Edmund didn't care. If they wanted to behave like commoners, let them.

Kyle was two miles ahead and had slowed his horse to a walk. He passed the first hill and decided against tracking them. If they expected Kyle to track them, they'd know it would slow him to a walk. So, if they were going to set up another ambush, they would have to set it up well. It wouldn't be a standard drygulch either. It would have to be imaginative and different. Kyle knew it would be a difficult nut to crack, so he tried to think like Claude and Louis.

They expected Kyle to track them slowly which would enable them to build up a sizeable lead. With that gap, they could then loop around the hill and come back to take the wagon while he was behind them tracking.

Kyle suddenly realized that he was no longer the primary target. It would be the wagon. In addition to the food, the Burleighs still must have money with them for their arrival in Yankton. They could hit the wagon, kill the Burleighs and take what they wanted. They'd have the added firepower of what he had left on the packhorse, too. Kyle knew then that he'd have to go back quickly.

But if that was going to be their plan, he could use that as a trap. He just needed to bait the trap.

Kyle wheeled his horse around and rode back toward the wagon, leaving a clear trail behind him. It didn't matter and it might be better if they found it. He spied the wagon and quickly rode toward it, arriving five minutes later, an idea for the bait in his mind.

He pulled to a stop before the wagon and hurriedly said, "Mister Burleigh, I want you to stop the wagon here. I want everyone to get out of the wagon. Quickly."

Kyle leapt from his horse and tied it off as Charles, Emily and Abigail exited the wagon.

Kyle slipped under the wagon and removed the jack, then slid it under the rear axle.

"What are you doing, Mister MacKenzie?" asked Charles, as Kyle began jacking up the wagon.

"I'm going to remove the wheel and make it look as if the axle is broken. They'll see the wagon and think you're easy game. Then I'm going to ride off and let them think I'm still trailing them. It should draw them in. What I'll need everyone to do is to stand around looking helpless and irritated. If they start coming, point at them and hide behind the wagon. Don't overdramatize it. They'll spot it as a trap, which is what it is. I'll have to hide my horse and then set up my own ambush."

As he was talking, Kyle had the wagon's wheel off the ground, then began removing the right rear wheel. After he removed the safety pin and pulled off the wheel, he lowered the wagon to the ground and leaned the removed wheel at an angle above the axle.

"From a distance, it'll look like a broken axle. Make sure when you're clustered around the wagon that you're behind it, so they'll get a good look. You may as well have some lunch, but I've got to go."

He climbed back on his horse and rode quickly to the south to get out of sight, just in case they were already approaching. He didn't think they would be visible for at least another hour or two as they'd have to realize that he wasn't trailing and then come up with their plan, but he wasn't sure.

Once Kyle was gone, Charles looked at the wagon and said, "It does look like the axle is broken, even up close. Shall we have lunch as he recommended?"

"I'll take care of it, Father," said Emily.

"I'll help, Emily."

"Thank you, Mother."

Edmund stepped down and looked at the wagon.

"I think he's actually abandoned us. He'll let them kill us and then kill them, so he'll have everything."

No one even acknowledged his absurd comment as Emily and Abigail made some lunch.

Edmund didn't care what they thought anymore. This was a silly plan, but he hadn't anything else to offer. He still kept his horse saddled, just in case a hasty exit was necessary.

———

An hour and ten minutes later, Claude and Louis had passed around the hill beside the stream and turned west.

"How far away are they, do you think?" asked Louis.

"If they kept rolling, not more than three miles."

"Let's pick up the pace. If he's behind us, it won't do us any good to wait. If he's not, we'll know soon enough."

"You don't think he's still waiting, do you?"

"That boy has Indian blood. He can wait all day, but I don't think so. Not this time. He's trailing us. I can feel him."

"If he's behind us, what do we do, Claude?"

"We take out the wagon. Kill them all. Get as much food as we can and take their money. They must have at least thousand dollars, Louis."

"That's what I was thinking, too."

99

"Just keep your eyes open. If you see any smoke, drop down. Then we'll have him. He can't reload that Sharps very fast."

"Okay."

They picked up the pace heading west toward the wagon with the unbroken axle.

———

Kyle had found his spot for keeping the horse from sight just a mile or so east of the wagon and left the gelding hidden in a deep gully before he took a long drink of water from his canteen.

He left his Sharps in its scabbard and had only his Henry and his two pistols with him. His bow and arrows and the Spencer were with the packhorse. He had a dozen extra rounds for the Henry but shouldn't need that many. It had all fifteen rounds loaded in its magazine tube and knew he wouldn't have time to reload anyway. He was pretty sure that neither of those two knew he had a repeater as its scabbard had a covering flap.

He left his horse and began jogging back toward a point about eight hundred yards in front of the wagon, looking for a spot in the heavy prairie grass where he would drop to a prone shooting position then wait for the sound of horses.

There was a good crop of prairie grass already, and he was confident that they wouldn't spot him until it was too late. He just hoped that they followed his trail to the wagon and were so anxious to get the food and supplies that they wouldn't be looking for him. His biggest concern was that Edmund might point him out to Claude and Louis, even if it meant that the others would die. He didn't doubt for a moment that the man would run.

He kept jogging at a good, even pace to get to a good shooting location.

"There he is, Father!" shouted Emily, pointing to the distant figure running through the grass.

"I wonder where he could be going. I don't see any places to hide ahead."

"I'm just going to watch," replied Emily.

She was excited watching Kyle as he sped across the ground and suddenly, just disappeared from view.

"He fell!" she cried.

Her father replied, "I don't think so, Emily. I think that's where he'll be if they show up. Well, lunch is over, let's pretend we're upset about the broken axle."

————

Claude and Louis had slowed down again when Claude suddenly spotted the wagon.

"There it is, Louis. About a mile and half southwest. Why are they stopped?"

"I don't know, but we don't have to worry about them. It's that green-eyed bastard I'm worried about. He shot that butler from six hundred yards. I don't see him anywhere, but I don't like it, Claude."

Claude turned in the saddle and said, "He's not behind us yet, Louis. I don't care where he is now. He won't have the time to catch us before we get to the wagon."

"Let's go, then," said Louis as they picked up the pace.

They continued to ride and when they were within a mile, Louis spied the wagon's problem.

"Claude, their axle is broken. They don't look very happy, either," he said as he grinned.

"So, where is MacKenzie? I don't see him anywhere."

"I think he's still trackin' behind us, Claude. Havin' to follow us in that stream would slow him down."

Despite the empty prairie, Claude was still skittish and said, "Wait a minute, Louis. This is too easy, don't you think?"

Louis thought about it and replied, "Maybe. Maybe not. I don't see his horse anywhere. I say we rush them. If he's nearby with that Sharps, it'll be an impossible shot and he'd only get one chance."

"That's true. Okay. That's what we'll do. We'll just rush them. Get your rifle ready. We'll fire once but we'll use the pistols when we get there."

"Shoot the men. I want the women."

"So, do I, Louis. Let's go."

The Burleigh party had seen them at the same time they had spotted the wagon and had been anxiously watching them approach.

"They're getting closer," said Charles as he pointed at the two men as Kyle had directed.

"Where is that damned Indian?" questioned Edmund loudly.

Emily wanted to scream at him for the remark but held off as they all watched from behind the wagon.

Kyle knew they were within a half mile and would be within range soon, so he reached over with his right thumb and cocked the Henry's hammer.

"They've spotted us!" Claude shouted. "Let's go!"

Claude and Louis began their charge from a mile out.

Kyle heard the shout and then the pounding hooves as they approached. He waited, listening and calculating the closing distance and estimated they'd pass just thirty or forty yards in front of him. He waited…waited…then it was time. He popped up and drew the Henry to his shoulder.

Claude saw him first and rapidly tried to swing his Burnside to bear on the sudden threat.

Kyle fired and levered in a second round as his first bullet struck Claude in the right side of his abdomen, just below the ribs.

Louis fired his rifle as Kyle fired his second round, but both missed.

Just after Louis had fired, Claude had fallen from his horse as Louis turned his horse quickly toward Kyle, dropping his rifle to the ground and pulling his pistol as he did.

Kyle took more careful aim as both fired his third shot. Kyle was levering in a fourth round when Louis toppled awkwardly to the prairie, the left side of his neck ripped apart by the Henry's .44 caliber round.

Kyle ran to Louis first and saw his glassy eyes before turning and jogging to a still-breathing Claude Bernard.

Kyle reached the dying man and looked down at him without sympathy.

Claude looked up at Kyle. "You killed me, mon amie. Will you bury us, me and Louis? Maybe say some words?"

"Aye, Claude. I'll do that."

"You are a good man, Kyle MacKenzie, even though I tried to kill you. At least now, I won't be hungry."

"No oysters in hell, Claude."

Claude laughed twice and then as blood gurgled from his mouth, died.

Kyle went through his pockets and found the fifty dollars that Charles Burleigh had paid him when they left Omaha City, then stuffed it into his jacket pocket. He picked up his pistol and removed his gunbelt, then he walked over to Louis, found his fifty dollars, and after pushing it into his jacket pocket, took his gunbelt and pistol as well. He left the Burnside carbines on the prairie, he never liked them anyway. Let them rust.

He walked over to their two horses, hung the gunbelts around the saddle horns and led them back toward the wagon. That threat had been eliminated, now it was just the Sioux he had to worry about for the next hundred and forty miles.

He reached the wagon and tied one of the horses behind the wagon with Bristol's horse and the packhorse as everyone just stared at him.

He looked at Charles and said calmly, "I'm going to mount the wheel and then retrieve my horse then I'm going to bury those two. You can keep going if you'd like and I'll catch up to you when I'm done."

No one said anything as he began jacking the wagon, then greased the axle while the wheel was off, slid it back on and put the nut and pin back in position and lowered it to the ground before storing the jack. He pulled a spare shirt out of Claude's saddlebag and wiped his hands clean before taking a spade from his packhorse. He mounted Bristol's horse because it hadn't been ridden hard and rode to where his horse was patiently waiting in the gully. He had to coax it out of the gully and then rode to the spot where Louis and Claude lay twenty feet apart.

Kyle dismounted, then hitched his horse to a scraggly bush and tied Bristol's horse to his. He took the spade and began digging. The wagon was approaching with Edmund riding outside near Emily. Kyle glanced at them and found himself jealous and wondered why he would be jealous of a man riding next to his wife?

He quickly dropped his eyes and concentrated on the job at hand as he continued to dig. After almost an hour, he had a hole big enough for the two men. He slid Louis in first and then Claude. At the last minute, before he started shoveling the dirt back on, he walked to their two rifles, tossed them on top of the bodies, then began shoveling and soon had them under the earth.

The wagon had stopped near the burial site and Charles held it in place with the hand brake while Kyle finished the job.

Kyle was sweating heavily and breathing hard when he finished, so he had to take a break. Then he ran his fingers through his long, jet black wet hair to straighten it out somewhat and laid down the shovel.

He stood over their graves, and fulfilling his promise to Claude, said, "Here are Louis Martin and Claude Bernard, Lord. They didn't start out as bad men. They just took the easy way, the lazy way, to get what they wanted. They were given a chance again to change their ways but came back to steal what was not theirs. They are yours now. It is in Your judgement, as it is for all of us, where they spend eternity."

Edmund was shocked when Kyle had finished. He had delivered the eulogy in impeccable French.

Kyle hadn't intended to do it to make a point with Edmund, he did it because the men were French, and he thought it was appropriate.

Kyle walked up to Charles, pulled the hundred dollars out of his pocket and handed it to him as he said, "This is yours I believe. They surely didn't earn it."

Charles took the money, then Kyle walked back, slid the spade onto the packhorse and mounted his own horse again.

He stopped at the front of the wagon and said, "I'll just ride about a half mile ahead again. We have about another hundred and forty miles to go."

Charles stared at the gravesite and said, "Mister MacKenzie, I'm sorry it had to come to this. I should never have hired those men."

"Mister Burleigh, that isn't what got them killed. It was their greed. Don't worry about them at all."

Then he wheeled his horse away and took his position at the point as the wagon followed.

He was almost four hundred yards in front when he finally pulled his canteen and emptied its contents down his parched throat. His clean buckskins were no longer close to being clean.

———

Even as the wagon was leaving the impromptu gravesite, word had filtered down from Yankton that the hated Walter Burleigh's relations were heading toward Yankton overland and reached the ears of Walking Buffalo, a war chief of the Santee Sioux.

CHAPTER 4

They were well into the hill country when Kyle pointed out the night's campsite. He unsaddled all the horses and tossed the saddles of the three spare horses into the wagon. The unexpected acquisition created a whole new option that he'd discuss with Mister Burleigh shortly. He unloaded the packhorse and set up the tent, figuring that taking it down was a task that they could handle.

He had the fire pit dug and ready for use when he approached Charles.

"Mister Burleigh, may I speak to you for a minute, please?" he asked.

"Of course. What do you need?"

"We now have enough horses and saddles for everyone. Now, it would be a lot faster to travel without the wagon, plus we'd have freedom of movement should we run into a problem. The only things that might be a cause of concern is that neither Mrs. Burleigh nor Mrs. Falstaff are dressed for riding and I doubt if they have riding attire with them.

"The other problem is that I doubt if either of them, or maybe even you have ridden for great distances. I leave it to you to decide which way we go. If we continue using the wagon, it'll take another eight days to reach Yankton, and that's if we don't have any problems like wide creeks or broken axles. If we ride, we can be there in four and the obstacles are less of a problem."

"That is tempting. I haven't ridden for long distances in quite a while, and I'm sure neither my wife nor daughter have either. But I'll broach the subject. Saving four days would be a real temptation."

"Let me know. I'm going to leave and set up my guard position, but I'll stop by and talk to you sometime tonight before you turn in."

"Aren't you going to join us for dinner?"

"No, sir. I'll just grab something while I'm keeping guard."

"Mister MacKenzie, I hope you don't think that we all hold the same wretched views that my son-in-law expressed to you."

"No, sir, I'm sure that you don't. I just don't wish to have to put your family in another uncomfortable position. I'll be back later."

Kyle turned and left the campsite then soon found a good observation location on a nearby hill that wasn't very large but gave him an unimpeded view of the campsite and both north and south for almost a mile. He sat on the summit with his field glasses, his canteen, some beef jerky and hard tack. He began scanning the terrain to memorize the shapes and positions of shrubs and trees, so if anything changed, he'd know.

Emily and Abigail were making dinner, and Abigail noticed Emily occasionally glancing at Kyle on the distant hill.

"Emily, as much as it pains me to tell you, you're a married woman now."

Emily continued to stir the pot as she said, "I know, Mother. But this is so very difficult for me. Being with Edmund was always boring, but I was a dutiful daughter and married him

109

because he was of good family. He was inoffensive at least. But now, I've developed a deep loathing of Edmund. Not just because of what he said to Mister MacKenzie, but because of everything else as his true nature is revealing itself. I cringe when Edmund tries to touch me.

"When I see Mister MacKenzie, I see everything I've ever imagined I would want in a husband. He's brave and strong, yet gentle and kind. He's intelligent and has a wonderful sense of humor. When we talk, Mother, we really speak to each other, and when I look into those marvelous green eyes, I see everything deep into his soul, and all that I see I find inspirational. I believe he feels the same way.

"But next week, we'll be in Yankton and we'll be civilized again. I'll be a married twenty-one-year-old woman who would rather be with someone not her husband, a man who would be hundreds of miles away in a place I won't even know. It will hurt, Mother. It will hurt for the rest of my life."

Abigail had seen it coming. It had begun as just admiration, but it kept growing quickly and deeply. She felt almost as bad for Emily as Emily did for herself and felt partly to blame for pushing the marriage with Edmund.

"Has Mister MacKenzie expressed any feelings for you?"

"No, Mother, he hasn't, and I haven't solicited any, nor will I."

"Emily, I really do understand. Marriage can be a terrible thing if you are married to someone you don't love. I have been fortunate because I love your father very much, and he loves me. I wish I had an answer for you, but I don't. All you can do is let the future arrive."

"I know, Mother. Thank you for listening. It makes it better."

"I'll always listen to you, Emily."

They finished cooking and were soon joined by Charles and Edmund.

"Where is the Indian? Off sitting in his teepee or something?" Edmund said as he chuckled.

A very irritated Charles snapped, "Mister MacKenzie, Edmund, is about a half a mile west on the top of that hill keeping us all safe. He isn't joining us for meals, so the rest of us don't have to worry about a confrontation between the two of you."

Edmund smiled and asked, "He's worried about confronting me?"

Charles was getting angry, and snapped, "No, Edmund, he was worried that he may get us all upset if he had to kill you."

Edmund's smile vanished as he asked, "He said he would kill me?"

"He said that if you had persisted in your diatribe against his mother much longer, he would have had to take action. You would be buried under the prairie if he did, Edmund. Do not doubt that for a second."

"What a crude buffoon! To threaten me with assassination just for making some comments which he found offense."

"We all found offense with them, Edmund. Mister MacKenzie's forbearance marked him as a true gentleman. Now I want to hear no more about it. I have something important to discuss."

Abigail quickly said, "Go ahead, dear."

"Thank you, Abigail. Mister MacKenzie has pointed out that with the demise of the three men, we now have an abundance of horses and saddles. If we decide to leave the wagon and ride to Yankton it would cut our remaining journey in half. The only issues would be the lack of appropriate riding apparel for the women and the lack of long-term riding experience by myself, Emily and Abigail. I'd like to know what you think."

Emily was truly torn about the subject. It would mean she'd be losing Kyle in less than a hundred hours, but if she were mounted, maybe she could spend some time talking to him. She held off making any decision until her mother had made hers, which came quickly.

"I'll ride a horse, Charles. Emily and I can adjust our clothing accordingly. It won't be exactly ladylike, but what has been on this journey?"

"What about the trunk?" asked Edmund.

"I don't know. I'll ask Mister MacKenzie when he returns in a little while. Emily?"

"I'll ride a horse. It's been a while and I know I'll be sore, but I get sore riding on that hard seat, too."

"Alright. I'll tell Mister MacKenzie in a little while."

Kyle had seen them talking and was already rearranging supplies in his mind. He could use the two draft horses as packhorses. He just needed to use the existing panniers more efficiently. He could use the leather straps and reins of the harness to fashion jury-rigged pack saddles. All three of the dead men had bedrolls which could serve as combination saddle blankets and panniers. He'd have to cut them in the middle. One half would be the saddle blanket and the other half would be a pannier. It would take some serious imagination, but it would work. He'd feel a lot safer knowing they could get away more quickly if they came under attack too.

Once he had the logistics settled, he found his mind wandering back to Emily. The rush of jealousy seeing her with Edmund had awakened him to his growing feelings for her.

He thought it was just a waste of emotion. She was such a wonderful person. Beyond her physical gifts, which were plenty, she was a considerate, thoughtful woman with a sharp mind, but he knew that he had to stop thinking of her that way. She was married to that horrid excuse of a man and that was the end of it.

He'd be taking her and her family to Yankton in a few days and then resupplying and heading to Fort Sully. That was all. But Kyle found himself still looking at her before he suddenly stood, angry with himself for useless mooning and turned to face the north.

———

In the Santee camp, Walking Buffalo was having a meeting with some of his war captains.

"The Indian Agent, Burleigh, has a relative coming across the prairie from the west. He had been on the boat that sank near Omaha City, but he hired a wagon and two guides and is coming to Yankton. It is not a big undertaking. His party has two women and two men. The guides are known to us and are no problem. I recommend we destroy this party to send a message to Burleigh. I will send a war party of eight warriors. Gray Hawk, choose seven warriors. We will send out four scouts. When they find the wagon, they will send up smoke."

"I will do as you order, Walking Buffalo. How many rifles may we take with us?"

"Four should be plenty. Make sure you select warriors who are good shooters."

"I will. I will have my war party ready to leave tomorrow. We will travel west and wait on the smoke."

After they had gone, Walking Buffalo called in four warrior scouts.

"When you find the party, send up smoke. The message should be simple. Gray Hawk will know the direction by whichever of you sees them."

"What if they have abandoned or lost the wagon?" asked Black Crow.

"Send the signal saying distance and on horse."

They all nodded with the instructions and left his lodge. This would be a simple, quick raid.

———

Kyle returned to the camp two hours after they finished eating and headed for Charles.

"Mister Burleigh, what's the decision?"

"They all voted to ride."

"Good. I've already come up with a plan to move things. It will take a couple of hours, but we'll make that up quickly."

"I was asked about the trunk."

"The trunk itself we leave behind, but we can take all of its contents."

"I'm sure that's all they were worried about. I think Emily left you some food in the pot. She doesn't think you got enough to eat."

Kyle smiled and said, "She's probably right. Tell her I appreciate it. I'll finish it off and then clean the pot."

"Thank you for everything, Mister MacKenzie."

"You're welcome, Mister Burleigh."

Charles smiled at the young man, then turned and headed for the tent.

Kyle took out a plate and filled it with the stew from the pot. It was very good, even though it was only lukewarm. He finished it quickly and took the pot and plate to the stream to wash them.

As he was washing, he kept his eyes on the pot and said quietly, "Good evening, Mrs. Falstaff."

Emily was startled that he had heard her quiet approach and identified her, but said, "Hello, Mister MacKenzie. Was the food all right?"

"It was excellent," he said as he continued to scrub the pot.

He knew it was clean, but he was afraid to turn around.

Emily knelt and then sat on her heels as she asked, "Mister MacKenzie, why did you speak French over the grave?"

"Because they were French. I felt it was the right thing to do."

"Edmund was very angry when he heard you speak French."

"Why? Was he afraid I would spread his secret?"

"Yes."

"Are you here to make sure that I don't, Mrs. Falstaff?"

"No. I'm here because I like talking to you."

Kyle, against his better judgement, turned and looked at Emily and soon realized that it was a mistake. Her eyes said it all, and he knew that his did as well, so he quickly looked away.

Emily knew at the same time and had a totally different reaction when she felt a flood of warmth rush through her that made her shiver.

After a few seconds to recover, she asked quietly, "Are we really going to be there in four days?"

"We should be. Even allowing for a run-in with some unfriendly Sioux."

"Do you think there will be a run-in?"

"If it's only one, then we'll be lucky."

"I suppose I have to get back before I'm missed. I said I had to use the privacy bushes."

"Father Lapierre would give you two Our Fathers penance for that," he said as he smiled.

"The good sisters would issue their own penance with their oak rods," she said and then laughed.

He was almost magnetically drawn to look into her eyes again and said, "Life can be difficult, Mrs. Falstaff."

She stared into his green eyes and replied softly, "It can be cruel, Mister MacKenzie."

She rocked forward and stood, looking down at Kyle one more time before trotting back to the tent.

Kyle watched her leave, blew out his breath, then stood with the clean pot and plate and walked back to the wagon where he put them both on the wagon's bed, then took his bedroll and walked fifty feet beyond the wagon and unrolled it. He didn't get inside, but just sat on top and thought about the next hundred hours.

———

The next morning, Kyle was hard at work early, before anyone was awake. He saddled all the horses, even Edmund's, which left the two draft horses as the only ones unencumbered. He began cutting the leather straps from the harness and reins, giving him a lot of material. Then he went to work on the three excess bedrolls. He sliced the top layer, not in half as it turned out, but closer to a sixty-forty cut. The forty would be the horse blankets and the sixty the panniers.

He used the straps from the harness to fashion straps for two of the makeshift panniers, running them completely around the pannier and through some slots he cut into them with his knife. He used two of the long reins to get the job done. Then he made a third strap for added strength in the middle from the harness. That gave one draft horse two heavy panniers. The second one had a pannier on one side and Kyle used leather from the harness to create loops for his spade, axe and ammunition pouches as a counterbalance for the last of the newly created panniers. He just needed to load everything after breakfast. He'd load the big tent on the draft horse carrying the spade and axe, then he'd cover both of the new, open panniers with the tarps. They'd been lucky with an absence of rain and doubted if it would hold up. He was surprised that he got it all done so quickly, too.

He walked over to the fire pit and restarted the fire, then took the coffeepot down to the creek, filled it and had the water heating as he took out food for breakfast. He was reviewing all he had done and wondered if he missed anything.

As he was making his inspection the Burleighs and Falstaffs began filtering out of the tent and heading for a private area.

A few minutes later, Emily and Abigail were making breakfast, as Charles examined Kyle's engineering and said, "You've been busy, Mister MacKenzie."

"Yes, sir. All we need is to have the trunk emptied, the remaining food from the wagon put into one of the makeshift panniers then pack the tent and your sleeping bags. We should be ready to start riding within an hour."

"That's outstanding."

"I was surprised how well it worked to be honest."

They ate breakfast, and Kyle found it almost impossible not to glance over at Emily. Whenever he did, he seemed to find her looking his way, which was disconcerting. He ate quickly and brought the plate down to the stream, cleaned it and headed back to the wagon.

After returning his plate, he headed over to take down the tent while the others ate. He slid both of the double sleeping bags from the tent, looking at the one that Emily and Edmund used and felt that twinge of jealousy again before he continued.

Kyle had the tent folded and ready for packing five minutes later then dragged it over to the packhorse. He began adding the small amount of remaining food and cooking gear into one of the new panniers before he emptied the coffeepot and took the cooking grate and put them in the opposite pannier before walking back to the wagon.

He approached Charles and said, "All we need now is to get the tent loaded and the contents of the trunk packed in the new panniers."

"Okay, let's get that done," he replied.

Kyle nodded, then leapt up into the wagon bed and slid the trunk to the back of the wagon before dropping lightly to the ground. He lowered the trunk to the ground and stood back to let them handle moving the contents.

Abigail opened the trunk, and Kyle was curious as what was inside, expecting tuxedos and ballroom gowns. She took out a leather satchel and handed it to Charles, then it was a series of velvet-wrapped items that he assumed were family treasures, as well as more clothing. They left much of the fancy clothes in the trunk even though there was room for some of it, which would have surprised him much more a couple of days earlier.

Charles, Abigail and Emily began packing what they had selected into the two panniers. Charles placed the leather satchel in last, and then wedged it in to keep it secure. Kyle assumed that it contained whatever cash he'd taken on the journey and had inspired Claude and Louis in the first place.

Kyle put the two sleeping bags on one of the draft horses and tied them down before he lifted the heavy canvas tent with a loud grunt and shoved it on top of the panniers. He covered them all with the tarps and lashed them down.

After checking that everything was balanced and secured, he turned to Charles and said, "Alright, we're ready to ride. If anyone gets uncomfortable and feels the need to stop, let me know. I'll be out front, but closer than before because you're on horseback."

They mounted the horses and Kyle led them northeast at a slow trot, but they still made much better time without the wagon. They continued riding at a normal, smooth pace as Kyle kept his focus on the front but would check their backtrail every ten minutes or so. They rode for four hours until Kyle found a nice stream and grassy area for a noon break.

The ladies stepped down gingerly, as did Charles, and soon each of them was stretching and rubbing sore body parts. Kyle noticed and smiled slightly, knowing that none of them would have dared display such discomfort when he first met them. He also caught a few malicious glances from Edmund, which surprised him somewhat because he hadn't said one word to Emily the entire morning. That would soon change.

Kyle just grabbed some beef jerky as he led his horse and the packhorses to the water, and while he was drinking, Emily brought her horse beside him. He knew he was pleasantly trapped because he couldn't just yank his horse away while its muzzle was buried in the water.

"How are you faring, Mrs. Falstaff?" he asked trying not to look her way.

"Better than I thought, Mister MacKenzie."

Edmund appeared on the other side but said nothing as Charles and Abigail arrived just seconds later.

"How are you and Mrs. Burleigh doing?" Kyle asked as he looked at Charles.

"I'm all right, but I believe Mrs. Burleigh is having a hard go of it."

"Will you both be able to go on or do you want to stop for a while?"

"We'll go on."

"That's good. We're making excellent time. We're already further this morning than we had gone in any day with the wagon. We'll be under a hundred miles to go when we stop tonight, I believe."

"That's very good."

He looked at Abigail, smiled and said, "Mrs. Burleigh, don't let the boys make your decision for you. If you want to stay for a little while, you just let me know. I believe that your husband will honor your decision, as will I."

Abigail smiled back and replied, "Thank you, Mister MacKenzie, but even though I'll admit to having a particularly painful posterior, I'll patiently plug along."

Kyle laughed lightly, then replied, "Perfect."

They had a quick, cold lunch and were on the trail less than forty minutes after stopping. Kyle had checked all of the horses' legs and shoes and thought that some might lose a shoe or two before they reached their destination.

In the mid-afternoon, Kyle saw smoke on the eastern horizon. It was ahead and slightly to his right about six miles away. He read the smoke, understood that they'd been spotted and would have visitors soon. He was sure that there was a line of scouts on hills with visibility covering a thirty-mile front. With the scouts out there keeping an eye on them, there was no way out without being tracked.

———

Each of the warrior scouts, including the one who had sent the signal, hadn't been told the details of the party, just that they were using a wagon. They were to report the distance and whether they had the wagon or not. If he had been fully informed or added more details in the smoke, he may have sent a signal that there were only five travelers, and they were being led by the Green-Eyed Devil and not the two Frenchmen. It was a fatal flaw in intelligence and initiative.

Kyle did a quick examination of the terrain ahead before he turned, rode back to the group and wheeled his horse next to Charles.

"The Sioux must have been waiting for us with the wagon. They just sent up smoke saying where we are and that we don't have the wagon."

"How would they know we're coming and have a wagon?"

"I'll talk about that later, but we have to act quickly before the war party arrives."

Charles nodded and asked, "What do you want us to do?"

"The smoke was about six miles away, so if we turn north, behind that hill over there, they'll lose us until we ride into the view of another scout. If he doesn't report us in view, they'll know we're behind the hill."

Edmund, Abigail and Emily had ridden nearby and listened to the exchange before Edmund said, "We should just go north and keep going until we can pass around them."

"They'll have scouts spread out across the wide area. If we go north, they'll just send up more smoke and drive us as far as the Missouri River if they need to. By then it'll be dark, and we'll be in much worse shape. Our best bet is to go behind that tall hill to the north and prepare a defense."

"We can't defend against a whole army!" shouted Edmund.

"It won't be an army, or even a company of warriors. I'd guess that they'll send no more than ten warriors. They probably only expect two shooters, but they don't know it's me. They think they're dealing with Claude and Louis."

"How would they know that, Mister MacKenzie?" asked Charles.

Kyle quickly replied, "They have intelligence networks just like any other army. They probably knew you were coming from someone in Yankton. Can I guess you sent a telegram to your cousin telling him that you were on your way with a wagon and who was leading the way?"

"I did. It was the last thing I did before we left."

"The news would probably be common knowledge in Yankton by now. The Yanktonai Sioux would know and pass that information to other groups. One group, probably the Santee Sioux, decided to act on it. We're in their area now. As I said before, the Santee aren't exactly pleased with your cousin. They claim that he was shorting them on their promised rations and money. They've filed complaints with the Bureau of Indian Affairs but haven't had any of the shortages corrected."

"Do you believe their complaints are justified?"

"I do. It's a common occurrence. We write treaties and promise all sorts of things. The Federal government doesn't really pay attention or doesn't provide the funding. The local Indian agents have been known to line their pockets with the difference between the amount they were authorized to spend and the amount they actually spent. Some don't but many do. For the Santee to go to the extreme of filing a complaint with the Federal government means it's almost guaranteed to be true."

Charles digested the information but then asked, "How will we set up our defense?"

"First, I'm going to need two of you to at least learn to shoot pistols. There are two extra revolvers now. I can load them with all six cylinders filled and leave them here. They're easy to fire, just pull back the hammer, point it at what you want to shoot and pull the trigger. Can I guess you and Mister Falstaff will be the two to handle the pistols?"

"I'll take one," Charles replied then turned to his son-in-law. "Edmund?"

Edmund thought about it and momentarily thought of shooting Kyle. He'd seen how Emily had been looking at him, but he knew he'd lose that contest. He'd never shot a pistol before because gentlemen didn't shoot pistols, not revolvers, anyway. They were so plebian and undignified, but he couldn't appear cowardly either.

"Yes, I'll take one."

Kyle had glimpsed that fleeting thought in Edmund's eyes and suspected that Edmund may take advantage of having a loaded pistol but ignored it for the time being. He had more important things on his mind.

"Alright. Here's what I'm going to do. We're going to tie the horses together, so none of them run off when it gets noisy. We'll strip them of their saddles and equipment to serve as a redoubt at the base of the hill. I'll hitch the horses about fifty feet away and up a bit from the base of the hill. They won't like it, but they'll get used to it. I'm going to go up near the top with my two rifles and the carbine, along with my bow and arrows. I'll stay just below the top, so I'll be within two hundred feet of where you will be and can still sneak a peek over the top from time to time. When I see them coming, I'll toss a rock down to you to let you know they're on their way, then I'll slide down closer to you, so I'll be more accurate."

He paused and asked if everyone understood the setup. Emily and the Burleighs nodded, but Edmund just stared past him looking at the horses. Kyle ignored him and continued.

"I'm going to wait for them to make the first move, then I need to be the first one to shoot and I'll take out as many as I can. Once they realize that they're dealing with me and not Claude and Louis, they'll concentrate on me, but they might send a couple of warriors in your direction as well.

"When they do, I want you both to hold your fire until the last moment, and only if you have to fire. If one of them gets past me, your job will be to protect the women. Wait until they're within twenty feet or less. For an inexperienced shooter, that's about as far as you could expect to hit a moving target. The closer they are the more likely you'll get a hit. Hopefully, neither one of you will even have to pull a trigger.

"I'll slide down just a bit with the Spencer or the Henry and start shooting long before they get that close. If I get half of them, they may break off to regroup. Once they start leaving, let them go. I'll take care of any stragglers, then I'll get back on top and see if any more are coming. They may try to send someone over the top to get at our rear, too. I'll take him out if he comes."

"Won't they have rifles?" asked Charles.

"Some will, but most won't. They don't have a lot to spare, and almost no repeaters like my Henry. For a job like this they won't have more than half of them armed with rifles, and they'll be single shot weapons, like the Burnsides that Claude and Louis carried. We'll actually have a considerable firepower advantage."

"Alright, Mister MacKenzie, let's start getting ready," Charles said.

They turned north and as Kyle watched the smoke announce their change of direction, he watched until the location was hidden behind the hill.

After a couple of hundred yards, he pulled up, dismounted and everyone else stepped down.

It didn't take long to get the horses stripped as all of them, even Edmund hastily began dragging saddles, packs and the tent to where Kyle thought was a good position. When finished, the saddle and supply redoubt was only about three feet tall and eight feet long, but it was better than nothing.

Kyle loaded the sixth chamber in Claude's and Louis' Colt New army pistols and gave one to Charles and the second to Edmund, then showed them how to cock and fire the pistol. He moved the horses about thirty yards north of their redoubt, pounded one of the tent stakes into the ground, then tied his horse to the stake and the rest to a trail rope linked to his gelding. He knew if they panicked, they could yank it out easily, but just hoped they would only get nervous. He knew his horse wouldn't panic and was counting on him to calm the others who may not have been near so much gunfire.

Then he took two trips to the top of the hill moving his weapons to an acceptably close position, took a glance back down the hill at the redoubt and the Burleighs, then he scrambled to the summit of the hill, spent almost a minute scanning the horizon but didn't see any movement. He was doing some quick calculations from the moment he'd seen the first smoke and estimated that the war party would arrive about two hours after being notified of their location.

He hadn't mentioned it to the Burleighs, but his biggest concern was that they might be angry enough to send two war parties and attack from both flanks. He knew that if they did, they'd all be dead soon.

Once he was satisfied that they had some time, he slid back down the hill past his rifles and bow, and soon reached the redoubt.

He popped to his feet and said, "There's no one coming yet, so we need to get something to eat and have some water while we can and keep your canteens near. I know that there's no privacy, but if you need to empty your bladders, now's your chance."

Emily glanced at Abigail, but neither took Kyle's suggestion.

"How much light do we have?" asked Charles.

"About three more hours, maybe less. They'll come soon, probably within the hour. They'll attack at night, but just like any army, prefer to fight in the daytime when they can see who they're fighting."

———

Gray Hawk was riding his horse in advance of the other seven warriors, proud to have been given the assignment. He knew that the Santee were discussing peace terms with the governor of the territory, but they refused to get rid of that Burleigh. They had even elected him to a higher office where he would have more power, and now they were bringing in another one.

Gray Hawk would strike a blow against him and do it gladly. He wasn't worried about the two Frenchmen and even knew what kind of rifles they carried. His party would only have to face two rifle shots before they were close enough for the guide to use their pistols and by then, it would be too late. With their four rifles, they would have the advantage. He had told his four shooters to wait until they fired and then shoot at the smoke.

Then it would get to close combat, and he and his warriors excelled at close combat. They had passed the scout an hour ago and had been told that the party had gone behind the hill that he was now approaching. He had thought of a two-pronged attack, one from the north and the other the south of the hill, but shifted in favor of a single wave, but in two stages.

First, the shooters would ride around the side of the hill and expose themselves, once Gray Wolf heard the two guides fire their rifles, then his four shooters would fire before the other four would charge around the cover of the hill with their war cries. Whites were always afraid of their war cries and with good reason.

―――――

Kyle was lying in the grass at the top of the hill and saw them approaching when they passed around the opposite hill, then slid back to his weapons, stopped, then tossed a fist-sized rock down toward the redoubt.

Charles looked up and Kyle showed him eight fingers. Charles nodded and whispered to the others that Kyle had counted eight Sioux.

Kyle took his Henry and cocked the hammer, then slid down the hill another eighty feet to a spot with a better foothold. It was also closer to the redoubt.

128

He saw Emily curled up near her mother looking up at him and smiled at her as she smiled back. Abigail smiled at him as well, and neither woman showed any sign of fear. Kyle was impressed with their courage as neither had any personal protection. He should have given them Louis and Clyde's knives, but it was too late now.

Kyle quickly shifted his focus back to the upcoming attack. There were eight warriors and they were all coming from the south side. He wanted all eight to come in one attack, not piecemeal, because if only some came in, the others would know they were dealing with a repeater and the Green-Eyed Devil, which would cause them to chance their tactics.

Gray Hawk had them riding slowly west in a line with a gap between him and the second warrior as they circled the southern side of the hill but looking to the north. The instant that he spotted the party hunkered down behind the redoubt, he pulled his horse back and they all turned and walked their horses a few yards away to stay out of view.

He was sure that he hadn't been spotted but was surprised that they had set up a defensive position. Seeing the hastily constructed redoubt had taken his attention away from a more detailed evaluation of their position, so he hadn't seen Kyle further up the hill, his buckskins blending in well with the tall grass.

Gray Hawk had his warriors in a circle and said, "They are waiting for us on the side of the hill behind a weak collection of saddles."

He Who Runs asked, "Did you see the Frenchmen?"

"No, but they are all bunched together behind their useless protection."

"Do you want me to go around the hill and look from the top?"

Gray Hawk thought about it, but the sun was too low in the sky to take the time for additional reconnaissance, so he shook his head and said, "No. It is not necessary. Our plan is a good one."

His decision made, he and his band moved closer to where he'd spotted the hated Burleigh people, then had his four shooters lined up then spread apart to begin the attack.

When their rifles were all cocked and ready to fire, Gray Hawk screamed his war cry and the first four warriors shot away while Gray Hawk and the other three waited for the sound of gunfire to add their voices to the mayhem.

The four rifle-carrying warriors were all echoing Gray Hawk's chilling cry as their horses thundered around the hill at the redoubt, now just a hundred yards away.

Charles and Edmund saw the Sioux start their attack and Charles held his fire as he was almost fascinated at the sight, but Edmund panicked at the pending danger and began to fire his pistol at eighty yards.

The Sioux, expecting a single shot, all opened fire on Edmund, and the ground around him exploded as the bullets all smashed into the earth, but none struck Edmund or anything else. The gunsmoke hanging around the redoubt was already impressive as Edmund continued to fire.

Gray Hawk heard what he expected to hear, two shots from the whites and four from his shooters and launched his attack of the second batch of warriors to support the first group. They added their voices to the sound of pistol fire and their brothers cries as they charged.

Kyle was seething over Edmund's premature firing but didn't wait for the second group of attackers because the first group was too close to the redoubt now. He began his defense by putting his first shot into one of the first four warriors. The one closest to Kyle grabbed his neck in shock before toppling off the left side of his charging horse.

Kyle fired again and missed, before cycling the lever and firing again. He didn't miss on his third shot, as the second Sioux warrior felt the bullet crash into his chest and fell to the prairie.

Kyle heard the second group getting closer, but still had work to do on the first four who were now just a few yards from the redoubt. His fourth shot struck one of the warriors in the hip, but he kept riding, so Kyle had to finish him off with his fifth.

It was then that Gray Hawk looked up on the face of the hill, saw Kyle's gunsmoke and knew he'd been given incorrect information. *The white-eyes had a repeater!* He shouted for them to regroup, but the fourth warrior had just fallen from his horse with Kyle's sixth shot, and now he shifted to the second group.

Gray Hawk had turned his horse and was hit in the left upper chest by Kyle's seventh shot. It wasn't immediately fatal, but he knew he would die yet was determined to kill Kyle or die trying, so he whipped his horse around and began riding up the hill.

Kyle's attention had already shifted from Gray Hawk to a second warrior of Gray Hawk's group when he saw the leader charging up the hill with his war tomahawk over his head.

Kyle could have shot him easily, but instead, laid down his hot Henry, pulled out his ten-inch long Bowie knife and just stood facing the oncoming warrior.

Gray Hawk recognized the challenge, slipped from his horse's back, letting the animal turn and stumble back down the hill.

The two remaining warriors on the flat ground recognized that only the man on the hill was a threat, so they pulled back from the attack, still fifty yards from the redoubt, and watched their captain advance with his war tomahawk raised and the white man with the long hair and green eyes face him with his knife. They both knew who he was and understood that Gray Hawk was fighting the Green-Eyed Devil.

"You are not one of the Frenchmen," Gray Hawk said in Sioux, his breath coming hard as blood filled his left lung.

"No, I am the Green-Eyed Devil. You are a brave warrior and I am sorry to have to meet you when you are not at your best."

"It is the only way. It is how it was written."

"Yes."

Gray Hawk screamed his last war cry and lunged at Kyle who plunged his knife into Gray Hawk with his right hand before he caught him with his left arm, then lowered Gray Hawk slowly to the ground.

He then looked down the hill and in Sioux, shouted, "Come and take your leader. I will not shoot either of you. The fight is over, and he needs to return to your village."

Kyle shouted to the Burleighs to hold their fire before removing his knife from Gray Hawk and wiping the blood on the warrior's buckskins. It wasn't a sign of disrespect, but to return it to the man who'd shed it.

The two survivors rode their horses to the base of the hill, slipped to the ground, and walked up the hill to where Gray Hawk lay still.

When they were close, he picked up Gray Hawk's war tomahawk and handed it to the one on the right and said, "It is the only way for a true warrior to die."

They both nodded but said nothing before the warrior handed Gray Hawk's war tomahawk back to Kyle. They picked up Gray Hawk's body and carried it down the hill as Kyle followed. When they reached the base of the hill, he retrieved Gray Hawk's horse and led it over to the two warriors.

"I will help you collect the bodies of your brothers. Tell Walking Buffalo that this man, Burleigh, is not as his cousin. This is a good man with honor. He listens to my words."

"We will tell him," replied He Who Runs.

It took another twenty minutes to get the other five bodies on their horses and secured for the ride back to their village. Kyle took some rope and made a long trail rope so the two could lead back the six horses and when he finished, they just rode off without ceremony.

Throughout the entire time, from Gray Wolf's charge up the hill to the departure of the last two warriors leading the line of body-draped horses around the hill, the two couples had stood watching, unsure of what was being said or why Kyle wasn't killing the last two warriors.

Kyle walked back up to the hill, retrieved his other weapons and then slid as much as walked down the hill to the redoubt.

He had already made up his mind not to say a word to Edmund about firing his pistol when he didn't need to shoot at all. Of course, Edmund had to make it hard to follow that inclination.

"Why did you let two of them go? They'll bring the whole tribe back on us!" Edmund shouted.

Kyle almost snapped, but managed to just grit his teeth and say, "No, Mister Falstaff, they won't come back. They'll take their leader and other dead back to their camp and honor them. I told them to pass the word to their chief that Mister Burleigh is a good and honorable man and their chief will listen.

"Do you know why I didn't shoot him, but chose to meet him with my knife? Because to shoot him would bring him dishonor. He had made a courageous charge on his horse up the hill to meet me. Shooting him would bring shame to both of us. I gave him a warrior's death, Mister Falstaff, an honorable death. He knew when he was dying that I was giving him this honor. That will be the last attack from the Santee."

He didn't wait for any response from Edmund, but just walked over to Charles, pulled Gray Hawk's war tomahawk from his gunbelt and handed it to him.

"Mister Burleigh, remember what you saw here today. These were brave and honorable men. They will know your name now and not blame you for what happened to their people. Keep the war tomahawk as something that will help you to remember this day, and perhaps it will be useful to show it to them when you need to talk to their chief."

Charles accepted the tomahawk and said, "I will. Thank you again, Mister MacKenzie."

Kyle nodded, then turned and walked to the two women, stopped and said, "Mrs. Burleigh and Mrs. Falstaff, I want to tell you both that I was very proud of you. You both showed no fear either before or during the fight. It let me concentrate on the danger and not be worried about either of you. You both showed true courage. You both have sand that would make any warrior proud."

They smiled at him, getting just an inkling of what 'sand' meant in his context, but not asking. They were both just pleased by his praise.

"We may as well camp here. I'll lead the horses to a stream that's about a half mile north and collect the canteens and fill them while I'm there."

Emily had her eyes fixed on his bright green eyes and could see the pain in his eyes for what he had just needed to do. After her initial surprise, she understood him even better and thought it made him more remarkable. He was such a rarity among men, and she was now certain that she loved him, but it didn't matter at all.

She watched him walk away, then turned to help her mother organize some form of cooking arrangement.

Kyle did feel bad about killing the six Santee. He knew it was retaliation for what they blamed Mister Burleigh's cousin for doing to them, but they had died for nothing. He knew it was necessary, but he couldn't stop them from making the attack by talking to them. He needed to kill them to drive that point home. There was no other way, but it was still such a waste.

He led the eight horses to the stream and let them all drink and as they did, he wondered if they were going to face any more troubles. If they did, it wouldn't be from the Santee, but the Lakota had been running raids into Santee territory lately and he hoped he didn't run into any. At least he wouldn't feel as bad about killing them as he did the Santee because they had killed his wife.

He just let the horses drink and tried to remember the face of Hesta 'se Vo 'e. It was so foggy, yet as he tried to remember her face, he would always find Emily's face in his mind and that bothered him as he felt as if he was dishonoring his beloved wife.

Back at the camp, Edmund was still fuming over what had happened. He had the pistol and had come very close to shooting Kyle when he had seen how Emily had looked at him. She never looked at him that way. When he had tried to fondle her last night, she had rolled away and curled into a ball. He knew why, too. *Was that backwoods bumpkin going to try to steal his wife?*

He sat on one of the saddlebags with the pistol in his hand and continued to stew about his wife. She wasn't the best of wives, and he had been very disappointed in Emily. She wasn't the subservient wife he had expected to marry, although it hadn't been apparent while they were courting.

He had wanted a beautiful young wife he could parade on his arm at the soirees and parties. She fulfilled those requirements but had seemed indifferent at best otherwise. He didn't mind all that much as long as she stayed quiet and knew her place. But she had a stubborn, rebellious streak that had occasionally erupted, but had really manifested itself on this trip, beginning in St. Louis. Now it had reached this level of open rebellion and he knew that she was infatuated with that heathen.

He was still boiling inside when he heard noise to his right, then saw Kyle bringing the horses back and slid his thumb over the Colt's hammer, knowing its power of life and death. It was justified, he told himself; the man coveted his wife, and the bastard wasn't necessary any longer. He said the Indians weren't going to attack, and it was only three days' ride away. Just a short ride northeasterly and they'd be at Yankton. They didn't need that unkempt savage anymore.

He stared northward at the approaching Kyle MacKenzie and decided to take action to defend his offended honor. He'd wait for him to get close, then pretend the gun had gone off accidentally. He held the gun close against him with his back to the others, cocked the hammer, then turned back to look at MacKenzie. He was hitching the horses, and he'd be close in another minute. Edmund's heart was already pounding in anticipation as he slipped his finger over the trigger.

Kyle paid no attention to Edmund as he walked to the group. His mood was still somber, but better than it was before he left. He saw Emily and Abigail preparing to cook and realized he had to make the fire, so he turned and picked up the spade to dig a fire pit as Edmund moved closer as he pretended to be looking at the pistol.

The only one who noticed Edmund's movement was Charles. He wondered why Edmund even had the pistol any longer as he had put his with Kyle's other weapons. Then he noticed that the pistol's hammer was cocked and was still wondering about it when the reason became apparent seconds later.

Kyle had the spade in his hand and was returning it to the pack as Edmund slid to his left until he was three feet from Kyle, pointed the pistol's muzzle at Kyle and pulled the trigger.

Kyle and everyone else heard the hammer's loud snap as the firing pin struck a discharged cylinder. His head snapped up and looked at a shocked Edmund who stood staring at Kyle with the Colt still pointed at him.

Kyle knew it wasn't accidental, as did Charles, but even though the women had only reacted to the sound, seeing Edmund standing there with the pistol's muzzle just three feet from Kyle was a shocking sight.

Edmund recovered and smoothly said, "I beg everyone's pardon. I was just examining the pistol and accidentally pulled the trigger. Luckily it wasn't charged."

"Yes, it was lucky for me especially," said Kyle as he took the pistol from Edmund and carried it over to the others and set it down.

Charles didn't know what to say. He had just witnessed a failed murder attempt and it had only been because Edmund had been so promiscuous in his shooting during the attack that Kyle was still alive. If he'd followed Kyle's instructions, that pistol would have discharged.

Edmund was losing all rational thought, and Charles didn't know how to approach this, so he decided to ask the intended victim.

He stepped closer to Kyle and asked, "Could I have a word, Mister MacKenzie?"

"Certainly."

Charles stepped away from the others and Kyle followed.

Edmund followed them with his eyes as Emily and Abigail watched as well.

Emily wasn't sure what had just happened, whether it was a true accident or not, but she was reasonably sure that her husband had just tried to murder Kyle, and her heart was still sick at the thought.

When they were thirty feet away, Charles stopped, turned to Kyle and quietly said, "Mister MacKenzie, I suspect that the misfire was not an accident. I had noticed that the pistol's hammer was back when he approached you."

"No, Mister Burleigh, I'm sure it wasn't an accident at all. It's not possible with those pistols to simply pull the trigger and have it fire. It had to be intentional."

"You knew yet you didn't retaliate. Why?"

"Why would I do that? He knows what he did, so do I, and obviously you do as well. He won't try again. Besides, I have no intention of letting him near any guns again anyway. In a few days, you'll all be safely in Yankton and I'll ride west and report to Fort Sully."

"Do you know why he tried to kill you?"

"I have my suspicions."

"It's Emily, isn't it?"

"I believe so."

"Could you tell me if he has reasons to be concerned?"

"It depends on who is making that judgement. Nothing has passed between us at all, Mister Burleigh and nothing ever will. She is married to Mister Falstaff and that is all that matters."

"I understand that, but just because I'm her father and got her into this marriage in the first place, could you tell me if you love Emily?"

Kyle studied Charles before replying, "Yes, I do, but as I said, it has no impact on the real world, does it?"

Charles wasn't surprised in his honest answer and replied, "No. Sadly, it does not. Believe me, I wish I could change all that. It was such a short-sighted and selfish thing we did to Emily.

"She was always such a free soul and a happy heart through all the years she was growing up and we wanted her to marry well, to get her accepted in the social circles of St. Louis. But we didn't pay any attention to what she wanted, and that was a true failing as parents. Now she's anchored to that despicable excuse for a man for the rest of her life. I'll burn in hell for what I did to my Emily."

"No, Mister Burleigh, you won't. The future isn't written yet. I'll return to my world and she'll return to hers, but I'll stop by every few months, and if it takes ten or twenty years, I'll be there when the future takes that glorious right-hand turn."

Charles nodded, then reached out and took Kyle's hand as he said, "You're the most remarkable man I've ever met, Mister MacKenzie. I'd be honored to call you my friend. Please call me Charles."

"I'd be honored myself, Charles. Call me Kyle."

They shook hands and walked back to the camp as friends.

———

Less than an hour later, Kyle had the fire going for supper. They were beginning to use Kyle's supplies, so the menu was different, but after ditching the wagon, it also meant they'd have enough for the remainder of the trip. It was when she was going through the tins of food for making supper that Abigail noticed the can of peaches.

"Peaches, Mister MacKenzie?" she asked as she smiled with the can in her hand.

He smiled back and replied, "It's a weakness. If you dig further down, you'll find some penny candy, too. I bought a nickel bag back at Omaha City and haven't indulged yet."

"You must not have much of a sweet tooth if you haven't had any yet."

"It comes and goes, ma'am," he said with a smile.

Kyle took the can and opened it with his knife and returned it to Abigail as he said, "I think the ladies should indulge."

"You don't mind?"

"Not at all."

As Abigail and Emily attacked the can of peaches, Kyle began to fill the coffeepot with water when he remembered something else that might interest the women. He went to the pannier and dug deeply, pulled out a small tin, then walked over to Abigail and showed her the label as he handed it to her.

Abigail's eyes had flown open when he had shown her the tin, then she reached reverently for the can, finished chewing the peach slice in her mouth and swallowed.

"*Tea?* You had tea and didn't mention it?"

"I had other things on my mind, Mrs. Burleigh. I only remembered it when you found the peaches."

"Why did you buy tea?"

"I like it every now and then for a change. My mother loved tea."

"Well, bless her for that. Could we have some of your hot water?"

"Yes, ma'am. I'll pour two cups of hot water before I add the coffee."

Kyle returned to the fire and sat on his heels in a much better mood than when he'd first returned from the stream. Somehow, seeing the joy on Abigail's face from such simple things like peaches and tea erased his somber temperament.

———

Walking Buffalo sat with the last two warriors in his lodge after they'd returned the bodies of their six comrades and made their report.

"You say it was the Green-Eyed Devil escorting this party?"

"Yes. He said to tell you that this Burleigh is not like his relative and is a man of honor."

Walking Buffalo nodded as the warrior continued.

"When Gray Hawk charged the devil, he put down his rifle and took out his knife to give him honor in death. He could have shot all of us but chose to honor Gray Hawk and allow us to bring him and the others back."

Again, Walking Buffalo nodded, then said, "Maybe we should not call him devil any longer. Allow them passage through our land to Yankton. Send the word."

The warrior nodded and left Walking Buffalo, who was saddened by the loss of the warriors and regretted his decision to send them to their deaths. He knew it was one of the burdens of being the chief, but it didn't make him feel any better.

———

Back at the camp, Kyle had assembled the tent and moved all the weapons to the top of the hill. He needed to clean the Henry and make sure it was full loaded, then clean and load the pistol that Edmund had used. He didn't expect any trouble from the Santee, which meant if he had trouble, it would come from behind him.

He sat on the hill as the sun set and knew he was safe here, but he wasn't worried about Edmund trying something different. He knew he had shot his wad. He was worried about Emily. That one look they had shared had told him everything. He knew he would have to be careful these last few days and began to curse Father Lapierre for instilling such a high level of moral character.

Then again, perhaps it was his mother instead of Father Lapierre, or a combination of the two who had turned him into such a rod-straight character. It certainly wasn't his father, he thought as he smiled. His father was a bit of a rascal. The only thing he was sure about was that his father never shamed his mother because he worshipped his wife.

Kyle wished he could just tell Emily how he felt and ask her to come with him, but he knew there was no chance of that happening at all. She was the legal wife of Edmund Falstaff, so there was no discussion and no gray area. But he would do as he had told Charles. After he was settled in Fort Sully, he would go to Yankton on occasion to see how she was.

That was provided that Fort Sully didn't kill him. He knew the location that they had chosen, and it wasn't very good. They were going to move it to a better spot further downriver on the other side of the Missouri. That was supposed to happen in a few months, and preliminary work had already begun. That's when they would be most vulnerable to attack by the Lakota.

Down at the bottom of the hill, they were preparing for sleep. Charles had been able to separate Abigail from Emily and Edmund and tell her about the conversation he had with Kyle after the failed assassination.

Abigail was stunned to learn that Edmund had tried to kill Kyle, especially in light of his value to get them to Yankton. She was just as enamored of Kyle as her husband was and felt the knife twist just as sharply as Charles had when he told Abigail of Kyle's feelings for Emily. She then told Charles what Emily had told him which only compounded their feelings of guilt. Now they both felt equally miserable, mostly because there was nothing either of them could do about it.

"Charles, do you think it would be appropriate to allow him to call me Abigail?" she asked, believing it was the only way she felt she could safely let Kyle know that she had accepted him as a friend.

"Yes, my love, I think it is not only appropriate but necessary. We owe that young man so much and all we can do is let him know that we see him as an equal."

"I'll ask him in the morning."

"That will be fine."

The Burleighs turned in while Kyle watched over them from his hilltop.

CHAPTER 5

Kyle slid down the hill with all of his weapons on his lap. Why make two trips? He reached the bottom while everyone else was still in the tent, then after carefully setting them on a tarp, began saddling the horses and putting the weapons where they belonged, including dropping both of the extra loaded Colts into his saddlebags.

He moved quickly to saddle all the horses, suddenly wanting this journey to end before he was even more tempted to breach his own moral dam. He didn't need to be reminded of what wasn't his and never would be.

He had everything packed and ready except for the food and cooking gear before he rebuilt the fire then waited for everyone to exit the tent. It seemed to be later than usual, so he finally decided to start cooking breakfast. This was the last of the bacon, so he'd have to hunt later for some fresh meat. He'd ride ahead and see if he could find some game after they began to move again. He'd spotted a few rabbits and a herd of white-tailed deer, so he didn't think he'd have a problem, especially now that he didn't have to worry about an attack by the Santee.

He had the bacon cooked before anyone left the tent and when someone did, it was Abigail. She waved and ran to the private place before returning a few minutes later. She strode toward Kyle purposefully and Kyle wondered what was on her mind. He thought it was likely that Charles had told her how he felt about Emily and she wanted to steer him clear and knew she would be right to do so.

"Good morning, Mrs. Burleigh," he said as he moved the skillet from the cooking grate.

Abigail dropped to her heels next to him and said, "Mister MacKenzie, I have a favor to ask of you."

Kyle already knew what to expect and replied, "Anything, ma'am."

"I ask that you please call me Abigail."

Kyle was relieved and a bit surprised, but smiled and said, "I'd be honored, Abigail. Please call me Kyle."

She smiled back, saying, "I wish things could be different, Kyle."

Again, he was surprised and realized that Abigail must have the same opinion of her son-in-law as her husband and replied, "As do I, but it's not in our power, is it?"

"No, it isn't. Do you want me to take over, Kyle?"

"If you would, Abigail. I'll need to do some hunting later, I believe. We're out of meat."

As Abigail moved the skillet back to the cooking grate, Kyle stood, just when the rest of the tent's occupants began slipping through its large flaps of canvas.

Charles exited first and was followed by Edmund. Then there was a two-minute pause before Emily trotted out. Soon, they were all around the fire accepting its welcome heat with open palms.

To make a point, Charles said, "Good morning, Kyle."

Kyle smiled and replied, "Good morning, Charles."

Edmund was shocked at MacKenzie's use of his Christian name but noted that Charles had offered first.

Abigail turned to Charles, "Kyle said he's going to have to do some hunting later today because we're out of meat."

Charles was enjoying Edmund's obvious discomfort and asked, "Is that right, Kyle?"

"Yes, sir. We may be able to move faster now that we don't have to worry about the Santee, but I think we'd all prefer some fresh meat."

"Yes, we would."

Emily was smiling inside at the obvious acceptance of Kyle by her parents, and although she knew there would be no real impact on her situation, it still meant a lot to her.

They finished their breakfast and after a quick cleanup, Kyle and Charles dismantled and packed the tent then saddled and packed the horses. With two men working it was much faster and Charles discovered how much he missed simple manual labor after years of office work.

They were riding an hour later and making good time. On horseback, they were able to skirt some hills quickly, and even when they had to cross the low passes, they were able to make them much more quickly than they would have if they were using the wagon. Everyone was in good spirits except Edmund.

After the noon break, Kyle rode a mile ahead and began to hunt. He was fortunate with an easterly wind and guessed they were only seventy miles at the most from Yankton. If things stayed this good, they could make Yankton the day after tomorrow.

Forty minutes later, he shot a young doe with the Henry and harvested enough meat to last the final two days. He stored the venison in his meat bags and returned to the other riders.

"Kyle, what is the smoke over there?" Charles asked as he pointed.

Kyle had already read the smoke and replied, "It says to give us safe passage."

"How soon do you think we'll be getting there?"

"The day after tomorrow, I would think," he answered before he looked at the sky and said, "But it looks like we're going to be wet for a while. We've been very fortunate to avoid rain so far. At this time of the year, it rains quite a bit. Our luck has run out, I believe."

After they rode for another two hours a light mist began to fall, so Kyle decided to set up camp a bit early before the rains descended.

After Kyle quickly removed the tent, he and Charles had it up before unsaddling the horses. He put the two sleeping bags inside then found his gray slicker and had to search a bit before finding the other two, then put them into the tent as well.

"Charles, the rain will be increasing shortly. I suggest that everyone get inside. I'll take care of the horses."

"I'll help you get them unsaddled."

"No, I'm used to this. Go ahead and make sure everyone stays dry."

"Are you sure?"

"I'm sure."

"Alright."

Charles rounded up Emily and Abigail and headed for the tent which was already occupied by Edmund as Kyle began unsaddling the horses. He had the two canvas tarps and put one on the ground and began stacking the saddles on top, then removed the guns and ammunition and put them on the tarp. The food and clothing panniers were the last to be unloaded, then he covered them with the second tarp before tying down the horses.

The rain began falling in earnest, so he found a corner of the tarp and sat under one corner and wrapped the same corner of the upper tarp over his shoulders, leaving his head exposed to the rain so he could see.

Inside the tent, there was a discussion about allowing Kyle to sleep in the tent and unsurprisingly, it was three against one.

"The tent is for family, and he is most assuredly not family!" snarled Edmund.

"He's my friend, and I say he comes in here," said Charles.

Emily knew better than to state her opinion as it would only make things worse.

"Edmund, what harm can it do?" asked Abigail.

"What harm, you ask? Why not let him sleep with Emil or yourself? You are not going to invite an unmarried man, a wild man, into this tent. I shall sleep outside myself if you do."

That was the clinching argument. Charles knew that Edmund's pride would get him to do just that. And like it or not, he was still family.

"Alright. Kyle should be all right. I just think it's a very unfriendly thing to do."

Edmund felt a measure of satisfaction but managed to hide his glee as they all prepared for sleep while Kyle sat under the tarp.

Kyle was actually quite comfortable compared to some of his other experiences. There were many nights where he'd had to sleep in sub-zero temperatures with strong winds blowing snow into his face as he covered himself with any protection he could find. These conditions were almost benevolent.

The rain continued unabated for most of the night, slowing toward morning. Kyle had just laid on his side when he needed to sleep but awakened early and noticed it was only misting when he slid out from under the tarps. The ground was a muddy mess, though.

He began to set up for the day's travel and was glad that he didn't have to shave today. The temperatures were a bit on the chilly side as he began to prepare the horses which was more difficult in the slippery mud.

He still managed to have all the horses dried and saddled, the packhorses loaded, and even a fire going before the Burleighs and Falstaffs began emerging from the tent.

Invariably, they would exit with their palms up, checking for rain. When Emily exited, she smiled at Kyle who returned her smile and lost it quickly when her husband exited right behind her and glared at him. He noticed that he was wearing one of the slickers. Both women were wearing one as well, so Kyle thought that he'd ask Charles about it when he saw him.

He had the coffee going when Charles reached the cooking area and asked, "How much is the rain going to slow us down, Kyle?"

"It'll have some impact, but we won't know how much for a while until we see if it keeps coming down, and I think it will. Gave up the slicker to Mister Falstaff, Charles?"

Charles grinned and replied, "I just didn't want to hear the complaints."

"If you want to rile him up a little, just casually mention that he's wearing mine," he said as he smiled.

Charles laughed as the others began to arrive.

As they ate their breakfast, Kyle would sneak glances at Emily and found that it was the same pattern that they had followed those first two days. They both would have to wait for Edmund to look down into his food and then they'd both look at each other momentarily and then quickly look away. Both Charles and Abigail noticed but said nothing.

———

An hour later, the group was moving through a steady rain that showed no sign of letting up. Kyle kept them moving slowly as they climbed and descended hills and thought they were making acceptable progress and should still make it to Yankton by tomorrow.

They stopped for a short, cold lunch and began again to add some distance before making camp for the night, which may be their last night as a group.

The skies didn't come close to clearing all afternoon, but actually went the other direction and soon solid sheets of drenching water engulfed the group and Kyle was beginning to worry about finding a campsite in this weather. If he was by himself, he wouldn't be concerned, but he needed to find someplace to set up that elephant tent.

As he looked around, he realized that might not be a problem after all. He had been here before, just a year earlier and knew that setting up the tent was no longer necessary. He turned them to the north, toward the Missouri River that separated Nebraska Territory from Dakota Territory. It was out of the way, but it would be worth it.

After another fifteen minutes of slogging he found what he was looking for, the half-hill with three caves. They weren't giant caverns, but they were big enough to suit their needs and keep dry for the night. He pointed to the caves and dropped back.

When he was beside Charles, he had to shout over the rain, "Charles, I'm going to bring the horses into the right-hand cave. It's the biggest, but I want you all to stay outside the caves until I get a chance to make sure they're all empty. It will only take a few minutes."

"Okay, Kyle," he yelled back.

Kyle then led the three packhorses toward the cave on the right, then when he reached the base of the cave, he stepped down and pulled his Spencer. It had the power to kill anything he might find, even a black bear. There weren't a lot of the bigger brown bears in the area, but there were cougars.

They sure weren't called mountain lions around here but maybe instead of cougars, they could call them hill lions. He laughed at the thought as he stepped into the darkness of the biggest cave. Once inside, he listened as his eyes adjusted to the low light. He had exceptional night vision, but it still took a minute to get acclimated enough to feel comfortable to enter deeper into the cave. It only took a minute to find it was empty of any critters as it was only thirty feet deep, but it would be good for the horses and saddles. He'd probably stay with them as well, knowing their body heat would make the cave warmer even without a fire.

While Kyle was waiting to get his night vision restored well enough to explore the cave, Edmund was growing frustrated and angry.

"Why should he be dry, and we all stay wet? He's just doing this to be annoying. There isn't anything in those caves. I'm not waiting!" he yelled against the pelting rain and he started forward.

"Edmund! Get back here!" shouted Charles.

Edmund either didn't hear him or ignored him as he stepped down off his horse and trotted up into the center cave. He took off his slicker and shook it out before he took a step into the cave and looked inside finding it empty, just as he expected.

But it wasn't empty, just dark. In the back of the cave was a female cougar who was watching the human enter her sanctuary with interest. She'd been injured earlier when she had slid off her wet perch when she'd been stalking a groundhog and smashed into some rocks.

She wasn't in a good mood and she was still hungry, not having caught any prey since the rains had begun. She was still watching the human but hadn't decided what to do about him. He was bigger than she was, and she knew that the two-legged creatures were dangerous, even if they didn't have claws or fangs. She would have run away from the man except there was no place to go. She felt trapped, trapped, hungry and in a foul mood as she weighed the risk of an attack on the human.

Edmund walked to the front of the cave, turned, shouted and waved, "Come in! It's empty!"

Kyle had begun to leave his cave when Edmund shouted, then was angered but not surprised by Edmund's actions. He was lucky this time, he thought, but knew that he wouldn't say anything to the arrogant bastard.

He was about to step out of his cave to move the packhorses in when the cougar, once she saw the human turn, recognized her advantage and sprang to the attack. She took three running steps and leapt, her ninety pounds of muscle slamming into Edmund's back and shoulders.

Edmund screamed as he tumbled from the mouth of the cave to the muddy hill below.

Kyle was stunned by the surprise attack, but quickly dropped the rifle and pulled his knife. He couldn't run because of the mud, knowing that with one slip, that idiot would be dead.

He took four careful steps and found the big cat with her jaws clamped on Edmund's forearm as he flailed. He was sliding slowly away from the mouth of the cave in the mud with the cougar on his chest when Kyle reached down with his left hand and scooped up a handful of mud.

He threw it underhanded at the cougar, and shouted, "Lgmuwatogla!"

The cougar, realizing there was a new threat, released Edmund and turned to Kyle, its ears back and teeth bared. It growled menacingly as Kyle walked toward it at a crouch, causing the cat to hiss loudly and back off slightly. Kyle advanced another two feet and showed the cougar his blade, then emitted his own low growl, letting her know he was the greater danger.

The big cat left Edmund entirely and now faced Kyle.

Once she stepped closer to him, Kyle suddenly stood tall and screamed his high-pitched war cry. The cougar was startled out of its defensive posture and bolted northward into the rain.

Kyle waited until she disappeared into the downpour, sheathed his knife, then stepped forward, grabbed Edmund by the collar, pulled him to his feet and helped him into the vacated cave. Once he was on the cave's floor, he turned and signaled for the others to come forward.

After they drew near, he shouted, "Take him inside. I need to go and check out the other cave, then I'll be back and take care of any injuries. Put your horses in the right-hand cave."

Charles nodded, then he and the women turned toward the horse cave as Kyle stepped back down into the mud but didn't bother going to get his Spencer.

He pulled his right-hand pistol, then stalked into the last cave, still hideously angry without showing it. Part of him wondered why he had even saved Edmund at all. The world didn't need his like. He was a sponge, living off the accomplishments of others and guessed that was his definition of a 'gentleman'. What made his actions even more unreasonable was that he not only was denying himself any chance of being with Emily, it was sentencing her to a life sentence with the bastard. With each step into the cave, Kyle questioned his own judgement in saving Edmund Falstaff.

The third cave was clear, so he returned to the middle cave and found everyone huddled around a moaning Edmund. They had already taken off his jacket and shirt.

"Let me take a look at his injuries," Kyle said as he approached.

Abigail and Emily stepped aside to let Kyle access his right arm. He found that it was bleeding from six puncture wounds, but not badly. The cougar had sunk her teeth in but hadn't had a chance to rip the muscle apart. Edmund had been very fortunate, but Kyle doubted if he realized it.

Kyle stood, turned to Charles and said, "He'll just need it bandaged. There wasn't much damage done. The cat just bit him and didn't rip the arm at all. He doesn't need any stitches, either. They're all just puncture wounds. The only worry would be from infection. If the cat had eaten, she could have tainted meat in her mouth. I can prevent the infection, but it's going to hurt."

"You're loving this, aren't you?" Edmund whined loudly, "You aren't even going to do anything except cause me pain."

Kyle looked down at him and said, "If you'd rather that I leave you as you are, then that's fine. It's your choice, Mister Falstaff."

Charles looked at Kyle and said, "Do what you need to do to stop the infection, Kyle."

Kyle nodded, then turned and left the cave, stepped carefully through the mud and rain to the now-full horse cave, entered, then found his saddlebags, pulled out an old shirt and a small flask before returning to the human cave.

Once in the middle cave, he began ripping strips of cloth out of the shirt and set them on top of Edmund's chest before he opened the flask, set it on the cave floor near his knee, then grasped Edmund's wrist tightly to keep it still. He then picked up the flask and, without warning, began pouring it onto Edmund's wound.

As expected, Edmund screeched loudly and tried to rip his arm from Kyle's vicelike grip as he flailed around. When he stopped wriggling, Kyle released his wrist then began wrapping the arm with the strips of cloth.

It was soon bandaged tightly, so Kyle stood, turned to Charles and said, "You can get him dressed again. I'll bring your sleeping bags and other things in here for you. I'll use the third cave to cook the venison."

He didn't wait for a response before he turned and left the cave. He was angry, and he was more than just mildly frustrated. Edmund had just acted as if he'd had both his arms amputated. Kyle had seen men lose limbs, either in battle or in the hospital tent, and few had made such a fuss.

This was the ignorant, useless man that would be taking Emily away tomorrow. It wouldn't bother him as much if he was losing her to someone that he respected but he had never respected any man less.

Kyle began unsaddling the horses and stripping off all the wet things, knowing that he'd have to make some form of clothesline to let everything dry, including his clothes. He felt thirty pounds heavier from his waterlogged buckskins and knew that it probably wasn't an exaggerated estimate.

He found the two sleeping bags and threw a tarp over them as he stepped back into the rain, then when he reached the cave's mouth, barely stepped inside, but simply unrolled the two sleeping bags before he turned and slipped and slid back to the horse cave to get the clothing panniers. Once he removed them, he again covered them with the tarp and carried them to the adjoining cavern.

When he finished with moving what they would need, he began bringing the venison and the cooking gear to the third cave so he could start cooking. That took several trips, glancing into the middle cave occasionally to follow their progress.

They had unrolled the sleeping bags and Emily and Charles had stripped Edmund's wet clothes and dressed him with dry clothes from the pannier before letting him slide into the sleeping bag as if he was a crippled invalid.

Kyle wanted to scream. The man had a few puncture wounds and nothing more. He should be up and walking around as if nothing had happened. As he entered the first cave again, he recalled the day he and his father had a personal encounter with a grizzly cow. She had left a four-inch scar on his chest that hadn't done much more than bleed. His father had sewn the gash and they had continued with the hunt. The grizzly had run off after her one swipe, and if he had moaned, his father would have commented unfavorably. He hadn't made a fuss because he always wanted his parents to be proud of him.

It was his father who had shown him the whiskey trick and had told him always to keep a flask on hand. At the time, his father had confided that he kept two, because one always seemed to be empty. So, just minutes after being slashed by a big bear, he and his father had shared a laugh.

The horses would have to go hungry for the night, but he found his own clothing pannier and set his dry clothes aside. He'd change after dinner.

It was difficult finding fuel for a fire, but he managed enough for dinner, and just two hours after the cougar's attack, had the venison steaks fried and put onto plates with some potatoes that he had fried along with the steaks. He had four plates of food stacked and under another upside-down plate as he left the cave and slipped over to the middle cave, almost losing his footing and the food in the process.

He handed the food to Abigail and said, "I'll get some water and utensils in a moment, Abigail."

"Thank you, Kyle," she replied as she accepted the plates, noticing there were only four.

Emily turned to her mother after Kyle had gone, and said, "This is all so wrong, Mother. He's doing everything and we're doing nothing."

"Emily, there is little we can do. He's the only one who knows how to survive out here."

"It doesn't make me feel any better."

"No, I'll admit to that. We're all pretty useless, aren't we?"

"Not useless, Abigail, just out of place. I wonder how Kyle would function in St. Louis?" asked Charles.

"Probably a lot better than we function in his world," replied Abigail.

Kyle showed up with two canteens and the knives and forks, then said, "After breakfast, we'll be pretty much done with the food. It's alright, though. We should reach the ferry around noontime."

"Won't it be shut down because of all the rain?" asked Charles.

"I don't think so. The rain is going to stop in a little while. The sky is already breaking up. The Missouri will be pretty swollen though, but I've seen them run that ferry in much worse conditions."

"How dangerous is it?" asked Abigail, her fear of water returning.

"It's not too bad. They have a steel cable that they have anchored on both banks. The ferry is hooked onto the cable and they have this wheel that they turn that rolls on the cable. The only restrictions might be on the horses. When the river is up like this, they don't like to have horses on the ferry in case they get spooked by the rolling movement. We'll see how it looks when we get there."

"What will we do if they won't let the horses on the ferry?" asked Charles.

"We'll decide what to do about it when we get there. It may not be an issue. I'm going to go back and eat my dinner before going back to the horse cave."

"Thank you for the food, Kyle," said Emily with a smile.

"Don't thank me until you've tasted it," he answered with a smile of his own, then waved and stepped back out into the diminishing rain.

As he ate his dinner, Kyle wondered about the ferry. *What would they do if the ferry wouldn't accept the horses?* The Burleighs probably wouldn't need the horses if they were in Yankton and doubted if they'd ride anywhere for a while. *But what would he do with eight horses?* He already knew that if the horses stayed on the Nebraska side of the Missouri, he'd have to stay as well.

He finished his steak and thought it was pretty good after all. He cleaned his plate and the frypan then stepped back out to examine the spitting sky. Even though the light was almost gone, it seemed as if the clouds were thinner now. It should be a clear day tomorrow when he said goodbye to the Burleighs.

He stepped past the middle cave without looking as he made his way to the horse cave. When he arrived, he found the animals sleeping and could understand why. They had a hard day walking through the deep mud, but it should be dry by morning. He walked to the back of the cave, lit a candle, and built a low clothesline out of the remaining rope, with the shovel and axe wedged between saddles acting as anchors. He stripped off his clothes and had barely gotten his dry pants on when he saw Emily stepping into the cave and was taken aback.

"Mrs. Falstaff, you'll have to give me a minute," he said quietly.

"I'm not embarrassed, Mister MacKenzie," she said as she continued past the horses.

She saw the long scar on his chest and asked, "How did you get that?"

"A female brown bear did that when I was fifteen."

"Did you moan as much as my husband?"

"Mrs. Falstaff, I'd rather not talk about your husband."

"Neither would I, Mister MacKenzie."

"What can I do for you, Mrs. Falstaff?" he asked as he shrugged on his shirt.

161

"I just wanted to talk to you for a little while. Is that alright?"

"Won't your husband be angry?"

"He's asleep. My parents know I'm here, obviously."

"They're good people, Mrs. Falstaff."

"I think so. So, tomorrow we'll be arriving at Yankton?"

"Around noon, I believe," he replied, already feeling uncomfortable.

"What will you do?"

"What I was supposed to do two weeks ago. I need to get to Fort Sully."

"Where is Fort Sully?"

"It's about two hundred miles west, north of Fort Pierre. It's on the Missouri River, too. If your riverboat hadn't sunk, it would have passed right by Fort Sully."

"Why didn't you just take the steamboat yourself?"

"I need to get a feel for the mood of the tribes in the area and need to know the country, too. It's part of my job. When I report to Lieutenant Colonel Carpenter, he'll ask me right away what I think is the biggest problem. He'll want an in-depth report before I have to go back out with his troops or on my own."

She had taken a seat on a saddle as she asked, "Do you go out alone very often?"

"More than most scouts because I have a lot of advantages."

"Are you afraid of dying?"

"Of course, I am. Fear is what keeps you alert."

"You never seemed afraid when you were fighting those men, or even facing down that cougar."

"Fear leaves when you have other things on your mind."

Then came the question that Kyle had been expecting.

"Mister MacKenzie, why did you save Edmund's life?"

"I had to, Mrs. Falstaff."

"But he's been so abhorrent to you. He hates you."

"I know. It doesn't matter."

"If the roles had been reversed, do you think he would have saved you?"

"No. But I'm not him. I do what I think is right and needs doing."

"So, tomorrow, I'll go back to my life and you will return to yours," she said with her eyes downcast and her voice low.

Kyle paused before replying, "Yes. As it must be."

She stood and faced Kyle just inches away, looked at those amazing green eyes and wanted him to hold her and take her away, but was certain that he'd do no such thing.

Kyle could read the desire in her eyes because it matched his own but knew how badly it would turn out and finally just said softly, "Good night, Mrs. Falstaff."

Emily felt her heart break as she whispered, "Good night, Mister MacKenzie."

Emily stepped into the family cave and then quickly turned and looked at the sky as stars began to appear through the clouds. Tears rolled down her cheeks in torrents as she struggled to keep from sobbing openly. It had been so close, so very, very close.

In the horse cave, Kyle was looking at the same sky and wondered if there was something wrong with him to send Emily away without telling her how he felt. He knew that her father had probably already told her but believed he should have. But his overwhelming sense of what was right and what was wrong had kept the words inside his heart, and he knew that tomorrow, when they parted, they'd still remain where they belonged.

He blew out his breath, then returned to his cave to get some sleep.

———

The next morning, the sun appeared over the horizon as if it had never missed a day. The ground was drying quickly as Kyle led the horses down from the cave and found a large pool of rainwater and let them drink it dry in less than a minute. He brought them to a grassy area and just let them graze as he built a firepit.

He soon had the fire going and began to cook breakfast, the last food they would share as a group. When it was ready, Kyle brought the food into their cave but brought his own as well this time. He needed to talk to Charles but admitted that his real reason was he wanted to see Emily for as long as he could before he started his long ride to Fort Sully. He wouldn't see her again until he made a visit to Yankton sometime in the future, if ever.

"Good morning, everyone. Here's breakfast," he smiled as he handed out the plates, "It's a little different this morning because we're pretty much out of food, but it shouldn't be a problem in a few hours."

He realized after he'd said it that it might not have been the right thing to say. As he handed Emily her food, he saw that it wasn't the right thing at all. She looked ready to break down in tears as she stared at the plate.

Kyle quickly turned away from Emily, looked at Edmund and said, "I'll get everything packed and the horses saddled shortly. How is the arm, Mister Falstaff?"

"It hurts, no thanks to you."

Kyle ignored the tone, and said, "It'll hurt for another week or so, but keep using it to keep the muscles from getting too tight"

He quickly polished off his plate and left the cave to get the horses saddled and the packhorses loaded. Because he didn't have to mess with the giant tent, he was able to get everything ready in less than an hour. He led the horses to the mouth of the middle cave and waited as the Burleighs and Falstaffs stepped out. Kyle was surprised by the somber mood that enveloped both Charles and Abigail. The only one who seemed chipper was Edmund, but at least he understood the reason why the poor excuse for a man was happy.

Despite the subdued atmosphere, they left the place and Kyle had to readjust his route because of the detour to find the caves.

"It may not be as quick as the steamboat, Charles, but it's not too bad," said Kyle as they rode along.

"No, Kyle, all things taken into account, we made good time."

"Getting rid of the wagon helped," he said.

Charles then asked, "Kyle, do you have to go to Fort Sully? I mean, you're not in the army, so they can't order you to go."

"No, they can't, but they need the help, Charles. I told them that I'd come, and I don't believe you would do less."

"I've never been asked to ride two hundred miles across hostile lands, either."

"It's what I do, Charles. Maybe after things quiet down, I can return home and see my parents."

"Do you think that will happen, Kyle? Do you think it will quiet down?"

"Not right away, but eventually, it has to, Charles. In a few years, the railroads will cross the area and the tribes will have to adapt. Right now, the army is still finishing that damned, stupid war. When they're done, they'll focus on the West. Even the Sioux won't be able to withstand the amount of firepower the army can bring to bear. They'll win some battles because the army will try to fight them with the same tactics that they used to win the war with the Confederates, but they'll eventually figure it out and they'll win. The Sioux, Cheyenne, Arapahoe, Blackfoot and Crow will all have to bow to the inevitable."

"Until then, you'll be out there?"

"Maybe. It depends on the commander. I won't work with some of them. That's the advantage of being a scout. I will only work with a competent commander who gives his men a chance to win. I've seen some very good ones sacked because they rubbed some general the wrong way or irritated some politician."

"Don't you feel some loyalty to the men?"

"In a situation with a bad commander, it doesn't matter. He wouldn't listen to what I tell him anyway. You see the same thing in the civilian world. It's just the costs that are different."

"Yes, you're right about that," Charles replied as he looked around to ensure Edmund was far enough away.

"Kyle, are you going to visit?"

"I will when I can."

"Good."

They rode parallel to the river, about a mile south of the Missouri and just before noon, Kyle spotted the ferry.

"There's the ferry, Charles," he said as he pointed.

They all could see Yankton on the other side of the river but with different emotions.

The ferry seemed to be operating, despite the Missouri's full banks and rapid flow.

"Kyle, how do the riverboats get past the ferry's cable?" Charles asked as they rode east along the river.

"They lower it to the river bottom. The steamboat blows his whistle about a mile away to let them know they're coming and the ferry operators have this large lever that pulls the cable out of the base. During this time of the year, it's not unusual for them to leave it down for a whole day because of more than one steamer, but it's up right now."

They continued to ride toward the ferry and soon reached its southern terminus and dismounted.

Kyle waved at the operator on the other side and he waved back, then they watched as he stepped on the large barge-like ferry with another man. They began turning a heavy wheel on the side of the barge with the cable and the boat began bouncing toward them, stretching the cable downriver as it moved.

Abigail's eyes grew wide and she turned to Charles and said, "Charles, I can't do it. It's as bad as that steamer."

Before Charles could respond, Kyle replied, "Abigail, remember what I told you after the Santee attack? When the Santee were attacking, I glanced down to where you were. I didn't see the slightest hint of fear and thought to myself, there's a woman with sand. You have an enormous reserve of courage, Abigail. You just need to realize what fear is. It's just a way of protecting ourselves, nothing more. Use that same courage and look at the far side and your destination. You'll be home in a warm house, having good food in just a few hours. It's worth it, Abigail."

Abigail looked at Kyle, and asked, "What's sand? You said that once before."

"It's more than just courage, it's the ability to do what has to be done, no matter the cost."

She nodded, then looked at the approaching ferry and took a deep breath before turning to her husband and saying, "Alright, Charles, I'll go."

Charles hugged his wife and smiled at Kyle.

The ferry bumped into the loading dock, the operator leapt ashore, approached them and said, "Howdy, folks. Crossing is ten cents apiece, but I can't take any horses today. It's too spooky for 'em. How many are coming across?"

Again, before Charles could answer, Kyle said, "Four. I'll be staying with the horses, but we've got some things that need to go across.

Emily's head whipped around and looked at Kyle, but he pretended not to notice.

Charles also looked at Kyle before he asked, "Are you sure, Kyle?"

"I can't leave my horse and packhorse, Charles. I've got to get to Fort Sully. Let's get what you need unloaded."

"Alright. All we need is the contents of the trunk."

"That'll be easy, then."

They walked to the improvised packhorse and Kyle unstrapped the two bedroll panniers and set them down.

Charles then said, "Kyle, I'm not going to insult you by offering you payment for all you've done."

"I wouldn't have accepted it anyway, Charles. You've paid too high a price for this trip already."

Charles glanced at Edmund who had stayed with Emily and Abigail, then said, "But not as high a price as you and Emily have paid, I'm afraid."

Kyle just shrugged before Charles said, "Just keep the horses, tent and other things. We surely won't be needing them."

Kyle again just nodded as talking was becoming more difficult.

Charles offered his hand and Kyle grasped it, then added his left, but neither said a word.

Charles then took both panniers, carried them to the dock where the ferryman relieved him of the large bags and put them in the small cabin on the ferry for safekeeping.

Abigail then walked close to Kyle and shocked Edmund when she hugged Kyle then kissed him on the cheek.

"Goodbye, Kyle. God bless you," she said softly with tears in her eyes.

"Goodbye, Abigail," he smiled which was closer to a grimace.

Kyle looked over at Edmund and said, "Goodbye, Mister Falstaff."

Edmund didn't answer but simply walked onto the barge and said loudly, "Come, Emily."

Charles and Abigail approached Edmund, and Charles said, "Edmund, could we talk to you for a moment," then turned him toward the front of the ferry.

Emily walked slowly toward Kyle, her eyes filling with tears.

Kyle wanted so much to hold her, but simply stood and tried to force a smile.

"Goodbye, Mrs. Falstaff," was all he could manage as he stared into those moist blue eyes and let his eyes tell her what his voice could not.

"Goodbye, Mister MacKenzie," she barely whispered in a shaky voice as she looked into his vibrant, green but incredibly sad eyes.

She knew he was in as much pain as she was, but he was able to hold it inside. She wanted so desperately to stay, but knew she had to leave now, or it would get even worse, so she turned then hurriedly walked to the barge and stepped onboard the ferry without looking back.

The two ferrymen began turning the wheel in the opposite direction and the craft left the southern shore to bounce across the hundred-yard wide Missouri River.

Kyle had been strangling his emotions in a mammoth choke hold as he watched Emily slowly rocking away. Charles and Abigail waved, and Kyle returned the wave.

Emily was under the scrutiny of Edmund and simply kept her eyes trained on Kyle. It seemed like just a long moment before the ferry reached the Dakota side of the river and they were ushered from the boat and soon disappeared into the town of Yankton.

Kyle watched them until they were out of sight and whispered, "Goodbye, Emily."

He eventually reverted to his normal demeanor but felt incredibly empty as he mounted, then led the other seven horses away from the ferry and headed due south to resupply.

It was going to be a long, lonely journey to Fort Sully.

CHAPTER 6

Kyle saw them before they saw him, which was highly important. The sixteen Lakota were painted for war and were leading two heavily loaded packhorses. Even with his extensive armory, it would be difficult to win an engagement with that many. They were traveling north to south, which means they must have gone to the shore of the Missouri for something. He didn't see any smoke in the distance, so they hadn't burned anything, but they sure stole a lot of something or bargained for it. He just stayed put in the trees and let them continue south.

Kyle was leading two horses now. One packhorse carried his supplies while the other lugged his armory. He kept the Henry in his scabbard and the two spare pistols in his saddlebags with extra ammunition for the Henry. Four loaded pistols were enough to let the packhorse hold the pistol ammunition. The Spencer and the Sharps were on the packhorse as well along with all their ammunition. He did have his unstrung bow and arrows with him though, and his knife, of course.

His first stop after leaving the ferry had been the Santee village to trade the extra five horses for food. He had also given up the giant tent and two double sleeping bags. The Santee were impressed with both and traded a new, more powerful bow, two more knives, and a war tomahawk for them. He had let them rob him in trading for the horses because they were unnecessary to him, but he needed the food. He had enough now for the long journey still ahead. Surprisingly, most of it was white man's food in tins. They didn't like the stuff and were glad to get rid of it, especially for horses. He tended to agree with them about the food. It wasn't as good as fresh, but it served its purpose.

He watched the Lakota Sioux disappear over the southern hill and then gave them five more minutes before he led his two horses out of the trees and into the clearing. He rode west until he picked up their tracks and followed their trail north to see where they had been. He knew it couldn't be very far because the Missouri was only three miles away.

Twenty minutes later, he found where they had been, and at first didn't know what it was except a single building with no defensive works at all. It was made of logs cut from the surrounding trees, but it wasn't going to be a farm, because there wasn't enough clear ground and it was too close to the river anyway. The Missouri's floods could be impressive.

The nearest settlement, Fort Randall, was six miles northwest on the other side of the river, so the location was a bit odd, too. After his brief reconnoiter, he started his gelding forward again at a walk and rode close to the front of the building, then stepped down. Once on the ground, he pulled his right-hand pistol, cocked the hammer, then walked to the door and swung it wide, expecting to see mayhem and blood but found neither.

"*Who are you?*" exclaimed a genuinely scruffy looking man who was about forty years old.

There was a second man with him, and both were staring at him as if he had caught them with their hands in the cookie jar. And that's exactly what he'd done, only it wasn't cookies that cause their guilty expressions. They had contraband in the room…deadly contraband.

Kyle glared at them as he growled, "My name's Kyle MacKenzie and you boys are going to leave now."

"Who the hell do you think you are?" shouted the bigger of the two, which was surprising given their situation.

"I'm the man with the pistol pointed at your gut. Now, I'd just as soon shoot the pair of you, but I'm going to give you an option. There's a canoe out near the river and I want you two in that canoe in two minutes. Now move!"

They looked at each other and the shorter man gave him a short nod before they turned toward the door and began to walk.

Kyle let them pass and just as they reached the doorway, they both suddenly whipped around and made a sudden lunge at Kyle.

Kyle pulled the trigger and then stepped aside as the smaller man hit the floor. The big man swiveled and snarled at Kyle, then must have figured that he'd catch Kyle by surprise by not running and quickly leapt toward Kyle who had already cocked the hammer of the Colt New Army and pulled the trigger. At four feet, the .44 slug did enormous damage, ripping through his chest, obliterating ribs, exploding his heart, and then leaving his back before burying itself in the log wall.

The big man still slammed into Kyle and knocked him back before he crashed face first into the floor, bounced and then after a loud gurgle, stopped moving.

Kyle regained his balance quickly, then cocked his hammer automatically as he turned his Colt to the thinner man, not sure if he was dead.

He stepped to the second body, saw his lifeless eyes staring into the roof, then lowered his pistol's hammer, slid it back into his holster, then shook his head and muttered, "Idiots."

Kyle knew why they had acted as they had because they were both going to hang, and probably didn't believe that they would be allowed to get into the canoe and just leave.

Oddly enough, Kyle was already realizing the issue that letting them go would have posed because they could circle around a few hundred yards downstream and let their Lakota friends know that they were in danger of losing their source of the contraband that he'd spotted. So, it was just as well that they decided to rush him. It was still stupid, but definitive.

He walked around the cabin and did a quick inventory of the contraband and realized just how bad the situation was and how much worse it could have been.

He found one full case of Henry rifles and one half-full case. That made eighteen repeating rifles that would find their way to the Sioux. He found two cases of .44 caliber rimfire Henry ammunition and hated to think how many these two 'entrepreneurs' had sold to the Sioux already. He had counted four cases on those horses that were being led by the Sioux and wondered why they hadn't bought all of the invaluable repeaters.

He guessed that the Indians didn't have enough cash to purchase them all. If the two gunrunners hadn't had a steady source of rifles, then the Lakota would have just killed them and taken them all, but the promise of more guns had kept the two white men alive, at least until Kyle arrived.

It was an ideal setup, really. Build a cabin a hundred yards back from the river, then bring the rifles in off a riverboat and the Sioux would know that when the riverboat comes by, there will be more rifles.

He examined the crates and noticed that they were stamped with AXE HEADS on the ammunition cases and SCYTHES on the cases that contained the rifles. There was another stamp near the end that read, LITTLE SHIPPING COMPANY, ST. LOUIS MISSOURI. He wrote the information down and yanked off the board as well for confirmation.

The name rang a bell and thought he'd send a letter to the owner of the company and let Charles Burleigh know that someone was using his business to conduct a gunrunning operation. He was confident that Charles knew nothing about it, though.

There was no shipping information, but because the Sioux had just left with their cases of rifles and ammunition, it had to have been in the last two or three days.

He found a pencil near the crude desk, then wrote today's date on the board that he'd pulled free: May 9, 1965. He'd have someone check and see which riverboats had passed this spot over the past few days.

He examined the rest of the cabin and found what they had received from the Sioux. It was Yankee currency in bills and gold that totaled almost sixteen hundred dollars, which was more money than he'd ever seen before.

He was surprised that there weren't any horses on the property and wondered where they got their supplies. He finally guessed that they used the large canoe to row upriver to Fort Randall when they were low.

He estimated that the Sioux had two cases of rifles and four cases of ammunition on those packhorses. If he were to buy them at a gun store back in Omaha, it would have cost him less than five hundred dollars. The Sioux overpaid, but he doubted if they cared. They had no use for white man's money other than what they just bought. He did wonder where they got the cash and examined some of the notes carefully, finding that they were genuine, at least as far as he could determine, and there was no question about the gold eagles and double eagles.

He stuffed the money into his pockets then checked the rest of the cabin. There was food, some clothes and one bed, but didn't have time to dally as he knew that the Sioux could be returning with more cash to buy the last of the shipment. He began unloading the rifles from their crates. He had eighteen of the Henry rifles that he'd have to pack on his packhorses then he'd see how much ammunition he could handle, but he'd have to start tossing things from the packhorses to make room. He started with the heavy things like the shovel and axe, then progressed to his cooking gear and the food that needed cooking.

Once he thought that he had enough room, he then tied the rifles into four groups of four and hung them over the pack saddles. He slid the remaining two into the empty scabbards on the packhorses, then he began moving as much ammunition as he could by taking them out of their wooden cases and dropping the smaller cardboard boxes of .44s into panniers. He was surprised when he was able to add both cases of cartridges into the panniers and still had room left over, so he gave in and put the coffeepot and frypan back on too. *What good was having two packhorses if he didn't make use of them?*

He checked the cabin one more time, found nothing else worth taking before he took their can of coal oil and splashed it all over the cabin then took the only lamp and walked outside.

Once out of the large cabin, he lit the lamp, then tossed it into the cabin. There was a loud whoosh as the flames took hold before he quickly mounted and was riding out of the clearing as the cabin turned into an inferno with the two bodies inside.

Before he left, he had restrung his new bow, nocked one of his personally branded arrows and fired it into a nearby tree, then turned west into the forest. Now the Lakota will know that the Green-Eyed Devil had returned. He'd returned, and they no longer had a source for the repeaters. He wasn't sure if that would stir immediate action or delay their plans.

After he left the trees and turned west again, he began to review what he'd just found and knew that Lieutenant Colonel Harry Carpenter would not be pleased with this piece of information. The Sioux were probably better armed than his own men were, and they were still in that horrid location.

He remembered when he'd first seen Fort Sully three years earlier and even then, had noticed how badly it had been positioned between those two hills. He understood why it had been placed there, too. It was to ward off the winter winds that blew across the prairie that the surveyors that chosen the site. But ironically, the location made those winds worse. The fort had the Missouri River to its east, then a tall hill on either side of the fort. That left the west end open and when the cold winds arrived, they'd rip down from the north and northwest and funnel through that gap.

He imagined that those surveyors had done their work in the summer and weren't accustomed to weather on the Plains, either.

Right now though, he needed to get as far away from the cabin as possible before the Lakota saw the smoke and knew that their personal armory had been closed.

As he moved, he began to wonder about the rifles he had with him. He hoped that Lieutenant Colonel Carpenter would be able to put them to good use. The army was generally stubborn when it came to firearms and balked at any change to more advanced weaponry.

The Henry had been available for most of the Civil War, but the generals had nixed the idea of buying them because they were concerned that soldiers would waste ammunition and they didn't have the trains to move the additional and different cartridges. They were also a much smaller caliber with a shorter range and the generals couldn't see the advantage to reducing the size of the bullet and decreasing the effective killing range. What they failed to see was that they could use fewer soldiers if the guns had a higher rate of fire and most effective fire was at much closer ranges than a hundred yards.

They were also not pleased with commanders that outfitted their soldiers with unauthorized firearms and that was what had brought the question to his mind. He'd ask the lieutenant colonel about it but didn't want to ruin the man's career, either.

He rode for another six hours to put as much distance between him and the Lakota and kept looking for smoke signals from the surrounding hills that would alert other Lakota groups of his passing, but the only smoke he saw was from the fire he'd set.

Once the sun went down with no alerts, he knew he'd cold camp rather than let anyone know where he was. With all those guns and ammunition, it would take some time to get them unpacked anyway. He found a good location and set up his camp. He still had a few more days of travel to Fort Sully when he turned in for the night.

————

Edmund was sitting at the newly built gentleman's club in Yankton. It wasn't a fancy club like the one he frequented in St. Louis, but it was better than staying at home with his wife. She had been absolutely useless since they had arrived in Yankton. It was no great loss, of course, but it was irritating.

He was sipping a brandy and reading a St. Louis newspaper as he relaxed in the sitting room. Granted, it was two weeks old, but it was the best he could do. He was still waiting for an appointment to the Indian Affairs office, but his father-in-law had told him to be patient as the government moved slowly.

"Excuse me, Mister Falstaff?"

Edmund looked to his left at the voice and saw a bespectacled man of medium height with no facial hair and light red hair.

"Yes. What do you need?"

"My name is Cal Coleridge. I'm a writer. Perhaps you've heard of me under my pen name of Abilene Jones."

"No, I can't say that I have."

"Well, that's understandable. I write what they call dime novels for the mass market. They're very popular and some of our characters have become very famous already."

"Oh?"

"Yes. You see, I was talking to some other members and they informed me that you recently arrived after a harrowing trip across the prairie and had encounters with robbers and wild Indians. Is that true?"

Edmund didn't know what to make of the man, but replied, "It is."

"Now, Mister Falstaff, I would be very excited to put your story down in print. There are some financial advantages as well if the novel sells well."

His interest piqued, Edmund said, "Go ahead."

"May I sit?" he asked.

"Yes, of course," he replied as the man slid a chair close to him and sat down.

"If you tell me your story and I find it exciting enough, I'll write it and we'll publish it in the East. I would be willing to pay you fifty dollars if the novel sells over ten thousand copies."

"Is that likely?"

"My last novel sold more than eighty thousand copies."

"Well, what if this one sells that many?" he asked, suddenly very interested.

"Then I would pay you another fifty dollars for each ten thousand sold."

"And all I would have to do is tell you the story?"

"Yes. Then it's my job to make it colorful, so it will sell well."

Edmund smiled, leaned back and after taking another sip of his brandy, said, "I don't think you'd have to embellish it very much, honestly. It is very exciting on its own. There were many times I was near death and only was able to extricate myself using extraordinary, and with all due modesty, courageous actions on my part."

Cal grinned, then said, "If you are amenable then, Mister Falstaff, I'll take out my notebook and begin listening to your tale."

Cal Coleridge removed his thick notebook and three pencils from his nearby satchel, then opened the notebook and took pencil in hand.

Edmund folded his newspaper, set it down, then started his tall tale by saying, "It began with the sinking of the riverboat *Bertrand* on the first of April…"

————

"Emily, you have to stop moping," Abigail said with a motherly hint of exasperation, "It's childish. The circumstances aren't going to change by your morose behavior."

"Mother, I'm trying to act properly. I truly am. It's just taking time to adjust back to living this way again."

Abigail sighed and said, "I know the cause of your difficulties, Emily, and it's not just adjusting to live in a civilized society, is it?"

"No, Mother, I'll admit that it's not, but I do understand that nothing will ever come of it, so I'm trying to do better."

"Just do your best and try to smile occasionally," she said as she smiled at her daughter, then added, "So, what do you think of your house?"

"It's very nice. It's not as big or as fancy as our home in St. Louis, but I like it better."

"What does Edmund think of it?"

"Naturally, he thinks we should have something grander, or at least as nice as yours."

"Where is Edmund, anyway? I haven't seen him around much."

"He's at the Yankton Club. He's there most days awaiting the position father is finding for him."

"I'm sure that will happen soon."

"Mother, there is something else that I think you should know about."

"Yes?"

"Remember during our journey, when I accused him of being a hypocrite for criticizing Mister MacKenzie for his Sioux mother?"

"How could I forget?"

"Well, the reason I made the accusation was because I had been told by one of my friends just before the wedding that he frequented the bordello in the colored section on Saturday nights. He also continued those visits after we were married."

Abigail was shocked, but recovered quickly and asked, "And why are you telling me this now?"

"Because of where he has gone the last two Saturday nights. When he returned, he smelled of alcohol and lilac water. When I asked him where he'd been the first time, he became very angry and threatened to punish me severely. I made the mistake of asking him about it last Saturday night and he carried out his threat. I will not ask again."

"He struck you?"

"Several times. He told me that I was being a disobedient wife and I deserved punishment."

Abigail sighed and hugged Emily before saying, "Try not to anger him again, my dear. Unfortunately, he's within his rights as the head of the household. Have you told your father?"

"Heavens, no! He would take that war tomahawk that Mister MacKenzie gave to him and use it against Edmund. I wouldn't want father to go to jail."

"Well, all you can do is try to be the meek housewife while he's at home."

"I will, Mother."

————

Kyle saw Fort Sully in the distance, and it made him cringe. It seemed even worse than he remembered. He guessed that the last Missouri River flood had filled the valley around the fort as could see how high the water had risen by the waterline it had left on the fort's walls. It wasn't a swamp, but it was close, and he looked at those hills to the north and south with new eyes. They looked like an even bigger invitation to an attack, especially with repeating rifles.

There had been no more adventures in the last four days of his ride. He'd caught sight of some Lakota and Yanktonai Sioux, but neither group had noticed him. Both were hunting groups anyway and there were only eight warriors in each band.

He'd moved one of the new Henry rifles into his personal scabbard and kept four boxes of the .44 caliber ammunition just in case the army took it all. He felt better having two of the repeaters instead of the Spencer. The Spencer had longer range and a bigger punch, but it only had seven cartridges and had to be manually cocked, slowing down the rate of fire. With two fully loaded Henry rifles, he could muster quite a lot of firepower.

He finally reached the gate of the fort and was stopped by a guard that looked old enough to be a noncom by now. He wasn't surprised that he had been stopped, with his long, black hair and buckskin clothes.

"What do you want?" he asked almost with a snarl.

"I need to see Lieutenant Colonel Carpenter."

"What would you want to see the colonel about?"

"About keeping your ass safe, Private. My name is Kyle MacKenzie. Colonel Carpenter has requested that I do some scouting for him."

The private had heard of MacKenzie but hadn't made the connection. Except for the green eyes, he almost looked like an Indian, and a young Indian at that.

"You're Kyle MacKenzie? The one the Indians call the Green-Eyed Devil? You're kinda young, ain't ya?"

"Old enough."

"Go on through. The colonel is in the commander's office."

"I never would have guessed," Kyle said under his breath as he rode through.

The private noticed the bunches of repeaters on the packhorse with a heightened level of interest.

Kyle headed for the headquarters building, drawing curious looks from several members of the post and was surprised to see several women walking about the fort.

He stopped outside the headquarters, dismounted, then tied off his horse before stepping up onto the boardwalk and going inside.

He was greeted by the corporal at the desk more courteously than the private at the gate…barely.

"Yes?"

"I need to see Lieutenant Colonel. Carpenter. He sent for me."

"And your name?"

"Kyle MacKenzie."

The corporal was surprised but didn't ask the customary, 'aren't you kind of young' question.

"Just a moment."

He left Kyle and walked to the commander's office, tapping on the door jamb before entering. He got as far as "Kyle" before Lieutenant Colonel Harry Carpenter interrupted him when he exclaimed, "*He's here?* Send him in! It's about time!"

The corporal looked out at Kyle and waved him in.

Kyle stepped around the corporal's desk, then passed the corporal before entering the commander's office.

Lieutenant Colonel Carpenter stood and shook Kyle's hand.

"What took you so long, Kyle? I was expecting you a couple of weeks ago. Have a seat."

Kyle sat and replied, "I got sidetracked and had to make a trip back up to Yankton. I remember seeing this place before, but it seems even worse now."

"It's pretty bad, isn't it? The mosquitoes are something fierce most of the year and the snows get even deeper here in the winter when that wind shoves the stuff into the valley. We had a bad flood last year before I got here, too. The new site is going to be much better. We're already making the move, but it'll take about a year. It's about thirty miles southeast and on a plateau. It's a great defensive position, too. So, what can you tell me about what you found on your way here?"

"First, I need to know how you feel about the army's stance on repeating rifles."

"It's abominable. The Sioux are getting repeaters and we aren't. Most of my men still have muzzle-loaders. Why?"

"I have eighteen Henry rifles and a couple of cases of cartridges on my packhorse. I already absconded with a rifle and a few boxes of ammunition, but if you could make good use of the rest, I'll leave them with you."

The command officer's eyes went wide as he asked, "How'd you come by so many rifles?"

"A few days ago, I caught some gunrunners on my way here. I noticed some Lakota Sioux heading south from the river with some packhorses. At first, I thought they'd just attacked some farmer or something, but there wasn't any smoke. I followed their tracks north and found a cabin where these two yahoos were selling cases of repeaters and cartridges to the Sioux. I cleaned them out and burned the place down."

"What happened to the two men?"

"I told them to take the canoe and leave, but they chose not to."

"That showed a shortage of brains. I'll be more than grateful to accept your gift and make sure they're put to good use. I won't be able to get any more ammunition through normal supply channels, though."

"I'll get you some more ammunition. I'll make a trip to Fort Pierre and tell them to order a couple of cases."

"I don't want to know about anything else that you might have found at the cabin. It would just make my report too wordy."

"We wouldn't want that," Kyle replied as he grinned.

The lieutenant colonel smiled back before Kyle said, "Colonel, the setup these boys had arranged looked like a riverboat would stop and drop the rifles and ammunition off and then continue on upriver. They were last supplied during the first week in May. I have all the information written down."

"Give it to me and I'll forward it to the adjutant general for action."

Kyle handed him a sheet with all the pertinent information, then said, "If you don't have anything pressing right away, I'll head down to Fort Pierre put in that order for cartridges and see if I can get you the name of that boat."

"Just drop off the rifles and cartridges with Sergeant Schmidt. What can you tell me about the tribes?"

For the next half hour, Kyle briefed the commander about what he had seen and heard on his passage from Yankton.

There was little good news, especially with the addition of repeaters into the mix.

"Colonel, is your wife with you?" Kyle asked when he finished.

He nodded and replied, "After Maddie was married and James went off to West Point, she didn't want to live by herself, so she's here. Doctor White's wife is here, and Captains Morrison and Parnell have their wives here as well."

"Are there any other women on the post?"

"There are the Sioux women in the laundry. It's run by Sergeant Isaacson's widow, Ruth. Looking for a wife, Kyle?" he asked as he smiled.

"No, sir. I was just wondering who needed protection."

"Well, I for one, am glad you're here. Don't tarry too long in Fort Pierre."

"I won't, sir. I'll get those cartridges ordered and see if I can ferret out the name of the boat they used."

"I'll hold that telegram until you can give me that information as well. It'll help. How long before you get back from Fort Pierre?"

"Four days, I think."

Lieutenant Colonel Carpenter stood and shook Kyle's hand again as he said, "It's good to have you here, Kyle."

Kyle nodded, turned, walked past the corporal at his desk, then went outside, unhitched his horse and led the three animals to the quartermaster building.

After tying off his horse again, he walked inside and found Sergeant Carl Schmidt at the desk writing an entry in a log.

As he stepped through the door, he said loudly, "Sergeant Schmidt, I've brought you some presents."

Schmidt looked up, saw Kyle and broke into a grin.

"Well, if it ain't the devil himself. How are you, Kyle?"

Kyle grinned back and replied, "I'm good, Carl. I do have some gifts for you outside."

"What do you have?"

"Seventeen brand new Henry rifles and a couple of cases of .44 cartridges."

"You're joking, aren't you?" he asked as he popped out of his chair.

"No, sir. Come on and we'll unload them. My packhorses would be grateful."

Sergeant Schmidt came from around his desk, and they quickly walked outside.

"Look at that, will you?" he exclaimed upon seeing the rifles, then asked, "Where did you get them?"

"I found some gunrunners selling them to the Lakota. I killed them both, took the guns and burned the place down."

"Well, let's get them inside before they start disappearing."

It took them two trips to move all the ordnance from the horses and soon they were all stacked on Sergeant Schmidt's desk.

"Does the colonel know about them?" he asked.

"He does. He told me to bring them to you."

"It'll do us a lot of good, Kyle."

"Unfortunately, the Lakota have a lot more, I believe. I don't know how long those two were in operation."

"Bastards like them are gonna get a lot of men killed."

"I'm going to go to Fort Pierre and get you some more ammunition tomorrow."

"Good luck with that."

Kyle then left the office, went outside and led his horses to the stables. There were only six other horses inside, and after he had them brushed down, fed and watered, he sought out the farrier and had him check and replace their shoes, sure that the three animals needed them badly.

He began moving his armory and supplies to the scout quarters. He was the only scout living in the quarters as the other two scouts were Yanktonai Sioux and preferred to live outside the enclave. Once everything was moved in, he cleaned up and had to figure out what to do with all the money that he'd found in the cabin along with the cash that he already had accumulated over the years.

It was getting to be far too much to carry around, so he set aside three hundred dollars and took the remainder to the paymaster. They had a large safe and stored all the officers' and noncoms' savings, but none of the privates ever kept enough to bother.

He walked in and caught sight of the paymaster, Sergeant Eric Saunders.

"Sergeant Saunders, I need to leave some cash with you. I don't fancy having it on me."

"Sure, Kyle. Let me get you an envelope. When did you get in?"

"Just a little while ago."

Sergeant Saunders brought a heavy envelope and wrote Kyle's name on a preprinted line.

Kyle pulled out all his cash and let Sergeant Saunders begin to count it.

"Lord, Kyle! Where'd you get so much money?"

"A lot of it came from the Pony Express, then scouting and other things."

"Your total is $2,160. That's more than everyone else combined."

"I don't have many expenses, Eric."

He wrote out a receipt for Kyle and wrote the amount on the outside of the envelope before sealing it and putting it into the cookstove-sized safe. Kyle didn't mention that he had a similar amount in a bank in Omaha. The fifteen-hundred-dollar gift from the gunrunners was a nice addition, though.

"Thanks, Eric. I'll be seeing you later."

Kyle put the receipt in his pocket and returned to the scout's quarters to relax for a while. He was tired after the long ride and needed a few hours to unwind before heading out in the morning to go to Fort Pierre.

———

"This is very impressive work, Mister Coleridge," said Edmund as he finished reading the sixty pages.

"Well, you gave me some very good material, Mister Falstaff."

"I do like the title, *Flinging Ed Falstaff,* although I'm not sure about the use of Ed instead of my proper Christian name."

"Our readers like something catchy, a name they can relate to."

Edmund nodded, reluctantly acquiescing to the very plebian use of his name.

"Do you do your own artwork as well?" he asked looking at the graphic pencil work he held in his hand.

"I'm rare in that I do. I wanted to show the dramatic end to your victory over the savages. See how your empty pistol is flying through the air, about to strike down that last Indian? I even used your trophy war tomahawk in the picture. It's just as you described to me down to the last detail; out of ammunition with one more attacking Sioux yet still needing to save your wife and in-laws. You had to fling your empty Colt revolver as a last resort, yet with uncanny accuracy, the barrel smashed into his face killing him. It's a thrilling story."

"It was very frightening for all of those around me, including that worthless half-breed I rescued, Kyle MacKenzie. You should have seen him cowering behind my wife. I, on the other hand, felt calm and in control, as I had to be."

"Well, I'll be sending out the manuscript to my publishers in New York. They should get it within a week, and it should be published two weeks later. Then, we'll see how it does."

"Wonderful. And these will be sold all over the East?"

"New York, Philadelphia, Boston, just to name a few."

"Excellent."

Cal Coleridge gathered up his manuscript and replaced it in a leather satchel. It was an outstanding effort, he admitted to himself. He knew that Edmund had exaggerated some of the facts, but that was the nature of the business. Of course, he'd added his own embellishments that Edmund hadn't disputed. He'd put it on the riverboat tomorrow, and it would be on the eastbound train in Omaha a few days later. He hadn't mentioned to Edmund that the novels also sold well in Chicago, St. Louis, Kansas City and even in Omaha.

———

"Why would the governor ask to see you, Charles?" Abigail asked.

"It seems that the Santee Sioux chief has asked that I be present at the new treaty negotiations. Have you seen my war tomahawk? I'd like to have it with me when we meet like Kyle suggested."

"I haven't seen it anywhere. I thought it was by the mantle."

"It isn't. Is Emily still here?"

"Yes, she's in the kitchen."

"I'll ask her."

Charles left the parlor and walked out to the kitchen where Emily was preparing lunch. She still seemed to want to remain the plains woman, although she had agreed to wear the corset again finally.

"Emily, have you seen my war tomahawk? It seems to have gone wandering."

"I saw Edmund taking it with him to the club several days ago."

"Edmund has it? Whatever for?"

"I'm not sure, Father. He doesn't talk to me very often."

"How are you doing, Emily?" he asked, seeing the perpetual sadness in her eyes.

"I'm fine, Father," she replied as she smiled but the sadness remained.

Charles leaned closer to his daughter and said quietly, "Emily, don't say anything about this, but I asked Kyle a day before we reached the landing if he loved you and he said he did, but knew there was nothing he could do about it. But he did say that he would stop by when he could just to be here, as he put it, when the future takes a sudden right turn."

The sadness flew from her eyes as she looked at her father.

Then she asked just as quietly, but with an undercurrent of unbridled excitement, "He really said that, Father? He said he'd be coming back to visit?"

"Yes. Your mother knows about the visits but doesn't know about the rest. I just thought you should know."

She hugged her father and whispered, "Thank you so much, Father. It gives me some hope."

"I owe you much more than that, Emily."

CHAPTER 7

Kyle departed Fort Sully at dawn, thinking that he might be able to make it down to Fort Pierre by three in the afternoon if he didn't have any problems. He was riding without any packhorse, so could move faster if he ran into a band of Lakota.

He was in a good mood, considering how he had been just a few days ago. The weather was good, and he was in his element.

It was midmorning and he was crossing one of the high points along the river, when he saw something that reminded him of an incident that he hadn't witnessed but had affected his life, a riverboat was beached on the opposite bank with its aft under the water. It was about a mile downriver from him and he could see the passengers clustered about the crew on the bank nearby, probably waiting for the next boat to pick them up.

Then his peripheral vision picked up motion to the southwest and he turned his attention to that direction and saw a much bigger problem. A party of Lakota was about two miles from the passengers, and they were heading in that direction.

Kyle cursed at the situation. It was just his luck to be on the wrong side of the river. This was no time for hesitation though, as he walked his horse down to the northern bank of the Missouri and let him enter the water. He had swum small rivers before with the horse, but this was the Missouri, not some creek trying to be called a river and it was still flowing quickly.

He knew the horse was a good swimmer, so just let him go and kept him pointed toward the shore. The horse was making headway and Kyle just let him swim as the current moved them closer to the passengers. They were moving east at around three or four knots with the current, so he began looking on the southern bank for someplace the horse could step up onto dry ground. He needed to find a place to get the horse ashore.

The horse was tiring from trying to fight the current instead of just letting the current take it, but it was only twenty feet from land now. He had to stay in the saddle if he was to keep the powder dry for his pistol reloads. The Henry's ammunition wasn't a problem, nor were the ten loads he had in his pistols, but he was already thinking ahead and might need that dry powder.

The horse finally began to feel the bottom and Kyle could feel his hooves gain purchase. Less than a minute later, the horse dragged them out of the Missouri and stumbled onto the ground. Now Kyle needed to get him moving behind the Lakota.

He dismounted, then led the horse up the bank and onto solid ground. He couldn't let the horse eat or drink, or even rest as he mounted again, all he could do was to give the gelding his thanks as he set him off to a medium trot behind the Lakota.

Once underway, he needed to come up with a semblance of a plan. He only had his Henry and his Colts, so he could fire fifteen shots from the rifle and ten from his pistols, but he'd never survive a gun battle with that many warriors. For once, he was outgunned.

Kyle rode behind the Lakota, still thinking as he watched the band less than a mile ahead. He set his horse to a fast trot and began making up the deficit quickly as they moved slowly but relentlessly toward their prey who were unable to escape.

He came over a small rise and saw the passengers in the distance and was only about three hundred yards behind the

Sioux and he realized that there was only one way out of this; only one and he didn't like the idea at all.

The passengers were in a state of true panic since they'd spotted the large band of Indians. The crew stood their ground in front of the passengers, but Kyle could see that they were woefully armed, with only three pistols among them.

Kyle wanted to do this with the most impact as the Lakota began to line up for their charge.

He leaned back and screamed the same high-pitched war cry that he had used on the cougar, then sat on his horse, his rifle on his hip and the blazing sun in his face as the Lakota turned en masse to see the source of the threatening cry.

Kyle then began trotting his horse forward to get within shouting distance as the passengers, crew, and most importantly, the Lakota watched as he approached.

When he was within sixty yards, he pulled to a stop and began to speak in Lakota Sioux, the language of his mother.

"Who are you, brave warriors of the Lakota that you make war on women? I am Kyle MacKenzie, the Green-Eyed Devil. I have killed many Lakota, but I only kill warriors. To kill women is without honor. Have you no honor? I am here to die to protect these people. But I will not fight men without honor. I throw down my rifle and pistols."

He dropped his Henry theatrically to the ground and then unbuckled his gunbelt, held it out on the other side and snapped his hand open with flair, letting the pistols hit the dirt.

He then shouted, "I have only my knife now. I will give one of you a chance to kill me, but I challenge you to face me. Show me that you have honor among the Lakota. Send me your strongest warrior. If I defeat him, you will return and cause no harm to the whites. If I am dead, then I can no longer prevent you and you will know that you have killed The Green-Eyed Devil at last."

He slowly drew his Bowie from its sheath and let it flash in the mid-morning sun.

The Lakota were both outraged and pleased. This was the chance to kill the famous Green-Eyed Devil.

Their leader, Night Bear, told the others that he would fight the devil and kill him, for he had stronger magic than the white man.

Before he rode to meet Kyle, he turned to his lieutenant and said, "If he takes my life, kill him."

His second in command, Howling Wolf, was shocked. *Where would be the honor in killing a man who had won a fight of courage?* He hoped that Night Bear would win to relieve him of this terrible decision.

Night Bear started his horse toward Kyle at a trot as Kyle stepped down, then took off his sheath and his shirt.

He had heard Night Bear's parting order and was beginning to question his decision as Night Bear slid from his horse when he was within twenty feet and pulled his own knife.

"You have been cut before, devil," he said, pointing to the long wound on his chest.

"It was a she-bear that cut me, not a Lakota. No Lakota or any other Sioux has ever cut me."

"You lie, devil. If not, then I, Night Bear, will be the first."

They began circling each other, each looking for the advantage. Kyle avoided facing into the sun by shifting to counterclockwise when he reached the north. Night Bear did the same as neither was prepared to give up that simple advantage.

Kyle made the first move, a quick thrust that he knew would be a miss. He just wanted to get this started.

Night Bear leapt aside easily and laughed but said nothing.

Kyle started a second thrust but just as he began to extend his right arm, jerked it back as Night Bear's blade slashed to where Kyle's arm should have been. Kyle continued his pullback and then began to turn in the same motion to complete a clockwise pirouette and slashed Night Bear across his chest, the big Bowie making a deep gash in his side.

Night Bear acted as if it was nothing but a scratch, but Kyle knew better as blood gushed down Night Bear's side. Kyle could have just waited for him to bleed to death, or at least start to get woozy, but he felt that it wouldn't be enough. He needed drama and needed to press his point to the remaining Lakota.

Night Bear knew he had already lost the fight, but he wanted to take the Green-Eyed Devil with him. He screamed his death cry and exploded at Kyle with his knife poised above his head.

Kyle let him come, knowing that the timing needed to be perfect. Night Bear had him as his blade began to come down onto Kyle's face, but just as Night Bear's blade began its downward arc toward him, Kyle fell backwards.

He could see the point of the blade just inches before his eyes and knew this was going to be close, then felt his back strike the ground and turned his head as hard as he could to the right as Night Bear's knife plunged into the prairie of Dakota Territory less than an inch from Kyle's ear.

Kyle wasted no time and rammed his big blade home into Night Bear's chest and felt the warmth of Night Bear's blood coat his naked chest, even as the dirt covered his back. He quickly rolled Night Bear's body from him and pulled his knife from the dead body. He didn't scream or do anything other than wipe his blade clean on Night Bear's pants before he walked to his horse, removed his canteen, took a long swallow and then used the water to wash off the blood to show that he hadn't been wounded.

When he finished, he turned and just looked at the remaining line of Lakota warriors, wondering what they would do.

Now, Howling Wolf had a decision to make. *Did he follow Night Bear's last orders?* He turned to his friend, Bright Owl and just looked at him. Bright Owl shook his head ever so slightly.

Howling Wolf shouted to his companions then they all turned back east toward Kyle as he stood beside Night Bear's body.

Kyle had replaced his knife in its sheath when he saw the Lakota approach and didn't pick up his rifle. It wouldn't matter now.

Howling Wolf said nothing to Kyle, but just slipped off his horse, as did Bright Owl. They picked up Night Bear's body and slipped it over his horse before he picked up Night Bear's knife, removed the decorative sheath from Night Bear and handed both to Kyle, then they mounted their horses, and rode west.

Kyle then blew out his breath, donned his shirt and put on his gunbelt, picked up his Henry, did a quick inspection to make sure that no dirt had found its way into the magazine tube, then slid it into his scabbard before walking toward the passengers, leading his exhausted horse. He was carrying Night Bear's knife in his hand, so he slid it into its sheath and then slipped the sheath under his belt.

When he reached the passengers, they just all looked at him at with some measure of trepidation as they weren't sure who he was.

He smiled at the crowd, then said loudly, "Morning, folks. Is everybody all right?", establishing himself as one of their own.

There was a long silence as Kyle looked at the still-stunned faces.

Eventually it was the captain that spoke when he stepped forward and asked, "Mister, who are you?"

"My name's Kyle MacKenzie. Is another boat coming by soon?" he asked.

"Your pa named Kyle MacKenzie, too?" he asked without providing an answer.

"No, sir," Kyle replied as he smiled.

"Then you're the Green-Eyed Devil we hear about?"

"I've been called that. So, what's the story on the boat?"

"Oh. We'll probably get picked up by the *Sheba* later this morning. She was shoving off early. Our boiler blew early this morning, but we got everybody off okay."

Then the dam broke and all the passengers wanted to know why he had done what he did, why the Indians left, and all sorts of other things. The most asked question was, "Will they be back?"

Kyle assured them that the Indians wouldn't be back, so it soon became almost a picnic atmosphere. There were six children in the group, so Kyle felt better about doing what he did. They had managed to get some food off the boat, and as Kyle sat on the ground, someone brought him something to eat.

More passengers came over to talk to him and thank him for what he did over the next two hours.

Around one o'clock, there was a sharp whistle followed by two short blasts from upriver.

"There's their ride," thought Kyle as the *Sheba* came into view.

Now that he knew they were safe, he mounted, then waved before he continued his ride to Fort Pierre on the wrong side of the river. It would be another river crossing for the horse, but it would mean a delay too as he wasn't going to ask the horse to cross twice in a day.

As he rode the horse, he told him that he was impressed by his performance and had earned a name. He told him he'd call him Neptune, which seemed appropriate.

After spending the night in a cold camp on the Nebraska side of the river, Kyle and Neptune crossed the river again and arrived in Fort Pierre in mid-morning. It was only a fort in name, like many were. The original builders of many trading posts erected defensive works and improved them as more people arrived to stay. The original fort would remain, but many of them grew into towns like Fort Pierre was doing. The original fort and trading post were still there by the river, but the buildings were spreading outward. He was walking his horse through the streets and had his old Henry in one scabbard and the Sharps in the other and was wearing both pistols, as usual. He left his bow and arrow and new Henry in his scout's quarters because he didn't want to be overly conspicuous in his amount of firepower, just marginally so.

He rode toward the wharf and when he was close to the docks, figured he might as well see if he could find out which steamboat had dropped off the weapons. He stepped down and tied off the horse at the nearest hitchrail. Before he'd left Fort Sully, he had his hair cut short for the mission to make him look less like an Indian and today he was wearing canvas britches and a flannel shirt to blend in as well.

He sauntered over to the shipping office and began perusing the announcements. Today was the sixteenth, and the oldest one posted was for the twelfth, so he walked inside.

"Morning. What can I do for you, young feller?" asked a heavily whiskered man of about forty who seemed affable.

"My brother was supposed to meet me here on the ninth, but I didn't make it in time because I had trouble with some Sioux. I don't even remember the name of the boat he was supposed to be on. I can't find him and I'm beginning to think his boat may have met with an accident or been attacked by the Indians."

"Well, mister, we've had a lot of both lately. You say the ninth? We only had two boats come by that day and one the day before. The one on the eighth was the *Missouri Queen*, they had problems with the Santee Sioux, but that was a few days ago. On the ninth we had the *Belle of Columbia* and the *Oregon*."

"Did any passengers get off here? My brother is shorter than I am and has brown eyes."

"Nope. No passengers."

Kyle scratched his head and said, "This is strange. Paul should have been on one or the other. Did either of them stop after they left Yankton?"

"The *Belle* didn't, but the *Oregon* was delayed with a boiler problem and had to put ashore south of Fort Randall. They were there a few hours to get the problem fixed."

Kyle knew that if the boat put in at the gunrunners' cabin, it had to be at the direction of the captain or pilot. A faulty boiler, while common, was probably a fabrication. They couldn't keep having boiler problems, though. A better way would be to rendezvous at night and offload them onto a barge.

There was something wrong in all of this. It seemed like such a good idea, if you consider gunrunning a worthy occupation, but having a riverboat actually stop there was pretty stupid. The passengers would even notice.

That was all true unless it was their first time and only then would it make sense. If it was the first shipment, they might not have had time to build a barge, so they came up with the boiler problem to offload the rifles and ammunition. In that case, it would indeed make sense. He should have checked for the presence of a barge near the water. All he had seen with his quick glance was the canoe. He had made a mistake, but there was nothing he could do about it now. But that also meant that if it was their first shipment, then the Lakota didn't get as many repeaters as he'd thought.

He stepped up on his horse and trotted him over to the trading post, firm in the knowledge that it was the *Oregon* that they had used for their gunrunning, but he was sure that it wouldn't be limited to that one steamboat once they had their operation fully established. He dismounted and tied off the horse, still deep in thought and didn't notice the two men who watched him ride up. They were walking quickly on his right side as he was stepping onto the post's porch.

"Hey, mister!" the taller of the two said loudly when they were within ten feet.

Kyle glanced at them and knew they were trouble. Why they wanted trouble was the question.

"Are you talking to me?" he asked in a normal tone.

"Who else am I lookin' at?"

"What do you want?"

"I was wonderin' what a breed like you was doin' with a repeater?"

"I bought it in Omaha a year ago, if it's any of your business, which it isn't."

"Oh, you wanna get feisty with me, do you?" he asked, as Kyle wondered if the shorter man could even talk.

"No, I answered your question and told you that where I bought my rifle isn't your business. Why is that feisty?"

"It sounds like you wanna get into a fight."

"No, I have no intention of getting into a fight with either of you or both of you."

"Afraid, are ya?"

"No. I'm just not in the mood. I have things I need to do before I leave."

"Gonna go back and hump your squaw wife are ya?" he laughed as his shorter sidekick giggled.

It wasn't a wise thing to say, yet Kyle held back his temper, but it was close, very close.

He gritted his teeth and the muscles on his jaws bulged as he growled, "You both had better leave. If you keep this up, you'll both be in a lot of pain in two minutes."

The combination of his green eyes and his threatening voice took them both aback, and if they'd been smarter, they would have taken his advice. But they had to push it because they weren't about to surrender their manhood to a damned half-breed.

Again, it was the taller man who snarled, "You're goin' too far, breed. We're gonna make you pay for what you just said."

"Leave now and stay healthy," Kyle replied as he tensed for what was to come.

They both pulled knives and advanced steadily, but slowly. Kyle knew they didn't have pistols, so he reached into his shoulder sheath and pulled out his huge Bowie that dwarfed their normal-sized knives.

They both were transfixed by the huge blade and it was the opportunity that Kyle needed. Without a hint of a warning, he suddenly rocked onto his left leg and snapped off a hard kick at the bigger man's knee. The sole of his boot and his heel smashed into the man's patella and snapped ligaments on the back sides of the knee, sending him screaming to the ground.

His partner wasted no time to lunge at Kyle with his blade pointed at Kyle's chest, but after he had kicked the first man, Kyle, expecting an immediate attack from the second man, simply dropped to the boardwalk, holding himself off the wood with his left hand as he struck upwards with his massive blade as the second man's knife hit the empty space where Kyle had just been. The Bowie knife slid effortlessly into the man's bicep and sliced it in half like a small roast.

The previously quiet man joined his partner in screaming as Kyle returned to his feet.

A crowd had gathered at the start of the fight and watched as Kyle cleaned his knife off on the shirt of the first man, slid it back into its sheath, then turned to the crowd.

"Does anyone know who these two men are?"

"Yeah," said a very short man with a very long beard, "that's Bobo Jenkins and the one with the arm cut open in Billie Parker. They're just a couple of bad boys. I reckon they ain't gonna bother nobody for a while."

"Do they deserve medical attention?"

"Nope," he replied.

Kyle looked down at the two, shook his head, then turned and left them howling on the street as did everyone else.

He entered the trading post and walked to the counter and approached the proprietor, who asked, "What can I do for ya', mister?"

"I need to place a large order for some .44 caliber rimfire ammunition for a Henry rifle."

"Sure. How much do you need?"

"Four cases should do it."

"Four cases? What you doin'? Outfittin' an army?" he asked with a laugh.

"Strangely enough, that's exactly what I'm doing. The 20th Infantry at Fort Sully, to be exact."

"Can't the army get 'em?"

"The army isn't fond of repeaters. At least not yet. They'll learn soon enough."

"That'll be forty-eight dollars."

Kyle counted out the cash and accepted the change.

"It'll take almost a month to get them in. What name should I put on the order?"

"Kyle MacKenzie."

"You're Kyle MacKenzie? For real? You seem younger than I figured."

"I'm old enough."

Kyle smiled and left the post, passing the two men who were still unaided on the trading post's porch. He climbed onto his horse to find dinner and then a room for the night.

———

Charles walked into the sitting room of the club and asked, "Edmund, do you have my war tomahawk?"

"Oh, yes, Charles. One of the fellows at the club wanted to see what it looked like and I didn't think you'd mind my showing it to him."

"That's fine, but I need it back soon. I've been invited to attend the treaty negotiations."

"Why you? Is it because your cousin was an Indian agent and is now a Congressman?"

"No, I believe it's because of what Kyle told their chief."

"Him again? Is there no escaping that man? He's been gone for almost three weeks now and his name keeps percolating into normal conversation."

"Edmund, just bring me the tomahawk to my house today, please?"

"I'll try. I left it with the other gentleman to examine, but he should be in sometime later."

Charles was getting more irritated with Edmund every day since *The Bertrand's* sinking. Charles had bought the house and was providing them with fifty dollars each month for expenses, but Edmund had done nothing but spend his time at the club.

"Just bring it by the house as soon as you can, please."

"I shall."

Charles left the gentleman's club and went home in a foul mood.

———

Kyle returned to the fort the next day and made his report to the boss, including the problem with the riverboat, which he already knew about, and then the problem with the two thugs in Fort Pierre. Once that was done, he took a day off to get everything cleaned up and organized before he made a three-day loop around the fort and found nothing that showed any unusual activity around the fort.

Now, Kyle was sitting across from Lieutenant Colonel Carpenter and was being briefed on a very different type of problem.

"Are you sure they're white men?" Kyle asked.

"That's what the Yanktonai scouts are telling me."

"Why are they doing it? Just to stir up more bad blood between the settlers and the Lakota?"

"That seems to be the idea. They've burned out two ranches and a farm in the past month. When we sent the scouts in, they checked each location and they told us it wasn't the Lakota. They're not too fond of the Lakota either, so I'm pretty sure they're telling me the truth. I just need to have you confirm their information. General Frobisher would be annoyed if I started accusing whites based on the word of two Sioux scouts."

"If I confirm the information, then what do you want me to do?"

"Use your best judgement about it."

"Alright. When do you want me to go?"

"How about tomorrow?" he asked as he smiled.

Kyle just nodded, before he replied, "I'll leave in the morning, then."

As he left the command building, he understood that in this case, using his best judgement was to make the problem disappear while making as few waves as possible.

————

Emily was tired of being the good, quiet housewife. She never loved Edmund at all, but now she positively abhorred the man, if one could call him that. She just wondered what his sudden swagger was all about. He'd taken to ordering her around like a servant. *Bring me a brandy! Get me some coffee!* He didn't know how close she'd come to spilling the last cup of coffee in his lap...accidentally, of course. But something was going on and she had no idea what he was planning.

She sat alone in her sitting room, closed her eyes and began to fantasize about simply buying a ticket on a riverboat to Fort Sully and finding Kyle. She would get off the riverboat and he would be there waiting for her. He'd take her in his arms and kiss her passionately before whisking her away to a private place, but still outdoors in the bright sunlight. They'd make love and say what neither could ever say before.

But now, even as she let her imagination fly, she realized that despite the looks they had shared and what her father had told her, she was sure that he wouldn't accept her even if she arrived at the fort. He was such an honorable man that he'd probably just send her back to Edmund. *Damned honor!*

She began to feel trapped all over again and as her thoughts of escape and finding Kyle dissolved, she went from exultant dream to crashing reality in seconds. Nothing would ever happen to Edmund. He just walked from the house to the club and back every day. The only other place he visited was one of the two bordellos on Saturday nights and wondered which one he used. Her biggest fear is that he would pass a social disease to her. Granted, he didn't bed her as often as most husbands did, but even twice a month was too often.

As she opened her eyes, she suddenly decided that she wasn't going to cry or mope any longer. Emily was going to be the same Emily that had looked up at Kyle as he prepared to fight off the Santee Sioux. She was going to have sand and make him proud of her.

———

In New York the manuscript submitted by Cal Coleridge, a.k.a. Abilene Jones, was on a lucky streak. It had hit the exact timing for the trains and had arrived in New York just eight days after he had put it on the steamer. Then the editor happened to have an empty desk when it arrived, so he read it in two hours, made three simple changes and sent it to the typesetter. The cover art was being tinted and two days later, the first printing run of five thousand copies was done. As per their policy, they packaged up the first five hundred and put them on a train for Omaha, the closest city to the story locale knowing it would appeal to the readers.

———

CHAPTER 8

Kyle was halfway to Fort Pierre by mid-morning. He was well-rested, well-fed, and eager to get the job done. He didn't see any new riverboats sinking, but he did see the upper decks of the one from his last trip to Fort Pierre which hadn't been salvaged yet.

When he arrived at Fort Pierre, the first thing he did was to casually ride around the growing settlement. It seemed even bigger than it was when he was there the last time, but thought it was just a misperception. It hadn't been that long, but he found that there were more rumors of gold in the Black Hills, and that was bad.

The Black Hills were sacred ground to the Lakota and even the rumors of gold were enough to attract a lot of the unsavory crowd. It also made what the white imposters were doing make some sort of sense as it would provide one more excuse to grab some land. So far, the rumors had been very faint, so there was the merest trickle of new troublemakers arriving into the area. If it were true and there was gold in the Black Hills, it would be a disaster.

He stepped down, tied off Neptune, then walked into the trading post. He noticed that there was a new, large sign that said DRY GOODS above the door. Maybe that's why he thought the place looked bigger. It was still the same place, though.

He found the proprietor, gave him a letter to post and asked, "Things been quiet lately? It sure seems quiet."

"Hardly that, Mister. We had a ranch burned out by them Sioux a few days ago, just east of here. They sure are raidin' a lot around here. Where is the army?"

"Fort Sully is just too far away where it is right now, but they're moving it a lot closer and that should help."

"Hope it ain't too late."

He left the self-proclaimed dry goods store, mounted his horse and wondered briefly what happened to those two thugs who tried to start trouble when he was here last. He may never know, so he turned Neptune east and rode out of the settlement. He was so heavily armed, and the weather was so cooperative, he decided before he left that he wouldn't stay in a hotel. He'd stay out of the built-up area and start scouting for the men burning out the farms and ranches.

He'd begin with the latest burnt out ranch. Finding it wasn't difficult as he just went east following the wagon ruts. He supposed if someone was generous, he could call it a road, but it was just a pair of often used wagon ruts.

Forty minutes later, he came to what used to be a ranch. There was a pile of charred ash where the house used to stand, but the only things that identified it as a house were the cook stove and the chimney and was surprised that the cookstove was still there. It must have been a tremendous blaze.

He stepped down and let Neptune stand with his packhorse as he began walking around the area examining the ground. He soon found both human and horse prints. All the horses were unshod. He found the family's footprints and saw two small sets as well and hoped those bastards didn't burn the family but didn't want to know.

Kyle widened his search and found the arrival hoofprints from further east, then followed them on foot for a quarter of a mile before turning back, constantly scanning the ground for clues. At first glance, and second glance for that matter, it would appear to be the work of the Lakota. But many of the moccasin-clad footprints showed him to be those of white men wearing moccasins.

They were used to wearing boots, not moccasins, so their patterns of movement were very different because they were uncomfortable in the moccasins. That and there were too many big feet. If the soil had been softer, it would have helped, because he'd be able to see how deep they were. He'd probably find that some of them tended toward fat, something never found in a Lakota warrior. He made his way back to his horse, mounted and began to walk Neptune following a set of the east-bound tracks. After half of a mile, more tracks joined the original group, returning the way they had come.

He walked Neptune for four miles before the trail made a sudden turn to the north, and he followed. After a mile, it began the expected westerly curve back toward Fort Pierre and he continued trailing, expecting them to go all the way to the growing settlement. He passed two intact farms, which further ruled out the Lakota. *Why attack a ranch closer to the settlement and leave more vulnerable farms untouched?*

When he reached the third farm, he saw the trail turn toward the farm's large barn, which surprised him. There were only eight sets of hoofprints, so eight men were causing all this.

He kept riding west past the farm, looking for a place to set up an observation post.

After he passed a low hill, he turned north and crossed behind the hill. It wasn't the best of places to wait and watch as the nearest water was a small pond about a half mile further north, but there was plenty of grass for the horses. So, he rode to the pond and let the horses drink before returning to the hill where he unsaddled both horses on the north slope of the hill and let them graze. He pulled in close to the hill, stretched out his bedroll and then just waited.

He set up a routine. Three times a day, he'd take the horses to drink, then brush them down and move their grazing location. He never made a fire, but he was all right with that. This was what a lot of scouting normally was, just waiting.

He spent a lot of the time thinking about Emily. The future looked so cloudy and unsure and many changes needed to happen, none of which were in his control.

For three days, Kyle had time to think about Emily and the confounded situation he found himself in. If she were just an infatuation, he could have just thrown it aside. But he knew it was much more than that after just a few days of that ride to Yankton. No one had ever touched his soul as she had.

Around midmorning on the fourth day, his patient waiting was finally rewarded when he heard hoofbeats of two or three horses passing and quickly scampered up the low hill to take a look. There were three of them and each had a rifle, but none were repeaters. They came from the east, probably from those other farmhouses that hadn't been attacked and watched as they turned toward the farmhouse.

He stayed in place and continued to wait when forty minutes later another four men arrived from the west and entered the house. All of their horses were left outside at a hitchrail. He was expecting them to return to their horses and remove the saddles before they attacked another place.

Ten minutes later, eight men dressed in buckskins with long black hair and feathers exited the house and walked to the barn.

218

Just a few minutes later, they rode out bareback on different horses. Kyle was initially surprised that they had more horses, but then guessed that they had stolen them from the ranches and farms they'd already burned.

They headed due south at a trot and Kyle could see them all laughing and talking as if they were going on a joy ride and not riding to destroy someone's home. He knew that he'd have to act quickly.

As soon as they were out of sight, he slid down the hill and saddled both horses. He walked Neptune toward the farm, trailing his packhorse, dismounted and tied off his horse at the crowded hitchrail, then stepped onto the porch and went inside the house without knocking, expecting it to be empty. But as the door slammed behind him, a female voice asked loudly, "Sam, what are you doin' back so soon?"

Kyle was momentarily surprised but recovered quickly, then quickly walked into the kitchen.

A woman of about thirty or so, plain of face but with a good figure was startled when Kyle stepped in.

"*Who are you?* What are you doin' in my house?" she shouted.

"Ma'am, I've come to stop what your man is doing."

"Sam ain't doin' nothin'. You get outta here!"

"Ma'am, I had aimed to burn this farm to the ground, just like your husband's been doing to try to rile up the army."

"Those damned Injuns deserve it. They killed my Jesse and burned down our first house. There ain't no hell hot enough for 'em!"

219

"Ma'am, there is no one with more vengeance in his heart for the Lakota than me. They killed my wife. But my war is with the Lakota and I would never harm a neighbor."

"But the army ain't doin' a thing! This'll get 'em goin'."

"You may think so, but it's not the way to do it. I'll leave your house intact, but I'm going to go and find those men. If they don't stop, then it'll come down to me against them."

"Then you'll die."

"Maybe," he said before he turned, walked quickly down the hall and exited the house.

He thought about leaving the packhorse, but didn't want to leave that woman anything, so he mounted Neptune and rode south. They had a half hour head start on him, but he would move faster than they could. He set both horses to a fast trot, following their easy trail and watching the horizon for their dust cloud. He didn't think their target was too close to home.

For once, he didn't care if they checked their backtrail. In fact, he was close to firing off a round to turn them around, but just continued after them instead.

———

The eight men didn't have to hurry. Their leader, Sam Wright, had wanted to do this job first, but he decided to wait until it looked like just another Lakota raid. The Jameson place appeared to be just another farm, and in most respects, it was. But it was the woman that made this job sweet. She was one of them…a hated Indian. It was why the farm was never threatened by real Lakota. They even let the damned Indians get food from them and probably gave them guns, too. This house would be different, because it would be occupied when it went up in flames. That Indian bitch, her squaw-loving husband and their three half-breed brats would all burn.

It was just another five miles away. In another hour, he'd watch that house and the Jamesons die.

———

Kyle saw the dust cloud a couple of miles ahead. He'd made up most of the distance and was still gaining. He pulled his Sharps out and slipped a percussion cap onto the nipple as Neptune kept up the pace. He had put the cartridge in place earlier when he thought that he may need its long range if he wasn't on time.

Then he spotted their target as the farmhouse appeared in the distance through the shimmering heat waves. There was no wind, so Kyle began doing calculations for the Sharps. The altitude was around fifteen hundred feet above sea level and the air temperature was already over eighty degrees, which was pretty hot for this time of year.

He pulled his canteen and took a long swallow of water knowing that it was going to be a hot day on the plains of Dakota Territory in more ways than one.

Ten minutes later, he could make out individual riders and was less than a mile away. He guessed that they felt secure and didn't need to check their backtrail. Overconfidence can be a dangerous thing.

Kyle kept closing the gap knowing that as long as they were riding, they wouldn't hear him. As long as none looked behind them, he could continue to get closer and would soon be in range.

———

Ahead of him, Sam Wright had his band slow down and spread out.

"We're gonna drive 'em back into the house if you see 'em. Jack, you and Maurice go wide right through the fields and make 'em run to the house. Henry, you and Al go left and do the same. We'll stay here and wait until we see you comin' back to the house."

"Okay, Sam," Jack replied, and the two pairs split from the others and began to make their looping rides around the farm to push anyone in the fields back to the house. They all knew of Sam's intentions and agreed with them.

Kyle saw them peel off and guessed easily what they were going to do. If they were just planning a fake Lakota raid, they'd just ride straight to the house and set it and the barn afire, but this was different. This was a killing raid and he didn't know the reason for the change, just that he knew that he had to stop it. He released the tie rope for the packhorse and let it drop.

As the two other pairs of riders departed, the immediate area around Sam Wright fell into silence.

Kyle knew he'd be heard as soon as the two groups had pulled far enough away from the center group, so he had slowed Neptune to a walk. He was only four hundred yards away and within the Sharps' range but wanted to get closer.

Out in the fields, Elijah Jameson and his wife Sarah and their oldest, eleven-year-old Joseph, had seen the riders and at first glance had assumed them to be passing Lakota, but Sarah noticed the difference in the way they rode.

"They're white men, Eli," she said loudly.

Eli and Joseph both looked at the two men and realized she was right.

"They're coming after us, Sarah!" Eli shouted.

"There are two more on the other side!" she shouted, pointing to the other riders.

Suddenly, both pairs began to ride quickly at them, waving their rifles in the air and screaming.

The Jamesons quickly began running toward the ranch house.

Sam Wright watched as the four men began their attack and was gratified when he heard them start whooping in a weak imitation of a Lakota war cry. It meant they were driving them into the house.

Kyle had seen the same thing and didn't hesitate as he cocked the Sharps' hammer, aimed at the rider who seemed to be giving instructions and pulled the trigger.

The Sharps erupted in flame and smoke as the .52 caliber projectile hurtled from the muzzle toward its target only two hundred and fifty yards away. Kyle rammed the Sharps into his scabbard and grabbed the Henry even as the Sharps' bullet slammed into Sam Wright, striking him high in the back, almost dead center, pulverizing his fifth thoracic vertebra and then exploding his aortic arch. He grunted, then fell forward onto his horse's neck, then rolled to the side and struck the ground four seconds later but didn't move.

Kyle screamed his mind-chilling war cry and set Neptune to a trot, his Henry held cocked and ready for firing.

As soon as the thunder from the Sharps had reached the men sitting beside Sam Wright as their leader fell to the dust, they turned and then had their neck hairs stiffen and a chill run down their spines as Kyle's cry reached them. They saw what appeared to be a short-haired Lakota coming at them, so they quickly pulled their rifles from their scabbards.

Kyle nudged Neptune's flanks with his knees as they charged, changing his direction slightly. The first man fired and missed wide before the second fired and Kyle felt the round pass through his flying buckskin shirt. The third man fired and hit Neptune's shoulder, causing the gelding to stumble while Kyle had to fight to maintain enough control to keep himself in the saddle.

Neptune stumbled to an awkward stop before Kyle leapt to the ground as the three men began to reload. They were sixty yards out and Kyle wasn't about to give them a chance to take that second shot. He quickly set his legs apart, brought his repeater level, picked his first target and began firing his Henry.

It was like a shooting gallery with three targets lined in a row. Kyle shot from right to left and didn't waste a shot. The first and third fell from their horses immediately after taking his first two .44s in the chest. The last one soon slumped over the front of his horse's neck, lifeless, by the time his Henry stopped sending bullets in their direction.

Kyle knew that Neptune was useless, so he ran to the dead men's horses as the four other riders gave up their pursuit of the Jamesons to counter the new threat. They had heard the firing and the war cry but didn't see the results as the house and barn obstructed their view, giving a huge advantage to Kyle.

Suddenly, a new variable was injected into the gunfight when the other two Jameson children left the house to see what was happening. When they spotted the horses and the four dead men, then saw Kyle running towards them, they thought he was the threat, so without any hesitation, they raced from the house heading to the fields and their onrushing parents and older brother.

They were both shouting for their parents, so Kyle never had a chance to warn them to stay in the house, nor could they hear the panicked shouts of their parents to return. Now, there were two sets of innocents between him and the other riders. He needed to draw the four riders away.

He had to gamble that the other four would view him as the only threat, so when he reached the bareback horses, he slowed enough to be able to lift himself onto the back of the nearest horse. He noticed that they still wore standard bridles which made him wonder why they bothered to disguise themselves at all. That alone would have identified them as white men to even a casual observer.

He wheeled the horse and rode north around the house, his Henry held in its right hand with eleven rounds remaining. As soon as he passed the house, he was finally spotted by the other four riders, and incredibly, they all initially mistook him for one of their own. It was a reasonable conclusion because no one else was there and he was riding Sam's horse, but that mistake lasted for just a few seconds before they realized he wasn't Sam.

Without any type of shouted coordination, they forgot about the family that had joined and was now running to the house and concentrated their attention on the stranger on Sam's horse. The two pairs of pseudo-Sioux almost simultaneously shifted their direction to the north as Kyle headed that way to draw them from the farmhouse.

Each man had the same thoughts. Whoever the man was on Sam's horse would be easy prey as it was four to one, and, *what had happened to the others?*

Kyle had the gelding at a gallop, then when saw the last four change direction toward him he felt a measure of relief, despite being the target of four rifles. After a few more seconds, he slowed the gelding to a medium trot and glanced behind him. They were still following, riding hard and gaining.

The distance to the house was enough, so it was time to take the fight to them.

He slowed the horse, then quickly turned the tired gelding to face the men. There would be no war cry this time. They all could see him in the open field, and he didn't want them to run. He wanted them to be committed and believe they had the advantage. His Henry was still rare in the territory and that was his only advantage in this straight-out gunfight. They had the advantage in range, but once they fired, he had them because they'd take too long to reload. He just needed to make them fire early and hoped that they missed.

The four men had slowed their charge to a trot and pulled their rifles but were now wary of the approaching stranger.

"Spread out!" shouted Jack Lawson and the other three suddenly veered away from him as they maintained eye contact with the lone rider.

Kyle had expected them to separate earlier, so when they did it was no surprise, but he slowed his horse to a walk to make a steadier shooting platform and let them get closer.

They may have spread apart to make his targeting more difficult, but each of them had maintained the same distance which made corrections for distance unnecessary.

When they were within two hundred yards, Kyle took aim at the second one from the left, then opened fire with his Henry, knowing it was ineffective at that range. He could hit a target if he was lucky, but the round wouldn't have the power to kill a man unless it hit a vital body part, yet it would have the power to make him fire in retaliation, which was his goal.

He fired just one shot and levered in a second round when two of them fired, including the one he had in his sights. He couldn't bother taking time to watch where there bullets landed. It was one of those mental tricks he'd learned long ago. There was no point in worrying about the shot because by the time he saw a muzzle flare, the bullet was either hitting him or it was already past.

But now, as the first two shooters began to reload, he needed to get the others to fire quickly as they were rapidly closing the gap, so he focused his next two on the ones with loaded rifles.

After quickly setting his sights on the first as they passed a hundred and fifty yards, he squeezed off his third shot, while the other one with a loaded rifle fired. Kyle didn't know where either of the shots landed, but he was getting close enough to make his shots matter as three of the four were reloading their rifles.

It was then that they realized that Kyle didn't have a single shot weapon when Jack yelled, "He's got a repeater!"

His secret exposed, Kyle realized that with three out of four men desperately ramming paper powder packets and balls into their muzzles on moving horses was the best he was going to get and wanted the ground under his feet, so Kyle suddenly whipped his left leg over the horse and began to slide from its back as the fourth rider fired.

Kyle was halfway to the ground when he felt the large caliber piece of lead crease his right shoulder but no more than that. He didn't have time to play the 'what if' game about where the bullet would have struck if he hadn't started to dismount but ignored the pain and blood when his feet were on the ground.

He quickly spread his feet apart, brought his Henry to bear and, just as he had with the others, began walking his shots from left to right. His only concern now was that they might ride away, but each one of them must have believed that he could finish his reload, find and insert a fresh percussion cap, and then aim and fire before catching one of Kyle's .44s, because none of them rode away.

Kyle took advantage of their determination, and after his first round slammed into the man on his far let, ripping into his upper abdomen and splitting his abdominal aorta, he took two more steps forward, then moved his Henry's sights to the man on his far right and squeezed the trigger.

The second rider felt the bullet slam into his chest high on the right side, then the burn and pain as ribs were shattered, his lung collapsed and then the bullet exited his chest, fracturing two more ribs in the process. He wasn't dead from the shot, but when he awkwardly fell to the Dakota turf, his head struck first, snapping his neck and finishing him off.

By the time he'd stopped moving, Kyle had already shifted to the third target, who was just pushing his percussion cap on his rifle's nipple.

His Henry cracked and the aerodynamic cylinder of lead spun down the rifled barrel, blew out of the muzzle at nine hundred feet per second, crossed the two hundred and sixty-three feet to Willy Corrigan, and hit him just above his Adam's apple before punching into the bottom of his skull and then riding the occipital bone's curving surface, expending energy and scrambling brain tissue as it passed until it buried itself in his sinuses on the front of his skull.

Willy never felt any pain as he slowly rolled to his right and flopped onto the ground, bounced once and then, after one roll lay unmoving on the ground.

The last man had finished reloading and was bringing his rifle to bear, so Kyle dropped to a prone position quickly before he fired and for the first time in the gunfight, he missed a shot that had been meant to kill.

He was levering in the next round when the man fired, and Kyle felt the bullet slam into his lower left side. He grunted, dropped his Henry, then felt his blood flowing onto the ground.

Jack Lawson exulted his apparent victory, but still began a hasty reload to make sure.

Kyle was gritting his teeth as he glanced at the last one as he was ramming home the paper-covered ammunition, then ignoring the pain from the second wound, picked up his Henry, then struggled to bring it to bear on the man who was concentrating on his reload fifty yards away. He knew that he couldn't afford to miss again, so he took an extra coupled of seconds to steady his sights.

Jack had just rammed home the ammunition and was reaching into his ammunition pouch for a percussion cap, when he glanced at his target and was stunned to see the muzzle of Kyle's Henry pointing straight into his eyes.

Even as he watched, almost mesmerized by the sight, he watched as a flash of light blossomed from the muzzle and a grayish-white cloud formed behind it, just as if it was a flower blooming in springtime.

It was the last sight that his eyes ever revealed to him when a fraction of a second later, the .44 caliber flower punched into the space between his eyes, then began its destructive path through his skull's frontal bone, his brain and then exited at the suture line between his left parietal bone and the occipital bone, leaving a much bigger hole as it left.

Kyle was already recycling his Henry when the last of the fake Indians flopped onto the ground and never even twitched.

He lay there for a few seconds, knowing that he'd taken some damage this time, it was just a question of how much damage. The shoulder was only a crease, but the second hit was not something he could avoid. He embarrassingly had to use his Henry as a crutch as he grabbed the hot barrel, placed the butt of the repeater onto the ground, then slowly managed to stand. Once he was upright, he quickly took his hand from the burning steel of the Henry's barrel, picked it up normally, then pulled his shirt up to look at the wound. It felt worse than it looked, which surprised him. It wasn't far enough from the edge of his gut to have hit anything serious and it looked clean but needed attention.

He began walking toward the house, leaving his borrowed horse and the others that had wandered away wondering how badly Neptune had been hit. He didn't realize how irrational it was to walk to the house, still four hundred yards away, rather than just take the reins of one of the horses that were no further away than twenty yards. His loss of blood, coupled with his sudden drop in adrenalin was having its effect.

He knew he was bleeding, but the shot seemed to have hit what little fat he had more than anything else. He had been lucky, very lucky, indeed. With the size of the round that those men had been firing, another inch would have been fatal. Of course, he thought, if it had been another inch the other direction, he would have missed entirely. He snickered at the thought as he continued to shuffle toward the house.

As he walked, he looked to the west to see if he could spot Neptune and wondered where the house was. *Wasn't there a house and a barn there?* As he grew more confused, he almost didn't notice the shadowy people running towards him.

When he finally understood that someone was coming, he figured it had to be the folks from the farm, so he raised his hand to tell them he meant no harm, then promptly fell face forward into the tilled Dakota field.

————

Emily had taken the letter that had just been delivered to her father along with a second letter that had been addressed to him and run to the spare bedroom, closed the door, and sat on the bed with her heart pounding. In all of her fantasies about Kyle, she had never even considered the possibility that he would write to her.

It was only when she looked at the envelope and saw the address that she understood why he thought it might be safe to write. The address was to her father, but in the return address, above his name he wrote: *For Emily.*

She eagerly, but carefully, opened the envelope and slipped out the two pages.

My Dearest Emily,

I thought that in the privacy of a letter, I could forgo the formalities of the spoken word and the prohibitions placed on them by society. Just writing your name gave me great pleasure.

As I go out into the prairie on scouting patrols, I am alone. I had grown accustomed to that in the past few years of my life and thought it was an acceptable way to live. Then, one day, after following some unusual wagon tracks across that prairie, I came upon a group of out-of-place city folk in the middle of Nebraska Territory. After a few days with them, for some reason, that view changed, and I no longer wanted to be alone. I wanted to be with you and not just for a few days but for the rest of my life. I knew it was impossible then and even now, but I haven't given up hope. Until that is possible, I will continue to go out on patrols alone, but not solitary in my soul. You will be with me then and will be with me always.

I know that the great castle wall of matrimony that separates us may never be torn asunder, yet I will be ever hopeful that one day it will crumble of its own accord. On that day, I will be able to look into your bright blue eyes and say, "I love you, Emily," without concern of social or moral retribution.

Ours has been the most restricted of love stories and perhaps that has made it stronger. When those societal and moral restrictions are lifted, my love, then all the stored love and passion will be released like a great dam crumbling before a torrent of unrelenting water. It will be a wonder to behold and even more to experience.

Until that day, I will continue to write, and if I am fortunate, to visit.

Tell Charles and Abigail that I think of them well and often. But I think of you, my Emily, most often and with every wisp of love in my heart.

Yours Always,

Kyle

Emily clutched the letter to her breast and smiled as one tear slipped from each eye. It made all the frustration and futility melt into nothingness. She no longer had limits to her hopes and fantasies as she was now certain that no matter how long she had to wait, she would do as Kyle said he would. She would let time handle the big problems because there was nothing she could do, but sooner or later, that wall would crumble, and they would be together. Once they were together, they would never part.

She trotted downstairs to her father's office, took out some paper and began to write.

———

Kyle had been awake for almost an hour now and felt much better. Sarah Jameson had sewn his wound closed while he was unconscious and had cleaned it with some medicinal brandy.

He had been gone from that place where the men had started for more than four hours now and knew he'd have to be leaving as soon as possible.

After he slid his legs from the bed, he sat and took a deep breath as Sarah entered, carrying a plate with some cold chicken, handed it to him, then sat in a chair near his bed.

"You are Kyle MacKenzie, aren't you?" she asked as Kyle began to eat.

"I am, but most Lakota refer to me as the Green-Eyed Devil. You are Lakota, are you not?"

Normally, that question was asked with an accusatory tone, but Kyle had used a normal voice, as she had expected because she knew of him.

She smiled as she replied, "I am Lakota. But I knew you as Kyle MacKenzie long before I heard you called by that other name."

Kyle then examined her more closely. Sarah was in her low to mid-thirties, very pretty, and very easily identified as Indian in her facial structure, dark eyes and straight black hair.

"Why did you know me?" he asked before taking another bite of chicken.

"I knew your mother before she left with your father. She was the most beautiful woman I have ever seen, and her bright green eyes were like nothing I had ever seen before until I saw you standing in the field firing at those men. It was then that I knew who you were and that my family was safe."

"You knew my mother?" Kyle asked in surprise.

"Not well, and not for very long, as she was older than I. But I remember her face and especially her eyes. Is she still alive?"

Kyle then smiled at the thought of his mother and replied, "Yes, she is. She and my father have a ranch about two hundred miles west of here."

"Good. I am happy for her. She was treated so badly by almost everyone in the village because of those eyes, but I always admired her. She had courage and acted as if she were a queen."

Kyle nodded and said, "I always thought she was a princess when I was growing up and now, I'll agree with you that she's a queen. I'd love to stay and talk to you about her, but I need to get back and I've got to dispose of the bodies, too."

"My husband and son have already put them over their horses and made a trail rope. Where will you take them?"

"I'll return them to Fort Pierre. They are still dressed as Lakota, so I want the people to see that it was white men, and not the Lakota who did this."

"Won't they get angry and try to shoot you?"

"I don't think so. I'll be ready if they do."

"I'm sure that you will. We've collected your horse and packhorse and they're waiting outside. The wound to your horse wasn't great, but I wouldn't ride him. My husband put two bodies on one of the horses and put your saddle on the other."

"Thank you for all your help, but I must go."

"You should really stay off your feet for another two days, Mister MacKenzie."

"I know, but I can rest on the way back to Fort Sully and then I'll rest when I get there. I'll be all right."

"They were going to kill us all, Mister MacKenzie. I think it was because I am Lakota."

"I think so. But this will be a lesson to them, I hope."

Sarah then looked into his green eyes and said quietly, "I have heard that you make personal war against the Lakota."

"Only their warriors, ma'am. Those that killed my innocent wife. No warriors should ever harm women and children, yet they killed her as if she was a threat. She was just a small, sweet Cheyenne woman who was carrying our child. No Lakota warrior is safe from me since that day."

"I hadn't heard that story, Mister MacKenzie, and I am truly sorry for your loss and understand why you would feel the need to avenge your wife and unborn child."

Kyle just nodded as she said, "Thank you, Mister MacKenzie for saving my family," then after a short pause, she smiled and added, "and my unborn child."

Kyle smiled then replied, "I am glad to have stopped them and hope that your baby is as beautiful as her mother."

She rubbed her stomach, then smiled back and said, "He will be a strong man, and if you would grant me the honor, we will name him Kyle."

Kyle nodded, then replied, "It is I who would be honored."

Sarah then stood, took his empty plate and walked from the room as Kyle gingerly rose to his feet.

His shirt was still a mess with the two bullet holes and the blood, but he had another in his saddlebags. He was a little wobbly at first, but soon stabilized and after making two loops around the room to make sure that he was ready, walked through the door, then headed for the front room where he found Eli and Joseph Jameson and the two little girls, Annie and Patience.

Eli shook his hand and thanked him for saving his family before Joseph shook his hand as well. The two girls each curtsied, as if he was royalty. Then he recalled that his mother was a queen, so maybe he was a prince. He smiled at them and bowed, which reminded him of his wound, then turned and left the house.

Kyle crossed the porch, stepped to the ground and approached Neptune. He had a poultice and some bear grease over his wound, and as he touched the gelding's muzzle, said, "I'm sorry for that wound, Neptune. I don't suppose it matters that I was shot twice, does it?"

He snickered after Neptune didn't reply, gave him a quick neck rub and then mounted the saddled, body-less horse, turned him west and set off at a walk, leading the other seven horses with their eight bodies along with his packhorse.

He didn't go straight to Fort Pierre though, but instead, headed for the Wright farm to let Mrs. Wright know that her husband was dead. And judging by her behavior in their last, very brief meeting, he expected that it might be wise to dismount with his hammer loop off.

He arrived after almost an hour and found the seven saddled horses that the others rode in on were still tied out front. He'd add them to his string when he left and select the best of the bunch to ride back to Fort Sully.

He reached the house, carefully dismounted, then after tying off the horse, walked up the steps, crossed the porch and pounded on the door.

Mrs. Wright soon opened the door and before she even said a word, spotted the bodies stretched out on the string of horses.

Her eyes exploded as she shouted, "You killed my Sam!" then slammed the door against the wall as she left the house and stood on the porch and stared at the bloody corpses.

Kyle had his hand on his Colt as he replied, "Yes, ma'am. I killed him and all of the others before they murdered an entire family, including two young girls. Did you know that was their plan?"

She turned, glared at him and snarled, "So, what? She was a damned squaw and had a bunch of half-breeds. She didn't have no right to be there."

Kyle's eyes narrowed as he looked down at the woman and calmly replied, "Well, ma'am, you've used up whatever sympathy I could possibly offer, and it wasn't much anyway. So, I'm going to take these bodies back to Fort Pierre, unless you'd like me to leave your husband's here."

"You gonna bury him?"

"No, ma'am. If you want him, you can dig the hole and bury him yourself."

She continued to glare at him then snapped, "Then you take him in, and I hope they hang you."

"Not likely, ma'am. I'm an army scout, and the army wouldn't be pleased with that."

Before she could respond, Kyle turned, walked down the porch steps and began to fashion another trail rope for the seven saddled horses that probably needed water after staying in place for so long.

She stepped to the edge of the porch and screeched, "What do you think you're doin? Those ain't your horses!"

"They will be. They shot mine."

"*What about me? What's going to happen to me?*" she screamed as spittle flew from her mouth.

Kyle was calmly threading the rope though the other horses' saddles when he said, "Ma'am, what happens to you is not my concern in the least. You'll probably find another husband who will want your farm and the pleasure of your gentle nature. But if you do find another bastard to join you in your bed and he tries to start something with the Jamesons or anyone else, I will come back here and burn this house to the ground."

She was seething in anger as she glared at Kyle while he finished attaching all of the horses, then stepped up and led the mass of horses to the trough. The horses had to take their turns, but soon, each had enough water for a while, then he led them out of the farm as he took one last glance at the hateful woman who had remained standing on the porch watching him.

Sadly, Kyle knew her attitude wasn't that unique or even the worst among the settlers. What made it so unfortunate was that too often, the whites and Indians who just wanted to live in peace were those who suffered the most.

He arrived in Fort Pierre almost two hours later and began collecting a crowd as soon as he passed the first buildings. He hunted down what passed for a mortuary, pulled his morbid parade to a stop, dismounted and tied off the horse.

He walked inside and found a heavy-set man with large jowls sitting behind a desk.

He looked at Kyle curiously, then asked, "Can I help you, mister?"

"The last time I knew Fort Pierre didn't have any law of any kind. Is that still true?"

"Yup. So, what do you need?"

"I've got eight customers for you outside."

His eyebrows shot up as he excitedly asked, "*Eight? What happened? The Injuns get 'em?*"

"No, sir. I got them. They were dressed as Lakota and were about to burn down another farmhouse. We got into a gun battle and they lost."

"You ain't sayin'!" he exclaimed as he popped to his feet, walked around the desk, then headed outside with Kyle following.

The undertaker examined the bodies and said, "I know most of those fellers, but they sure are dressed different. They're all dressed like Injuns."

"That was the whole plan. They were burning farms and ranches to try to get everyone all riled up so the army would have to come in. This time, they decided to add murder to their list of crimes and burn an entire family, including three children. How much to bury them all?"

"That's a heap of work, mister. That'll run you forty dollars."

"Alright. Let's get them off those horses and I'll pay you. Where do you want to put them?"

"Bring 'em around back. I've got a wagon."

Kyle untied the first horse, then led his long line of animals around the back, where he, the mortician and his assistant began to slide the bodies off the horses onto the undertaker's wagon. Kyle doubted if he'd do anything more than have someone dig a hole and dump all eight bodies into it, but he didn't care and wouldn't have cared if they were left out on the plains for the critters. He paid the money and decided he'd lead all the horses away from Fort Pierre rather than stick around.

After checking at the new dry goods store on the off chance that his ammunition order had arrived with no luck, he departed Fort Pierre heading north to Fort Sully in the late afternoon. He still had almost three hours of daylight left, so he kept riding and wasn't sure he wouldn't be dragging unwelcome visitors in addition to the horses, so he'd ride until after dusk and even after keeping a close eye on his backtrail, would make a sudden change to the north for a mile or so should anyone follow.

He finally pulled up two hours after sunset, then unsaddled his horse and the packhorse. He had some water and some cold beans and smoked beef before he unsaddled all the others. As he did, he did a quick inspection of the animals and found most to be in good shape, but a few needed new shoes. If the army wanted them, they could buy them. Once he had the stack of saddles in a big pile, he led them all to a nearby creek and let them drink before just tying off the lead horse and letting them graze as best they could. He guessed he had another four or five hours ride ahead of him tomorrow.

His side was pounding from all of the exercise and he noticed that there were spots of fresh blood on his nasty shirt. He'd sleep in it tonight but wash in the creek and put some clean clothes on in the morning. His britches had picked up some blood, too, but he'd see if they could be salvaged with a good washing in the creek.

He finished the day's work by cleaning and reloading his Henry and the Sharps. When he did, he was grateful that he hadn't needed to take a second shot after taking the hit. When he dropped the rifle, a lot of dirt had found its way into the slot in the bottom of the magazine tube and if he'd tried to lever in a new round, it probably would have jammed. As it was, the cleaning took more than three times what he normally spent to make sure the repeater was safe to use.

When he unraveled his bedroll for the night, he just lay on top rather than risk getting blood on the inside of the bedroll. He thought that he'd stay awake for hours after having been out for so long, but after only a few minutes of Emily-inspired fantasy, he drifted off to a deep sleep.

————

Kyle was startled when he awakened to sunlight with a heavy coating of dew on everything, including his clothes.

He sat up, experienced no dizziness, then stood and walked away from his cold camp a few feet, answered nature's call, then returned and began preparing for the day's ride.

First, he stripped down to birthday suit, then walked past the still sleeping horses to the creek with a bar of white soap, a towel, and his bloody britches and shirt.

He washed his face and hair, then inspected and gingerly washed his gut wound before washing the rest of his body, taking a quick inventory of any damage he may have missed. He couldn't see the crease on his back, but when he washed it with the soap, he knew where it was and how long it was.

"Just another half-inch," he said aloud as he snickered.

He then scrubbed his dark canvas britches as best he could, and even though the blood stain was still noticeable, he kept them because they were still useful. The shirt was still nasty-looking when he finished, but he kept it as well.

He tossed them on some bushes to dry while he had a cold breakfast of just smoked beef and hard tack washed down with water and after putting on some clean underpants, began to saddle the horses while his damaged clothes dried. Kyle spent over an hour saddling the horses and loading the one packhorse. After everything was secure, he checked Neptune's wound, then he noticed that his own wound had begun to ooze blood again, so rather than ruin a clean shirt, he walked to the bush, felt his washed clothes, and deemed them dry enough to wear.

After he dressed in his damp and still-bloody clothes, he mounted his selected horse for the day, a deep-chested black gelding with a black mane and tail and a white star on his forehead as his only marking.

He had the herd moving a little more than three hours after waking and was pleasantly surprised when the only thing he encountered that was threatening on the rest of the journey was an irate brown bear cow with her cub. He just stopped until she was satisfied that the horses weren't a threat to her cub, and after she moved off toward the river Kyle had moved ridden on.

He picked up Fort Sully a little past noon and was soon entering the gate with the horses. Soldiers not on duty, and some who were, watched the parade enter the fort, and Kyle realized that he might have made a wrong impression with his shirt looking as it did, but at least they'd know he hadn't been out on a joy ride.

He pulled the horse train to a stop and dismounted in front of the headquarters building but didn't bother tying off the horse. He wasn't going anywhere, not with that group lashed to him.

As he walked into the office, he almost bumped into Lieutenant Colonel Carpenter who was hurriedly exiting after being told of Kyle's return leading a bunch of horses.

He spotted his bloody shirt and said, "Kyle, get in here and sit down," then turned to the soldier at the desk and said, "Corporal Wheeler, get the doctor in here."

"Yes, sir!" the corporal all but shouted the automatic and expected reply before Corporal Wheeler ejected himself from his chair and the building.

Kyle smiled at the young soldier's reaction then walked ahead of the commander and gratefully took a seat in front of the large desk as Lieutenant Colonel Carpenter passed by and then sat in his chair.

"I gather by your shirt and the horses that you had a confrontation with the Lakota white men?" he asked with raised eyebrows.

"Yes, sir. I used my best judgement and I suppose it should have been to simply return with the information I had gathered, but that changed when they rode to murder an entire family and I couldn't let that happen. It turns out there were eight of them involved in the raids. They'd meet at the leader's farmhouse about two hours' ride north of Fort Pierre, change into buckskins and wigs, and then swap to unshod horses.

"You know, those morons still used their bridles? All that work to hide the fact that they were white men, and they still used bridles. Well, anyway, I trailed them and was going to just threaten them, but they had decided to add murder to their list of charges because the mother in the house was Lakota. They were herding the family just like cattle and driving them into their house, where I assumed that they'd burn them alive. So, I engaged them and left all eight bodies at Fort Pierre."

"How bad was it?"

"Honestly? The first four were just like target practice, and after I had the other four chase after me, it wasn't too bad. At least they all got shots off."

"It seems like you took a couple of them too, Kyle."

"One was just a burn, though. Mrs. Jameson, she was the Lakota wife of the white farmer, sewed up the other. It looks okay."

244

"That's just your diagnosis, but I want to hear it from Doc White, then I want you to lay off doing anything for at least three days."

"Then I'll go back to scouting?"

"We'll see. So, what's with the horses?"

"Oh, that's right, the horses. Eight are the unshod horses they used in the raids and the other seven were the ones the others rode in on. I figured that rather than let the witch of a woman in the ringleader's farmhouse keep them, I'd bring them along. Neptune took a hit and he's off duty for a while, so I'll take a couple of the others. You don't have a horse, do you, Colonel?"

"I don't, now that you mention it. Are you offering me one as an incentive to get what you want?"

Kyle grinned then replied, "Colonel, I'm a scout. I get what I want anyway. But after I take two, that'll leave thirteen and six saddles."

"I may take you up on that offer. Why do you want two more? Not that I'm begrudging you the right to take them all, I'm just curious."

"One is to temporarily replace Neptune. But I'm not going out anymore without a backup. If Neptune had been shot and I was out in the middle of nowhere, which I am most of the time, I'd have to do a lot of walking."

"That makes sense."

Doctor Alphonse White then entered the office and without saying a word, took Kyle's elbow then escorted him out of the headquarters building to the dispensary.

Once there, he set Kyle on his examination table and had Kyle take off the shirt and his knife harness and examined both wounds.

"Lord, Kyle, I swear that you are the luckiest son of a bitch God ever put on this green earth. If either of those big slugs of lead had been just another inch closer, you'd be lying dead on the great plains of Dakota Territory."

Kyle smiled and replied, "C'mon, Doc. You know the counter argument to that logic."

Doctor White snickered as he looked at Sarah's suturing job and said, "I know, but I love the idea of not having to repair wounds or amputate limbs."

Kyle didn't reply as he knew that the doctor had served two years with the Army of the Tennessee before being sent to Fort Sully and he'd been at Shiloh having to tend the aftermath of that slaughter.

After his examination was done, the doctor pronounced the wound well-sutured and told him he needed to have them removed in ten days.

As Kyle stood, the doctor said, "I have one recommendation, Kyle."

"What's that?"

"Change that god-awful shirt."

Kyle was laughing lightly as he left the dispensary, and by the time he stepped out into the sunshine, the horses, including his packhorse and Neptune had been moved to the barn at Lieutenant Colonel Carpenter's direction.

Kyle walked to his quarters, left his pistols on his bed, then finally donned a clean shirt. He walked to the barn, found the horses all brushed, and already knew which two he would take. One was the black gelding with the black mane and tail he'd used that day. He was the most powerful of the group and was less than six years old. The second was another gelding, a dark, chestnut brown with lighter brown mane and tail. He had no markings at all and was even younger at about five years.

Both were ideal scout horses in coloring, but he wasn't sure of their disposition, despite having ridden the black gelding that morning. He had watched the gait on the chestnut as they rode back and found him to have a nice motion. Both horses were taller than Neptune, but he hadn't paid attention to them during the gunfight, so he didn't know how each would respond to close gunfire. He chose one more saddle and let the farrier know which were his animals and asked that they have their shoes changed.

Once his transportation needs were met, he began pulling his weapons out of their scabbards and carried them to his quarters where he carefully laid them down on one of the empty beds.

He skipped lunch and just stretched out in his bunk for a nap which turned out to be a little longer than he expected but was awake when the all-important bugle announcing evening mess call was sounded.

———

While Kyle was sleeping, the first editions of *Flinging Ed Falstaff* arrived in Omaha and were soon being snapped up by voracious readers, most under the age of sixteen.

———

Kyle spent his two days of forced rest to clean and condition all his weapons but did take some time to establish a relationship with his new equine friends. He still spent some time with Neptune to inspect his healing wound and estimated that he'd be back to full strength in two more weeks.

His own wound should be well-healed by then because he knew that he was always a fast healer.

The black gelding, which would be his primary ride, at least until Neptune was healed, was named Duke and the dark brown gelding was christened Baron. He was close to renaming Neptune with a higher level of royalty but figured that being a god was better anyway.

———

Kyle did routine scouting for two weeks and, after Doctor White removed his stitches, felt almost normal again. He was still stiff, but he didn't have to worry about yanking out stitches anymore and began to work at returning his body to full flexibility, which could be critical to a scout with his aggressive nature.

Six days after having the sutures removed, he was out on patrol and had ranged south about eight miles, following the river when he spotted signs of a large Lakota war party. It had been following the Missouri, but where he found their trail, they had shifted almost due east, away from the river. It was easy to discern that it wasn't a hunting party just by its size alone. He estimated that the group was over a hundred warriors, which gave him serious concern.

He followed their trail for another hour before the group split, with the larger group continuing east, while the smaller one headed due north toward Fort Sully. The smaller group numbered around twenty warriors, and the logical thing for him to do was to follow the bigger band, but he suspected that the smaller one was the greater danger as it was heading straight to the fort and the memory of seeing those Lakota carting off those repeaters and ammunition flared into his mind.

Kyle turned Duke north following the smaller group and picked up the pace. As he followed their tracks, he pictured the terrible location of Fort Sully and immediately understood the damage those repeaters could cause to the soldiers in the fort if they were on the nearby hills.

They wouldn't even have to do the killing, but just keep the soldiers' heads down for the large group to make an assault on the gates to the fort or scale the sixteen-foot high log walls. It wasn't even difficult to predict the war chief's strategy.

The two groups size was the largest mass of Lakota he had seen in some time, but it still wasn't large enough to attack Fort Sully in a frontal attack, but with those repeaters, everything changed.

As poorly situated as the fort was between those two overlooking hills that created the valley that housed the fort, there was one other aspect of the terrain that made the site even more tenuous. The lower hill to the north had been denuded of pines to build the fort, and was totally bald, but the taller hill to the south had only lost the trees in the lower half, was sixty to eighty feet higher than the fort walls and still had most of its trees making ideal hiding locations. They should have at least stripped the taller hill of those trees, but he guessed that once they had enough wood to build the fort, they'd stopped work. It was probably built by the same idiots who'd selected the location in the first place.

As he rode following the twenty warriors, he pictured the entire setup in his mind.

After this bunch climbed over the back of the southern hill and snuck in among the pines with their repeaters, they'd need to have targets.

So, the first trick would be to lure the soldiers out onto the walls to try and reduce their numbers and that, he guessed, would be the job of the larger group. They would feign an attack from the east and draw the soldiers to the walls where they would either be picked off by the small group in the trees with their repeaters or sent scurrying into defensive positions.

He didn't know how accurate the Sioux would be with those rifles but assumed that they'd depend on volume more than accuracy. He knew that they didn't like to engage in target practice because they couldn't afford to waste ammunition.

Regardless of their accuracy, once the soldiers were decimated and had to keep their heads down, the big group would attack in earnest and either break through the gate or start fires to burn the fort to the ground. Then, the killing would start in earnest.

Kyle may have figured out their strategy, but he still had to stop it and make good use the only two advantages he had: surprise and his reputation.

———

At Fort Sully, Private Henry Witherspoon was the first to notice activity to the northwest and called down to the sergeant on duty.

"Sergeant Jones, I've got something moving in the northeast. It looks like a large party of Sioux!" he shouted.

Sergeant Michael Jones quickly climbed the ladder to the parapet and took the field glasses that were hanging from a nearby nail.

As he scanned the riders he said, "You're right, Henry. It looks like about eighty of 'em. Sound the general alarm."

The bugler was notified, blew the call to action and within seconds, the troops began to grab their Springfields except for those marksmen who had been assigned the new Henry rifles that they all called the Kyles. Each had a box of ammunition in his pocket as they made their way to the east wall to face the threat. Theirs was an undermanned regiment even before they had to assign men to make the move downstream to the new fort. Instead of the book anointed size of ten companies of one hundred men each, there were only six companies of fifty men each. With illnesses and injuries, there were only two hundred and thirty-six effectives assigned to the fort that day. It should still be enough if they hadn't been in the process of moving the fort. Sixty men were either at the new location or enroute. But as they began to mount the walls, each man believed that one hundred and seventy-six should be enough.

Lieutenant Colonel Carpenter had mounted the eastern wall and was watching the large group of Lakota to the northeast through his field glasses.

"Sergeant Jones, does this make any sense to you? Why are they riding in the open like that? They must know we can see them."

"Well, sir, there's just no accountin' for what they're doin'. We're just gonna have to find out, I'm thinkin'."

"You may be right. Send Captain Arthur to see me. I'm going to want his company moved from the eastern wall to the western wall in case they come from that side, too."

"Yes, sir."

Twenty minutes later, Captain Arthur had his forty-eight men lined up on the western wall. Like the eastern wall, every seventh man was armed with a Henry rifle.

Lieutenant Colonel Carpenter felt he had his men deployed as best he could, but he was still uncomfortable. He wished he had Kyle MacKenzie with him to advise him of their intentions or plans and swore that Kyle knew the Lakota better than they did themselves.

––––––––

Watching Eagle had his warriors dismount well before the southern face of the taller south hill. After tying off their horses in the trees, they took their rifles and one extra box of ammunition apiece, then began to enter the trees that began at the Missouri River and continued up the hill. They knew that none of the soldiers in the fort could see them and that even if the hill was as bare as the other one, their attention would be focused to the east.

He gave the signal and the band melted into the trees then began to slowly move up the hill to the tree-covered face of the hill that overlooked Fort Sully, the fort that would soon be overflowing with targets.

––––––––

Kyle had reached the base of the hill, quickly spotted their horses, then dismounted, and led Duke closer to the trees and found a good spot where he could graze and still be safe and unseen. He tied him off to a branch, pulled his Henry from its scabbard, then emptied a box of .44 rimfire cartridges and put them in his jacket pockets. He thought about taking his bow with him, but stealth wasn't going to be necessary in this engagement. Satisfied that he was ready, he began the same climb that the Lakota had made almost thirty minutes earlier.

The main group under war chief, Little Wolf, was watching for a signal from the second group to let him know they were in position. When they were in place, they would flash a signal with a mirror. Then the main group would feign the frontal attack that the soldiers expected. They'd make a lot of noise and then, as soon as the soldiers fired their first volley of their single-shot rifles, Watching Eagle's group would begin their killing fire from their flank.

With the repeaters, there would be little chance to escape. Each of the warriors had enough ammunition to keep up fire for a long time, and then when he received a second signal from Watching Eagle, the main group would close and shoot their fire arrows, putting an end to Fort Sully.

Kyle continued to climb the hill and finally reached the summit and lay prone on his stomach, not for a shooting position, but to catch his breath. A minute later, he crawled over the top of the hill and slid down a little on the opposite side. He was in the grass wearing his buckskins, so he was nearly invisible as he began to identify targets. They were spread out, but not as much as they should have been.

Each warrior was behind a tree but aligned in what appeared to be seven columns of three rows. He'd be able to pick off the nine on his end without too much problem before things got interesting. He'd have to wait for them to start firing, though, so it would take a while before they realized he was behind them. He had enough ammunition for all of them but doubted that his Henry would still be firing when this was over. He'd be down to his pistols if he was lucky, and his knife if he wasn't. He also had to plan a reload on the Henry when he could afford the time because it took some care to get more .44s into that magazine tube.

When the shooting started, he'd start firing at the back row, right-hand column and then move to his left, taking out as many warriors as possible, then if he was lucky, he'd start on the next row, again, right to left. He wondered how many he could hit before they realized that they were being attacked from behind and suspected that it was unlikely that he'd even get an entire row of nine. That would be extraordinarily lucky. He also didn't have a lot of wiggle room with ammunition. If he got six, that left fourteen warriors, and he'd only have nine rounds left in his Henry. He sure wished he had the second repeater, but it was too late now.

He calmed and waited for the action to start as he stared at the backs of the men he was about to kill, just twenty yards away.

———

Watching Eagle signaled the go-ahead to the far-right warrior; Kyles last column, first row. The warrior took out his mirror and angled the sun's light to Little Wolf.

Little Wolf saw the flash, then had his warriors line up in attack formation, shrieked his war cry then launched the mass attack.

The disciplined soldiers had been expecting the assault and waited until they got in range. The Lakota knew the range of the Springfield was good and the rifle was accurate in trained hands, but they only had one shot and it was awkward to maneuver. The chief was prepared to sacrifice a few warriors in the faux charge to ensure the much larger victory.

They kept charging and when they were within two hundred yards, Sergeant Jones shouted, "Fire!"

A heavy fusillade of flame and smoke erupted from the wall as six warriors crashed into the ground and the soldiers quickly began reloading their muskets.

Watching Eagle's band didn't need another signal, so as soon as the soldiers had fired, his warriors opened fire with their repeaters.

Kyle already had his man targeted and as soon as the firing started, he squeezed his trigger. As the warrior crumpled to the ground, blood pooling onto his buckskin shirt around the hole in the center of his chest, he quickly levered in a second round, refocused to his left slightly and fired again. The second Lakota spun clockwise, sending his repeater flying before he rolled down the hill slightly and Kyle quickly moved his sights to the left.

———

Meanwhile, down in the fort, Lieutenant Colonel Carpenter suddenly realized how vulnerable he was as the hill to the south erupted in gunfire and some of his men already fell from the walls. He ordered Captain Arthur to move his company to the southern wall to protect them from the enfilading fire of the repeaters firing from the trees.

The soldiers on the west wall began to file down the steps but Watching Eagle's warriors began picking them off and a general panic began. Men began leaping from the twelve-foot high wall walkway onto the ground to escape the rain of .44s as the officers tried to regain some semblance of control, but it was utter chaos.

Kyle had just finished off his fourth warrior when he realized that the disaster that was happening in the fort was worse than he had anticipated, so he knew that he no longer had time to keep picking off unsuspecting warriors one at a time. He had to attract their attention from the fort and then do as much damage as possible, hoping that their accuracy wasn't as good as his.

His mind settled, he took a breath, knelt, then peeled off his shirt quickly and took a few precious seconds to reload his Henry. He had his eyes on the magazine and when he slid the last cartridge into the tube, he turned and slowly released the holding mechanism. Now that he had fifteen rounds available, he stood, raised his Henry high above his head and using every bit of air in his lungs, screamed the most horrifying war cry imaginable.

To a man, the warriors in Watching Eagle's group turned and saw the Green-Eyed Devil behind them, and each one was beyond surprised; they were stunned. *How had he gotten behind them?* Many were more than just stunned as they recalled the stories that they'd heard about the fearless white warrior who terrorized the Sioux; they were terrified. *Was his magic so powerful that he could just appear wherever he wished?*

The firing suddenly died down by Lakota and soldier alike as Kyle shouted loudly enough for those in the fort to hear, "I am the Green-Eyed Devil and I am here to kill all of the Lakota who are on this hill. Come, my brothers! Sing your death songs! I do not have one for I will not die! Come!"

Several of the warriors quickly turned their rifles toward Kyle but his green eyes, those terrifying green eyes almost glowed in the afternoon sun as he looked at them and made their rifle's sights dance. Three fired and all three missed sending their bullets somewhere that didn't matter.

Kyle saw the smoke, brought his Henry level and began firing. He stood on the top of that hill and just fired his rifle and levered in new rounds, hitting anyone who shot at him or those who were visible. He didn't shoot rapidly, but methodically began to eliminate the Lakota, even as they returned fire. He didn't hit one with every shot and he knew he was running low on ammunition but didn't care. He had done his job and bought the soldiers time.

He had moved his hand up the hot barrel of the Henry when the magazine's tube thumb tab had reached the lower end of the spring-loaded tube which told him he was low on ammunition. The barrel was burning his left hand as he continued to fire.

He hadn't been surprised that not a single Lakota warrior had slipped behind a tree trunk for protection because he was standing in the open and to do so would be an act of cowardice.

His hammer finally came down on an empty chamber and he gratefully tossed aside the hot but now useless rifle, then pulled both pistols. He cocked the hammers and began to slowly walk down the hill toward the remaining seven Lakota, only three with any ammunition remaining in their repeaters. One kept levering and pulling the trigger on an empty chamber, hoping that a cartridge would somehow make its way into firing position.

Kyle began to fire with his right hand when he was within range, killed another three, including the one who was firing an empty rifle. With four remaining, including Watching Eagle, the leader decided to attack in their own way and tossed aside his own rifle, then pull his war tomahawk from his leather belt, and shrieked his war cry before launching himself at the Green-Eyed Devil. When the other three saw Watching Eagle make his attack, they did the same and soon four Lakota warriors were charging up the hill.

Kyle knew better than to get into a hand-to-hand fight with four Sioux warriors, and this wasn't a fight of honor, this was a killing fight. He fired once more with his right hand, killing the furthest warrior to his right, then suspected his pistol was empty but didn't wait for a confirming click. He just dropped it into his holster, pulled his left-hand pistol, transferred it quickly to his right hand and fired three times more killing the other two. leaving only Watching Eagle still coming, now just thirty feet away. He suddenly slowed, glared at the man who had ruined their attack, dropped his war tomahawk, and slid his knife from its sheath.

He met Kyle's green eyes with his own fierce browns and said, "I will kill you, Green-Eyed Devil. I will…"

Kyle interrupted his soliloquy when he just squeezed the trigger of his Colt New Army.

Watching Eagle dropped to his knees in disbelief, then with his eyes still wide, fell face forward to the ground.

Kyle looked at his prostrate form and said, "This is war."

Kyle then lifted his eyes and scanned the warriors scattered all over the hill. Several were wounded, but not dead, so he began walking among the Lakota picking up the priceless repeaters and making a stack near his own Henry. It took about ten minutes.

While Kyle was cleaning the aftermath of his own fight, order had been restored in the fort.

Little Wolf had seen and heard much of what had happened on the hill. Like many of the warriors, he too wondered how the Green-Eyed Devil had appeared behind his men.

Kyle returned to where he'd left all of the guns and shouted, "Colonel, I need some troops to come up here and get these rifles. There's ammunition, too."

Lieutenant Colonel Carpenter shouted back, "They're on their way. Glad to see you made it back!"

Kyle then picked up his own Henry, climbed to the top of the hill and yelled in Sioux, "You have dead and wounded on the hill. You may retrieve them when I fire my pistol."

He turned to the fort and yelled again, "I told them to come and get their dead and wounded after I fired my pistol. Let them pass!"

He sat and waited until the soldiers had removed all the rifles and ammunition and had to stop one from taking his rifle. When they had returned to the fort safely, he stood on the top of the hill and fired his pistol.

He waited on the top of the hill, still standing with his reloaded Henry as he watched as a line of Lakota separated from the main group.

He reached down, picked up his shirt, shook out the dust, then quickly donned it as he saw the column of unarmed Lakota trot past the fort, then ride around the hill to get the horses of the smaller group.

It took almost an hour to get all the dead and wounded from the hill and Kyle remained on the top of the hill watching until the Lakota rode off before he finally walked down hill and found Duke. He pulled his canteen and emptied it before he mounted then rode around the hill to the fort and through the open gate.

Lieutenant Colonel Carpenter greeted Kyle as he stepped down.

"Welcome back, Kyle. You sure were a welcome sight."

"How many did we lose?"

"Eight dead and about forty injured, but a lot of those are broken bones from idiots trying to jump down from that wall."

"They almost had you, Colonel."

"Kyle, they almost had Madeline. I should never have let her come here."

"I think she might argue the point, Colonel."

"I know. I don't know what moron chose this spot, but at least we'll be out of here next year. Do you think they'll attack again?"

"The fort? No, I don't think so. They lost too many of their rifles and ammunition, not to mention the loss of twenty of their warriors."

"You know what you did today would win you a Medal of Honor if you'd been a soldier."

"If I'd been a soldier, I'd have been inside the fort."

"True. I've got to go and check on the men and make my report to General Frobisher"

Kyle looked at the commanding officer and said, "You know he's going to blame you for this."

He nodded and simply replied, "I know."

———

Cal Coleridge and Edmund were sitting across from each other at the club, and Cal had a problem.

"I don't see what the difficulty is at all," said Edmund.

"I just discovered that Kyle MacKenzie is real and not an invention of your imagination."

"I never claimed otherwise."

"That's my problem, Edmund. Because I thought your story was mostly embellishment, I made the rather poor assumption that Mister MacKenzie was also fictitious."

"Why would you think my story was embellishment?"

"Because, Edmund, no one man could do all the things you claim to have happened in just a single, two-week period. It's impossible."

"I beg to differ. I did all of it, and Mister MacKenzie was as portrayed."

"That's another issue. Mister MacKenzie, it seems, has a rather extensive record as an Indian fighter of some repute. Now, you see, that presents two problems. One is legal, and the second is my own safety."

"What is the legal issue?"

"Libel, Edmund. If we use someone's legitimate name in one of our books, he must be portrayed accurately. If the man was honorable, but the novel makes him out to be as your Kyle MacKenzie was, a coward and villain, he would have an excellent case of libel against the publisher and myself. I would lose my job at the very least."

"I see your difficulty. What is the safety problem?"

"Those novels are available all over the West already. It is only a matter of time before they come to the attention of Mister MacKenzie. Now do you see my problem?"

"Not only yours, Mister Coleridge, but my own as well. I do have several safeguards, however," Edmund said as he smiled.

"Whatever they are, you had better be prepared to use them. I am booking passage on the next riverboat to Kansas City. It was much safer there."

"And I, Mister Coleridge, shall return to St. Louis. It seems that my darling wife had been holding back some information," he said as he grinned, "It seems that she has a tidy sum of her own in a bank in St. Louis, and as her husband, I have the right to that money. So, I will go back to my house and announce to her parents that I am returning to St. Louis and taking my wife with me. They can say or do nothing. Nor can she."

"I thought you didn't even like your wife."

"I don't. But you see, the beauty of this situation is that Mister MacKenzie does. As long as I have her with me, he can do nothing. I will be safe, wealthy and, as your novel is selling well in St. Louis, I assume that I am now famous as Flinging Ed Falstaff."

CHAPTER 9

Six days after the attack, Kyle was returning from a patrol to the north. He'd been out for three days and encountered several large bands of Lakota. He knew that something was brewing, but he hadn't heard any rumors.

He led his packhorse into the fort riding Duke. The big gelding had become his favored mount as Neptune, while healthy, had a more jarring gait after the injury. Even Baron wasn't as smooth or as powerful as Duke.

He stepped down outside the headquarters building, tied off Duke, then entered the office and asked the corporal if the colonel was in and received an odd response.

"They're both in, Kyle."

"Both?" Kyle asked.

The corporal nodded and made a face to let Kyle know he wasn't happy about it.

"Could you let Lieutenant Colonel Carpenter know I'm back and have some intelligence for him?"

"I'll do that."

The corporal stood, walked to the office and knocked on the door jamb.

"Colonel Carpenter, Kyle MacKenzie is back and has some news for you."

"Send him in, Corporal Sheffield."

"Yes, sir."

He waved Kyle into the office and Kyle was wondering what was going on, but suspected it was due to the Lakota attack. He was just surprised that the army was moving this quickly.

He stepped into the office and saw Lieutenant Colonel Carpenter sitting in a side chair and a full colonel sitting behind his desk, confirming his suspicions.

He ignored the full bird colonel, looked at Lieutenant Colonel Carpenter and said, "Colonel Carpenter, in the past few days, I've spotted three different bands of Lakota. Large bands of over a hundred each and they were all heading west. Something is happening, but I haven't picked up any indications of what it could be."

"Thanks, Kyle. Perhaps you need to make your report to Colonel Johnson. He's the new commander of Fort Sully. I have been relieved and will be returning to Washington City."

"Under what pretense?" Kyle asked.

"I am under investigation for the attack on the fort that left eight dead and forty-two wounded."

Kyle snapped, "*And how are you responsible for that?* You didn't choose this abominable location and you'd only been in command for three months."

Colonel Johnson interrupted, saying, "Mister MacKenzie, that is none of your concern. That is the army's concern. You are a scout, nothing more. I expect you to follow my orders explicitly and provide me with detailed, accurate reports. I do not wish

264

you to engage the enemy on your own, either. That is the job of the soldiers. Is that understood?"

Kyle looked at the colonel and said, "Yes, sir."

"Good. Your presence is no longer necessary. I will send for you when I have need of your skills."

"Thank you, sir!" Kyle exclaimed then snapped a salute which confused the new officer and his old commander as well.

He turned, glanced at an astonished Lieutenant Colonel Carpenter and winked before he did a commendable about face, then with a smile on his face marched from the office, passed a grinning Corporal Sheffield and exited the headquarters building.

After leaving, he headed to the paymaster's office, and once inside, walked to the desk and said, "Eric, I need my cash. It's time for me to be moving on."

"I'm not surprised, Kyle. I guess you've met our new commander."

"Yup. It's just about all I want to see of him, too."

"We're gonna miss you, Kyle."

"You'll be safe anyway. The Lakota won't come back until you're in your new fort and it'll be a lot better."

Sergeant Saunders opened the safe, slid out Kyle's thick envelope and handed it to him. Kyle signed the receipt and slid the heavy envelope into his jacket.

He then left the paymaster and led Duke and Baron, who was the packhorse for the mission, to the stables where he asked

265

that they and Neptune be reshod as he was leaving in the morning and received the same 'met our new commander' comment.

After he left the stables, he returned to his scout's quarters. When he entered, he saw some papers on his bunk, then set his two Henry repeaters, his Sharps and his Spencer in the corner before he set his bow and arrows on the bunk next to his. One was an envelope and the other was a piece of paper.

The envelope was a letter from Emily, which excited him as he hadn't heard from her since he said goodbye at the ferry. He'd read it after he read the telegram.

It was a telegram from Charles and read:

KYLE MACKENZIE FORT SULLY DAKOTA TERRITORY

**NEED YOU TO RETURN AS SOON AS POSSIBLE
EDMUND TOOK EMILY TO ST LOUIS
AGAINST OUR WISHES
WE HAVE NO LEGAL RIGHTS TO KEEP HER HERE
SOMETHING IS NOT RIGHT
WE NEED YOUR HELP
OTHER PROBLEM HANDLED**

CHARLES BURLEIGH YANKTON DAKOTA TERRITORY

He didn't read Emily's letter yet but left his quarters and went to the telegraph room.

"Corporal Winters, I need to send a response to this telegram."

"Write it up, Kyle, and I'll send it out."

Kyle wrote quickly:

CHARLES BURLEIGH YANKTON DAKOTA TERRITORY

WILL LEAVE TOMORROW FOR FORT PIERRE
ON FIRST STEAMER TO OMAHA
TRAINS FROM OMAHA TO ST LOUIS
WILL LET YOU KNOW WHICH BOAT
WILL NOT BE RETURNING TO FORT SULLY
SCOUTING DAYS OVER

KYLE MACKENZIE FORT SULLY DAKOTA TERRITORY

He handed the sheet to Corporal Winters who read it, then looked at Kyle and said, "We all figured that you'd be leaving after you met the new commander. I think we all wish that we could, too."

"Sorry, Pete. You should never have signed those enlistment papers."

Pete snickered, then began tapping out the message. When he was finished, and received his acknowledgement signal from the receiving operator, he handed Kyle back his copy.

"Thanks, Pete."

"Good luck, Kyle. We're all gonna miss you."

"Stay safe, Pete."

Kyle left the small office, jogged back toward his quarters and began to pack. Just as he'd expressed in his telegram, he was done with scouting. It wasn't the battle, or even the futility of watching Lieutenant Colonel Carpenter bear the brunt of the army's wrath without cause that made that decision. It wasn't even the possibility of finding Emily. It was just that he didn't see

267

an end to it. He expected that with the War Between the States coming to its costly conclusion the wars against the Plains tribes would last for decades.

His quick packing almost complete, he sat at the small desk in the scouts' quarters and wrote a letter to his parents that he would post in Fort Pierre.

Finally, he closed the door and pulled out Emily's letter and waved it under his nose and could smell Emily's light lilac scent.

Then he carefully, opened the envelope, slid out the two pages and unfolded them, reading her delicate script.

My Dearest Kyle,

You're right. Just writing your Christian name gave me a thrill.

I received your letter today, but don't know how soon I can respond because of a difficult state of affairs that has risen. But when I first opened those miraculous sheets of paper and read what you had written, it made me the happiest of women, despite my situation. I have waited for so long to hear you say those words but reading them may even be better. I can hear your voice say them to me each time I read them, and I will read them hourly.

Edmund has taken to wearing a pistol and acting as if he is a man of the West. I don't know what has caused this dramatic change, but it has something to do with a man he meets at the gentleman's club. He's become both more indifferent and more abusive to me. It sounds impossible, but it is true.

Do you know how soon I came to love you? Not when you saved us from those guides or the Lakota. I came to love you when we talked. I could see all of you in your eyes which were windows to your heart and soul. It was all open to me, Kyle, as

I'm sure mine were to you, and I was shaken by the discovery. I had been told so many things about love that were wrong. The greatest lie was that love takes time. Marry first, they would say, and let love grow. But when I gazed into your marvelous eyes, I knew without question that I loved you. Love was already there, Kyle, and it was looking right back at me. I felt it flow through me and let it fill my very being.

I know it is possible we may never get to complete our love, but if we do get that chance, my love, no matter how long we must wait, I will do everything possible to show you the depth of my love for you.

I pray that the day may come when you hold me in your arms and hear you say those words that I read in your letter, and I would whisper to your ear, "And I love you, Kyle."

You are forever in my heart,

Emily

Kyle read it once more, then slowly lowered the letter to his lap. Now, for some inexplicable reason, his precious Emily had been taken back to St. Louis by Edmund, a man who not only treated her indifferently, but now hurt her.

Kyle didn't care about rules and complications any longer, he would go and find Emily and take her away from that despicable human being. If it meant that they'd be labeled as adulterers, so be it. He was tired of society, a society that allows a man like Edmund Falstaff to have complete control over a woman like Emily. A society that finds fault with a man like Lieutenant Colonel Carpenter for something that was not of his doing simply because they needed someone to blame.

Kyle would handle Edmund and then see if he could help Lieutenant Colonel Carpenter somehow. He wanted to start making things right for the people who mattered to him.

———

"What did you say your name was?" asked the bartender.

"Ed. Ed Falstaff."

"Are you really him? Flinging Ed Falstaff? The one from the book?"

"In the flesh."

"Well, Mister Falstaff, the next one's on the house. Why, you're already a celebrity in town and it's an honor to meet you."

He shook Ed's hand and Edmund felt his pride soar. He had already had free drinks at two other establishments, then become the center of attention as men gathered around to hear his story. After the first time, he had stopped calling himself Edmund and just referred to himself as Ed and let the others add the 'Flinging' part to his name. Ed had also stopped wearing his collar and tie, adopting a more casual dress that the others, his worshippers, seemed to favor.

And this was just an overnight stay in Omaha, so he couldn't wait until they reached St. Louis. He'd decided that they should take the train to get there sooner. He'd never have to buy a drink again, he thought as he snickered. But now he could afford it, thanks to that insipid wife of his back in the hotel room. He wondered if the ladies in the colored whore house had heard of Flinging Ed Falstaff. If they hadn't, he'd give them one of the twenty copies of the dime novel he'd purchased. He even autographed a few, for a fee of course.

THE WAKE OF THE BERTRAND

———

The next morning, Kyle ate in the general mess and then returned to his quarters and finalized his packing before he went to the stables where he saddled Duke and Baron with riding saddles then tossed the pack saddle on Neptune. He led them outside the stables and began to load his things onto Neptune. He slipped the Sharps and the new Henry in Duke's scabbards and the other Henry and the Spencer in the Baron's but kept the bow and arrows on Neptune.

He was getting ready to mount when he heard a gruff voice and recognized it, even though he'd only heard it once before.

"Where do you think you are going, Mister MacKenzie?"

Kyle turned around and replied loudly, "That, Colonel Johnson, is none of your damned business. I am though with scouting and I am through with you."

The colonel was shocked and exclaimed, "I'll have you up on charges for desertion!"

"Colonel, have you any idea how stupid that sounded? Men like you who climb their way up in the ladder of promotion but are afraid to do anything that might upset their bosses are a dime a dozen. I've seen your type before, and every time I do, I leave. In your case, it's so bad, I'm leaving the service of the United States Army for good.

"All the problems that ensue are on your head now, Colonel. Either you buck up and handle them with some of Lieutenant Colonel Carpenter's leadership skills, or you'll soon be wallowing in the guts of the men that will die because of you."

"You are under arrest, Mister MacKenzie!" he shouted.

Kyle mounted then turned Duke away and shouted over his shoulder, "Go back into your quarters and abuse yourself, Colonel. It may be the only thing you're good at."

Kyle then began walking his horses away from the seething senior officer.

Colonel Johnson knew that he didn't have the authority to arrest the man, but by God, he had the ability to shoot him! He began to remove his pistol and when he looked up to target the receding Kyle MacKenzie, he saw MacKenzie's pistol already aimed at him.

Kyle said loudly, "I figured you for a back shooter, Mister Johnson. You should be grateful I let you live."

Those were the last words spoken by Kyle MacKenzie as he departed Fort Sully. He knew he had just eliminated Colonel Johnson's ability to command, but he also knew that he had very little to begin with.

He then headed south, setting a rapid pace to Fort Pierre.

————

In Yankton, Charles and Abigail were also packing. They had purchased two new trunks and had them filled, had checked the riverboard schedule and guessed that Kyle would be on the *Warwick*, which would be arriving in two days.

"How did Edmund find out about Emily's inheritance?" Abigail asked.

"I have no idea. I know she wasn't about to tell him."

"What do you think Kyle will do? He's been so damned honorable about this whole thing."

"I'm not sure, but I know what I'm going to recommend what he does about this," he said as he tossed the copy of *Flinging Ed Falstaff* that had found its way to Yankton from Omaha.

Charles continued, saying, "He'll be able to shut down that publisher. I'll have him talk to Horace when we get to St. Louis."

"I can't believe this thing," Abigail said, after picking up the dime novel, "At least he didn't use our names."

"I wonder if Emily has seen it?"

"I hope not. She's liable to kill him."

"Abigail, are you sure you're all right with the boat?"

"No, I'm not all right with the boat, Charles, but I'll handle it. Like Kyle said, I have sand," she replied as she smiled.

———

Kyle reached Fort Pierre in plenty of time, rode straight to the dock area and arranged passage for him and his three horses on the *Warwick* leaving the following morning for St. Louis. The next stop would be in Yankton, then it would be on to Omaha where they could take the train to St. Louis.

He walked to the dry goods store and asked that the four cases of ammunition be sent to Fort Sully and had to pay an extra six dollars to get them delivered to the fort. There was no sense in depriving the troops of the cartridges.

———

Edmund and Emily were eating breakfast in the dining car as they crossed Missouri. Emily hadn't said a word since Edmund had told her in no uncertain terms that they were returning to St.

Louis. He still wore his pistol, and she wasn't convinced he wouldn't find some excuse to use it on her since he found out about her money.

She, like her parents, had no idea how he had found out about her inheritance. She was the only grandchild of Ralph Little, the founder of Little Shipping, and when she had been born, he had left her the rather tidy sum of twenty thousand dollars in a trust.

Over the long term of its existence, the money had grown into a staggering $57,442.50 as of the date she had departed St. Louis. She had never spent a dime of the money and preferred to keep it secret, especially from Edmund. As her husband, he could spend the money and leave her destitute. Laws were being passed to prevent that from happening and one had been in the Missouri legislature before they had gone. She hoped they had made it into law.

Edmund had discovered the existence of Emily's money through sheer happenstance. He was alone in their house while Emily was with her mother and decided to have a cup of tea for a change. He never drank tea but wanted to see why women liked it so much. He pulled out the tea container and found a small bank book inside. He curiously opened the first page, saw the name of Emily Burleigh, then turned the pages as the numbers changed until he reached the last page and stared at the numbers.

It was Emily's inheritance and he was stunned. *That bitch had been holding out on him!* He had slipped the book back into place and was determined at that moment that they would return to St. Louis where he would have it all now. Fame as Flinging Ed Falstaff and now a lot of money. He wouldn't even have to buy a house as he and Emily could live in the grand Burleigh estate. It was empty anyway.

The next day, he had told Emily they were leaving, and her parents had tried to convince him to stay, but he had overruled their demands. He had let it slip that he knew about the inheritance, but it didn't matter if they knew or not as they could do nothing. He had all the cards now because their daughter was now his property, as was all of her money.

Now, as their train rocked and clacked eastward across Iowa, Edmund knew that in less than a day, he'd be in St. Louis. Before they left Kanas City, he had seriously thought about wiring ahead to his parents to have them notify the *St. Louis Post* that their famous son was returning.

———

Kyle was up early after having spent a restless night, worried that he might miss the riverboat. He was dressed and took his saddlebags and weapons with him to the livery shortly after sunrise. He had his horses saddled and his long guns loaded, then led them to the café, had his breakfast and then walked them to the dock. The gangplank was down, so he followed the stock manager onto the *Warwick* and led his horses down to the stock deck where he and the manager put them into their stalls.

"Are my guns safe down here?" he asked.

"Safer than a bank. They can't go anywhere," he replied as he grinned.

Kyle smiled back and left all his long guns with the horses after they were stripped. He returned to the deck as the other passengers began boarding, then climbed the port stairway and found his cabin, unlocked the door and left it open. It was kind of small, but it would only be for a few days. He wondered if Charles and Abigail would be joining him when the boat arrived at Yankton. A lot depended on Abigail and her fear of waterborne transportation.

275

After the *Warwick* got underway, Kyle took a stroll around the upper deck and then walked down the starboard stairs to the bottom deck. He walked to the front as the pilot navigated sternwheeler down the waterway. In just three more days he would be on a train heading east across Iowa and then they'd head down to Missouri. A long day on the train, but just four days altogether, which wasn't bad when compared to the length of time he'd taken just going from Fort Omaha to Fort Sully.

He stayed on the deck until lunchtime then walked to the dining room, found an empty table, sat down and was served his lunch. As he was eating, he spied a man reading. It was what he was reading that caught his eye.

The man must have just finished, because he had a satisfied look on his face as he put the thin book down on the table and began to eat.

Kyle finished his meal quickly, then picked up his cup of coffee and approached the man's table.

"Excuse me, sir. Would you mind if I join you for a few minutes? I'd like to ask you about your book."

"Sure. Have a seat. This isn't really a book, just one of those dime novels. I didn't buy it, either. It was left in my cabin. It's quite entertaining, but I'm sure it's just outrageously exaggerated fiction. Why did it interest you?"

"The name on the title, *Flinging Ed Falstaff.*"

"Yes, that's the name of the hero, Ed Falstaff. In the book, he saves his wife and in-laws from robbers, Indians and some cowardly type from a cougar while he leads them through hostile Indian territory."

Kyle should have been stunned but just a glimpse of the cover and the title had prepared him for the contents, so he simply replied, "You don't say. And what is the name of the cowardly type that he rescues?"

"Kyle something-or-other."

"Kyle MacKenzie, perhaps?"

"That's it! I thought you hadn't read the book by your questions."

"I haven't. My name is Kyle MacKenzie."

The man stared at Kyle, who was still wearing his pistols, swallowed, then said, "At the risk of jumping to conclusions, Mister MacKenzie, you hardly appear to be the type of man depicted in the novel."

"Mister...what is your name, by the way?"

"Oh, excuse me. My name is George Overton."

"Well, Mister Overton, I was on that trip and Mister Falstaff was hardly the hero depicted in the novel. Among the Lakota, I am referred to as the Green-Eyed Devil for a very good reason. I have been a thorn in their side for five years now."

"Then, Mister MacKenzie, you surely have a case of libel against the publisher. Your character and name have been severely damaged by the book's publication."

"That is my intention, Mister Overton. I'm on my way to St. Louis right now to find Mister Falstaff."

"Because of the book?"

"No, it is a different issue entirely and the novel will only add to the discussion."

Overton smiled and said, "By the looks of you, that will be some discussion, but I have a feeling it will be very one-sided."

Kyle smiled back and replied, "That's possible."

"Please, take this copy. I surely won't read it again. It only takes an hour to read."

"Thank you. I'm sure my attorney will spend much more time with it than I will."

He laughed and they shook hands.

Kyle slipped the book into his jacket pocket, right beside Emily's letter.

———

Late the next morning, the *Warwick* was docking at Yankton and Kyle thought he'd go and pay Charles and Abigail a visit. So, he was waiting on the deck for the gangplank to be set in position when he spied them both waiting to board. He waved, and they waved in return.

Charles looked at his wife and said, "Well, Abigail, Kyle's here, so things are looking better."

"Except for the boat, Charles."

"It wouldn't dare sink with Kyle on board," Charles said with a smile.

Kyle waited for them to board and soon engaged Charles in a firm handshake and then received a hug and kiss on the cheek from Abigail. Their two trunks were being taken below as Kyle walked with them to the upper deck.

"Charles, what happened?" he asked.

"Edmund somehow found out about Emily's inheritance. As her husband, he has the right to spend the money. Once he found out about the inheritance, he told Emily that they would be returning to St. Louis immediately. She didn't want to go, but she had no say in the matter and neither did we. I don't wield the power of the purse over him any longer."

They reached the steps and Kyle stepped aside to let Charles and Abigail go up the stairway. The thought of Emily being wealthy had never occurred to him and it made him surprisingly uncomfortable.

When they reached the top, they walked to their cabin, unlocked the door and placed their travel bags inside.

Charles turned to Kyle after they exited the cabin, and said, "Kyle, there's something else, and it's one of the reasons that Edmund left so abruptly, I believe."

"The dime novel, *Flinging Ed Falstaff*?"

"Yes. When did you find out about it?"

"Yesterday. I read it last night. It was well-written, but the facts were a bit askew."

"You aren't angry?"

"Of course, I'm angry. I'm livid. But it does no good to show it now."

"You're an amazing man, Kyle. I have a wonderful attorney in St. Louis. If you have no objections, he'll file a libel suit against the publisher and the author when we arrive."

"I was going to do it myself, but I'll accept your offer. Another thing, Charles. How is your standing with your cousin?"

"It's all right. He thought before I accepted the position that I might not do as he wished."

"Let me explain to you about Fort Sully. There was this attack by the Lakota...."

When he had finished, Charles smiled.

"I don't think we need to bother my brother, Kyle. After I received your letter about the gunrunning operation, I sent a letter to the Secretary of War. I had met him on several occasions before we left St. Louis. In my letter, I told him about the smuggling of rifles to the Sioux and how it worked. He wrote back and thanked me profusely and said that he would have the army handle it immediately.

"In that letter, I had told him of your role, and he wrote back and said your reputation was already well known even in Washington City. If you'll tell me the detailed story of the attack this time, and don't hold back your single-handed rescue of the fort from the hill either as it's an oft-repeated legend already. Give me the details and I'll write another letter to Stanton with your recommendation. That should help Lieutenant Colonel Carpenter."

Kyle felt relieved as he replied, "Thank you, Charles. I'll give you all of the details and we'll see if we can't correct that error."

"I still have to find out the source of that illegal operation when we get to St. Louis, too."

"I figure it'll take some time for them to set it up again, but it's the source that's the problem."

"Not for much longer, Kyle," Charles replied as *The Warwick* pulled away from the dock and was soon on its way south to Omaha.

———

Emily looked out the window of the train as it traveled through Missouri. It didn't look any different than Iowa, but it was all irrelevant anyway. They'd be arriving in St. Louis in a few hours and she'd become a prisoner.

"When we get to St. Louis, Emily, we'll take a carriage to your family home and live there. It's unoccupied and there is no reason for us to live elsewhere."

Emily didn't bother to say anything as he couldn't care less about what she thought or how she felt. She was so depressed and disconnected she just didn't care anymore. She knew she'd never see Kyle again and with Edmund in control of her money, there was little she could do. She doubted if she'd be going to any balls or soirees, either. She had hated them before but now, Edmund seemed to behave like a celebrity and an unmarried one at that. She still had no idea why he was acting as the important man, but really didn't care anymore.

Edmund continued his monologue, saying, "After we're established in the house, we'll hire a cook and a maid. I will hire them and a new butler as well, but I will be in charge, Emily. You will not speak back to me nor will you make any appearance of dislike and will be punished if you do. But at least I will relieve you of your wifely duties."

He then snickered before he continued.

"You were so boring in bed anyway, so I'll choose my own entertainment on that front. If I bring any of my escorts to the house, you are to make yourself scarce. In fact, you and I will sleep in two different rooms as far apart as possible. I am going to be a gentleman again, Emily, but I shall continue to wear my pistol as a reminder of who I am."

Emily didn't have a clue who he thought he was. At least not yet. She recalled the last time he'd held a pistol in his hand and tried to shoot Kyle in the back and wished she had a loaded pistol in her hand at that moment.

———

The *Warwick* was pulling into the docks in Omaha and Kyle, Charles and Abigail were already packed. The boat would stay overnight, but by then they planned on being out of Iowa and into Missouri.

Kyle looked over at a surprisingly peaceful Abigail and asked, "Abigail, I have to admit, you have impressed me yet again. You did very well on that voyage."

Abigail turned to Kyle, and said, "It was my intention to impress you, Kyle. I had to show to you that I had sand."

Kyle smiled and nodded before replying, "You did that, Abigail. I hope Emily has enough sand to handle the next few days."

"What will you do, Kyle?" asked Charles.

"I've had it with the rules, Charles. I'm not going back to my life as a scout. I'm going to take Emily from Edmund for her own safety and I'll return her to you. What happens between me and Edmund is up to him."

"You can't kill him, Kyle. You'd hang."

"I know that, Charles. I won't, either. He knows that and in knowing that, he may be foolish enough to draw that pistol he keeps with him now. If he does, then I'll shoot in self-defense."

"But you could get killed!" Abigail exclaimed.

"I know, Abigail. It's a risk I'm willing to take for Emily. She has no life now and I will get her away from Edmund."

"But he'll still have her money, Kyle."

"I don't care about the money. I care about Emily. In fact, I wish she didn't have the money at all. I want to be there for her and to provide for her. I want to give her everything I have. If it takes my life to give her back hers, then so be it. I just don't believe it will happen that way."

"I hope not," said Abigail.

Four hours later, they were sitting on board a Union Pacific train heading east. Kyle's horses were in the stock car and the Burleighs' two trunks were in the baggage car. It was just about four hundred miles to St. Louis. They were scheduled to arrive in eighteen hours and would have to change trains twice. It would be a long and tiring trip, but they would still arrive two days before the steamboat.

———

The Falstaffs had moved into the Burleigh estate, and as he had promised, Edmund had set up his room on one end of the house and let Emily occupy a bedroom in the other wing. They would sleep over a hundred feet apart, which was fine with Emily. She had moved her clothes from her old bedroom, which was just two rooms from Edmund's chosen room which had belonged to her parents.

As she moved her things and was putting them away in the drawer, she was preparing to slide one garment into the drawer and stopped. She then held the corset out at arm's length and smiled, hearing one of Kyle's first pronouncement that 'the women are wearing corsets and petticoats and have their hair up'.

She slowly began removing hairpins until her long brown hair cascaded down her back, then began to disrobe. To hell with Edmund.

After she was corset-less and free of petticoats, she laid down on her bed and pulled Kyle's letter from her travel bag. She had read it so often that she could quote it word for word, but reading it gave her strength. *Would her parents tell him what had happened? Where was he now?*

She began to believe that Kyle would come for her, knowing that he wouldn't let this happen to her. He loved her and that was all that mattered.

As Emily was reading, Edmund was preparing to go out for the evening for the first time since they'd returned. He wanted to see how much his fame had spread in St. Louis, and he'd start in his favorite place where they already knew him as Edmund Falstaff. But did they know him as Flinging Ed Falstaff? If they did, then maybe those colored girls would fawn all over him and maybe even give him free ones.

He hadn't hired any help yet, so he saddled his own horse that was still on the grounds and kept in fine condition by a service hired by Charles Burleigh.

He mounted, then rode out of the estate and headed for the colored section to his preferred bawdy house. It only featured the classiest whores and catered to the white gentlemen, like himself, that preferred the adventure. There was no risk of disease there, either. The owner ensured that the girls were clean, or they'd find their way to the docks.

He rode along in complete confidence with his pistol on his hip. Flinging Ed was about to make his entrance into the St. Louis arena.

He arrived at Mary's Parlor around seven o'clock, dismounted and had a groom take his horse before he went inside and was greeted by the madam, Mary Jefferson.

"Good evening, Mary," he said with a grin.

"Well, welcome back, Mister Falstaff. I hear you've been having adventures out West."

Edmund was enormously pleased and said, "Yes, I must admit. It was difficult at times, but I prevailed."

"Well, we have two new girls you might want to sample. You might really like Marie. She's very special."

"You pique my interest, Mary. Is she available?"

"She is. Marie!"

A few seconds later, a very beautiful young woman of perhaps twenty entered the room and Edmund was most assuredly interested.

"Marie, this is Mister Falstaff, an old customer. Mister Falstaff, this is Marie. Is she not as special as I suggested?"

"Very special, indeed, Mary. Perhaps I should give Marie the special attention that she deserves. Do you speak French, Marie?"

Marie looked at him with her dark eyes, and whispered seductively, "Oui, Monsieur."

Edmund was instantly hooked, then smiled at Marie and took her by the arm. They left the sitting area, and Edmund began to try to impress Marie, as if she was a girlfriend, with his exploits on the plains of Nebraska.

———

Emily knew he was gone, so she relaxed, then walked down the stairs and went to the kitchen and could cook herself something to eat. There weren't any fresh foods, but she knew how to make the best out of canned foods now.

Again, she smiled at memories of Kyle and the trip across the Plains. For all the hardship and danger, she would always remember them with unrestrained joy. It was where she met Kyle and now, she was convinced that Kyle would come for her.

She was already sound asleep in her bedroom when her husband returned.

Edmund entered the big double doors after midnight in an excellent mood. He'd sleep late and then, tomorrow night, he'd go back and see Marie. She had seemed very interested in the exploits of Flinging Ed, and it showed in her lovemaking. She had even asked him to return because she had told him that he had excited her. If she wasn't colored, he'd make her a concubine. But he couldn't be seen with women like that. They were for fornicating and little else.

———

As their train rolled through the night, Abigail was sleeping with her head against the window as Charles looked at Kyle.

"When we get to St. Louis, we'll just hire a cab to go to our house. I imagine that's where we'll find them. The question is how do you want to handle this? The only advantage we have is that I have the authority to kick him out of the house, but not to keep Emily there."

"I know, but all we can do is to get a read on the situation. I have a feeling that Edmund, or Flinging Ed, would try to blackmail you into giving him more money for a divorce."

"I'd pay it, Kyle."

"No, Charles, you won't. I may not care about Emily's money, but I sure don't want that weasel to get it, not even a single dollar. If we find Emily without Edmund, just take her to a room that you know is safe while I talk to Flinging Ed. I can be quite convincing if need be."

Charles said, "I'm sure you can, but we have to make sure that everything is legal, Kyle. His family is well established in St. Louis society."

"Oh, it will be legal. Trust me."

"Okay. We'll be getting in early in the evening and should be at the house by seven o'clock tomorrow night."

"Charles, I think we'll be able to handle this to everyone's satisfaction, especially Emily's."

"I hope so, Kyle. I really hope so."

CHAPTER 10

Edmund was up at ten o'clock and as he walked to the bathroom, was loudly demanding breakfast from his wife down the hallway.

Emily was soon in the kitchen trying to avoid being hurt until Kyle arrived, so she made what she could from tins, but knew it was a culinary disaster.

Edmund looked at the food on his plate, glared at her then, stood and smashed her hard with the back of his hand across her face, knocking Emily to the floor.

"You had better do better than this slop tomorrow morning. In fact, I want a cook in here in three days and I want a proper gentleman's breakfast. Right now, I'm going to go to the restaurant and have something that I can digest."

He slid the food to the other side of the table, then turned and stalked off, slamming the door as he left the house.

Emily picked herself from the floor and sat at the table and slowly ate the food, thinking that it wasn't bad at all. Her shoulder hurt from hitting the floor, and she noticed that for the first time, Edmund had hit her face. She suddenly realized that he finally didn't care any longer if her parents or anyone else saw her with bruises. That epiphany made her understand that her treatment was only going to get worse. She knew that she would die her parents' house unless Kyle came.

She finished eating and cleaned up, then returned to her room, took out her letter and sat on the bed, all the while thinking, "Please come quickly, Kyle. Please."

———

Edmund ate a good breakfast at the gentleman's club and regaled his fellow gentlemen with stories about how he had vanquished the savages and how that pathetic half-breed Kyle MacKenzie had cowered before him. *What else could you expect of a man whose mother was a savage and had married another?*

The other gentlemen agreed as the thought of mixing races was too horrible to contemplate. One told a ribald joke about colored women that Edmund though hilarious. Perhaps he'd tell it to Marie tonight.

Edmund returned to the house after a large, late lunch, knowing that the bitch wife of his wouldn't be able to satisfy him. Then he snickered at his own double entendre.

———

The train carrying Kyle and the Burleighs pulled in a little early at 5:20 and Charles went to hire a carriage while Kyle walked to the stock corral to retrieve his horses and their armory.

Twenty minutes later, Kyle was riding Duke behind the hired carriage trailing Baron and Neptune as it headed for the Burleigh estate. Kyle felt a bit out of place in the highbrow neighborhood but didn't let it show. He was going to see Emily, and despite the situation, it was all that mattered.

The carriage turned onto what looked like a small castle's entrance as Kyle followed and was already excited with the prospect of seeing Emily again. With each hoofbeat, Kyle found his anticipation growing and tried to contain himself.

He had already modified his original plan and instead of heading for the carriage house, he decided he'd just tie up his horses and go in the back entrance, mainly because he wanted to see Emily sooner.

————

Emily had walked downstairs to make herself some dinner while Edmund had just finished dressing for his night to go and see Marie. He was stepping down the wide staircase when he thought he heard a carriage approaching but was anxious to leave and ignored it.

He walked out to the kitchen and saw Emily getting ready to cook, which irritated him, but to make it worse, she was dressed like a commoner again.

He glared at her and snarled, "Wife, the next time I see you, you will be properly dressed, and that includes a corset."

Emily snapped and shouted, "I will not! I will wear what I choose and where I will go. This is my parents' house, you, pathetic bastard, not yours!"

Outside the back door as he pulled Duke to a stop, Kyle heard Emily's explosion and quickly dismounted, not tying anything to anywhere as he jogged to the large back entrance and took the six steps two at a time.

Edmund was furious as he screamed, "How dare you! You are nothing! You have nothing! I have everything now!"

He grabbed her by the hair and tossed her across the room as the door flew open and Kyle stood in the entrance, his eyes pouring mountainous hate at Edmund. But when he saw Emily crash into a chair and slump to the ground, Kyle didn't have time for Edmund as he raced to Emily.

He shot past Edmund, giving him a quick shove to get him out of the way.

As Kyle reached a shaken, but unhurt Emily, Edmund saw his chance, and was reaching for his pistol, his loaded pistol this time, he thought.

But Kyle suspected he might try something and the moment he knew that Emily wasn't injured, had pulled his right-hand pistol, cocked the hammer and had it pointing at Edmund before Flinging Ed could get his out of his holster.

His green eyes flared at Edmund as he growled, "Give me an excuse, Falstaff. Please! Or should I call you Flinging Ed now, you, lying son of a bitch?"

Edmund quickly threw his hands in the air and began to back toward the kitchen door.

"You can't shoot me, MacKenzie. You'd hang. You have to let me go."

Then as he continued to backpedal toward the open door he said, "And you'll never have her, either. I'll see to that. You lose, MacKenzie. This isn't a world where you can just gun down anyone you want. This is civilization, MacKenzie. This is my world. The world of gentlemen."

He reached the doorway, turned and quickly jogged to his horse, mounted and rode quickly down the long, graveled drive.

Charles and Abigail had heard the commotion and walked quickly to the kitchen to find Kyle leaned over Emily.

291

Kyle heard Edmund's horse race past, knew he was gone, but he was no longer his primary concern now.

Emily looked up and saw those bright green eyes looking at her from just inches away, then smiled as if she had never smiled before.

She touched his face with her fingertips and said gently, "You came for me like I knew you would."

He smiled at her and replied, "Yes, I came for you. I'll always be here for you now. But this won't be over with Falstaff hovering about."

Charles and Abigail could see the bruising on Emily's face from Edmund's first blow and knew that the injury might drive Kyle into killing the man who had hurt her.

Charles walked close and said, "Kyle, I'll get lawyers. We can solve this all legally. Don't do anything rash. Please."

Kyle turned his eyes from Emily to her father and calmly said, "Your civilized society allowed that man to just throw his wife across the room and not even worry about punishment. It will allow him to take everything from her unless he's stopped. Well, Charles, I've had it with civilization."

Kyle looked down at Emily, then rose to his feet and unbuckled his gunbelt. He took off his pistols and laid them on the table, leaving his massive Bowie knife as his only weapon. It was all he needed and was the instrument he wanted to use for Flinging Ed.

"Kyle, please don't do this," begged Abigail.

"There's right and there's wrong, Abigail," Kyle said, "I'll take care of this the only way I can."

He then helped Emily to her feet, and held her face in his hands as he asked, "Where did he go, Emily? Trust me to do this the right way."

Emily looked into those marvelous green eyes and knew she had to trust him, or it all would mean nothing.

"He's gone to Mary's Parlor on 14th Street. Turn left on the road and then it's four streets down on the left."

Kyle smiled at Emily, knowing that she had told him simply because she trusted him.

He turned, left the kitchen, then walked to the horses and untied the trail rope. He mounted Duke and set off for Mary's Parlor and his meeting with Flinging Ed Falstaff.

———

Even as Kyle was mounting his horse, Edmund had already entered the whore house and had asked for Marie again. He was impatiently waiting as Kyle made the turn out of the Burleigh estate, but soon Marie swayed her way toward Edmund and led him back to her room.

———

Back at the house, Charles and Abigail were talking with Emily, but none knew for certain what Kyle intended to do.

"Mother, I had to tell him. I had to trust him without question."

"I know, sweetheart, but I wish I knew what he was planning. Kyle told us that he would give his life to allow you to live yours and now, I think he's going to do that one way or the other."

"Mother, doesn't he understand that I will have no life without him?"

"He just knows that what was happening to you wasn't right and he said that you deserve more."

"Why didn't I just leave when I had the chance? I could have gone to him before it came to this."

"He wouldn't have let you do that, Emily. You know that. For the same reason he never could call you anything but Mrs. Falstaff. You were married and he would never let you violate your vows."

Emily looked at the back door and quietly said, "Mother, I never ever even heard him say my name. I wanted so much for him to look at me and call me Emily."

"I know, sweetheart, I know."

———

Marie was standing in front of a naked and very aroused Edmund. She wore a white silk robe that was open in the front, revealing her dark curves.

Edmund was entranced as he studied her glorious body and had tried to grab her several times, but Marie had delayed their lovemaking to make it more exciting and it was working.

Marie's hair was still up as she took two steps closer and spread her robe apart slowly, revealing its hidden treasure, inch by incredible inch.

"Monsieur," she began as she let the silk robe fall gently to the floor, "you have told me all these stories, but you know nothing of me."

THE WAKE OF THE BERTRAND

Marie slid closer to him and straddled an aroused Edmund who laid back and let his eyes travel across her lustrous skin.

She pulled her one, four-inch long hairpin and let her long, black hair fall in cascades across her back and breasts as Edmund watched in breathless anticipation.

"You do not even know my name," she whispered as she leaned forward, letting her breasts slide across his chest and began kissing his neck.

"Close your eyes, monsieur, and let me pleasure you."

Edmund closed his eyes and Marie leaned forward again.

When her lips were just inches from his right ear, she whispered, "My name is Marie Martin, Monsieur Falstaff. My father was Louis Martin and you killed him."

Before Edmund could protest and deny the accusation, Marie slipped the long hairpin into Edmund's left nostril and rammed it upwards into his head. Edmund's eyes went wide.

Marie sat back and picked up Edmund's pistol as Kyle walked into Mary's Parlor.

"Welcome, Sir..." was all Mary said when there was a pistol shot from a nearby room, which was immediately followed by a second. Kyle ran to the room with Mary running behind him.

He opened the door and found Edmund sprawled on the bed beneath Marie, their blood mingling on the silk sheets beneath them. The gunsmoke still hung in the room, the acrid smell overpowering the normal, flowery scents.

"Marie!" cried Mary.

Kyle was stunned as he looked at the scene. *What had happened?* He had come to kill Edmund, but he was already dead.

Mary quickly walked to the bed, hurriedly examined both bodies, then turned to Kyle and said, "Marie must have killed Mister Falstaff. Her hairpin is in his nose, then she shot him before she killed herself. Why did she do such a thing?"

Kyle looked at Mary and said, "Maybe he beat her."

"No. He hit them, but not as bad as some. She said something about her father understanding last night when he left. I don't know what it meant."

"What was her last name?"

"Martin."

"Oh," was all Kyle said, making the connection immediately.

"Mister, you'd better leave as there will be policemen all over this place soon."

"Alright. Maybe some other time."

Kyle then quickly walked out of the establishment and found Duke himself, as the groom had gone into the building to see what had happened. He mounted, then rode away from the bordello at a reasonable pace still shocked by what had happened.

He knew that Louis Martin was a Cajun, but didn't know he had a wife, much less a daughter.

———

Charles, Abigail and Emily could do nothing more than wait for either Kyle or the police.

Abigail had made coffee and Charles told Emily about Kyle's request to help the commander of Fort Sully and then told her the other stories which astounded her.

When he finished, Charles said, "He told us he was done with scouting now."

Emily stared into her coffee and said quietly, "Father, he will be done with everything after tonight if he kills Edmund."

"Don't worry, sweetheart. Everything will be fine," Abigail said although she was an emotional disaster as she anticipated the worst.

They suddenly heard hoofbeats from the back yard and they knew that either Kyle or Edmund was back, but none believed it was Edmund.

Emily knew that no matter what happened, she would spend as much time as she could with Kyle. If they were going to arrest him and take him to prison or worse, hang him, she would go to his bed tonight, not caring what anyone thought.

———

Kyle stepped down, still a bit numb from what he had witnessed. This had to be the end of it. There could be no more tragedies.

He opened the door and saw three pairs of blue eyes looking at him with concern.

He closed the door and walked toward Emily, who rose and stepped toward him, a slight, hopeful smile on her face.

He stopped and took her hands, then as he gazed into her blue eyes, quietly said, "Hello, Emily."

She tried to speak, but just moved her lips. The second time, she managed to say in a hoarse whisper, "Hello, Kyle."

Then he just enveloped her in his arms and held her as she began to cry.

Charles had to ask, "Kyle, is he dead?"

"Yes, Charles. He's dead," he replied as he felt Emily shuddering.

"I'll get you a lawyer, a whole team of lawyers, Kyle. You are not going to hang!"

Kyle felt Emily still shaking, but turned his eyes to her father and said, "No, I won't hang and the lawyers won't be necessary, either. He was murdered, but I didn't do it. He was killed by a prostitute."

Emily heard his words, instantly stopped shaking, and felt a rush of relief flood through her as she realized that she was not only free, but free to be with Kyle.

She still had tears streaming down her face, but for a completely different reason as she looked into his green eyes and asked, "What happened?"

"It was the strangest of circumstances. He was bedding the young woman and she pushed a hairpin into his nose, then she took his pistol and shot him before she killed herself."

"Why?" asked Abigail.

"He had been bragging about himself as if he had done all those things in that sorry novel. He didn't know that she was the daughter of Louis Martin, and he had claimed to have killed her father. I didn't even know that Louis was married."

"So, if she had known the truth, she would have tried to kill you," said Charles.

"Maybe. But she only knew the story and was living here in St. Louis. If the book had never been published, or Edmund hadn't decided to take Emily to St. Louis, none of this would have happened."

"Now, what will we do, Kyle?" asked Emily.

"Now, Emily, we wait until your parents graciously leave the kitchen," he said as he smiled.

Charles and Abigail took the hint well, then stood and as Charles took Abigail's hand, said, "I'm going to pull the trunks inside."

"I'll help," Abigail added, knowing she wouldn't be needed.

After they left the kitchen, Kyle looked into Emily's now-smiling blue eyes, and said, "Now, Emily, this is what happens next."

He pulled her closer and kissed her softly, but the soft aspect gave way to a full passionate kiss that lasted for a full minute as Emily lifted her feet from the floor.

When that long kiss finally ended, Kyle asked, "Emily Burleigh, will you marry me?"

Emily could only nod as her face threatened to crack in two.

Before they kissed again, Emily asked, "Can you tell me now?"

Just as he had before he left to find Edmund, he cradled her face in his big hands, looked into her eyes and with as much passion as he could, softly said, "I love you, Emily."

Emily took his hands from her face, her eyes never leaving his, then touched her lips to his fingers and whispered, "I love you, Kyle."

They then shared one more long, meaningful kiss before they separated, smiled at each other, then Kyle put his hand around her waist, and after she put her arm around his, he leaned over and whispered, "No corset, Emily?"

Emily giggled lightly, then replied, "Never again. Did you want to make sure later?"

"I'll make sure to check thoroughly, ma'am."

Emily hoped that he meant it as they strolled out of the kitchen and walked down the long, wide hallway to the front parlor.

When they arrived in the room, Kyle had to leave Emily to help Charles with the two heavy trunks. Once they were where they needed to be, Kyle quickly trotted to the settee where Emily was waiting with a big smile.

After he sat next to her and took her hand, Charles asked, "Well, Kyle, have you proposed yet?"

"Yes, Charles, as soon as I could get my breath."

"Did you respond appropriately, Emily?" Abigail asked.

300

"Sort of, Mother. I couldn't talk so I just nodded."

"Well, now that all things are sorted out, let's go and finish our coffee and figure out what we need to do about this whole affair."

Charles and Abigail walked down the hallway holding hands.

As soon as they disappeared down the hallway, Kyle and Emily stood, but Kyle quickly scooped Emily into his arms again and then kissed her before she could say anything.

Emily felt her toes curl as he held her close and understood immediately that he wanted her as much as she wanted him, and even though he wasn't going to hang or even go to prison, she wanted it to be tonight. No more lonely nights in bed with fantasies, she wanted the real thing and was sure that it wouldn't take much of a suggestion to get him there.

She pulled back slightly and whispered, "I want that corset inspection tonight. Is that understood?"

Kyle kissed her quickly, then replied, "I can only feel cotton between us, ma'am, but I do feel the need to make sure that you're not hiding a whalebone or two somewhere."

"You'd better make sure that I'm not, mister. I'm not sleeping alone anymore."

Then he answered more seriously, "Never again, Emily. I'm never going to let you go."

Emily sighed then after he released her, took his hands and they made their delayed walk down the hallway.

———

After almost thirty minutes of conversation about what had happened at Mary's Parlor and what they would do over the next few days, Abigail and Charles excused themselves.

As they walked out of the kitchen holding hands and preparing to enjoy some private time of their own in their own bedroom, Kyle and Emily sat at the table, holding both hands as they talked.

They waited until they heard the upstairs bedroom door close before Emily asked, "Do you want to hear something odd?"

"I'd be surprised if it could be anything more unusual than what's already happened tonight."

"Ever since we met, I've dreamed about being with you. I've made up so many fantasies and let my imagination loose about how exciting it would be to make love to you. But now, when I know that it's so near, I'm nervous."

As much as he wanted Emily, Kyle said, "If you want to wait until we're married, that's alright."

Emily quickly shook her head as she said, "No, no, that's not what I meant at all. In fact, it's just the opposite from wanting to postpone our first night together. What was odd was that I felt as if I was a schoolgirl before her first kiss. I'm so excited that I'm almost giggling inside. I've never felt that way before and yet, here I am an old married woman who is behaving like a teenager."

Kyle stood, took her hand and said, "If it makes you feel any better, I've been thinking about you the same way and have that same nervousness. I want so much to please you."

Emily smiled as she slowly stood, then said, "You already have, Kyle. Take me upstairs now and we can please each other."

As they walked up the wide staircase hand in hand, Kyle was surprised at his nervousness. He'd faced death more often than he wanted to count but now, as he was about to make love to Emily, he felt his heart pounding.

They passed the big bedroom and pretended not to hear anything as they walked down the long hallway and entered the bedroom where Emily had slept alone the night before.

Once inside, Kyle closed the door as Emily surprised him by lighting a lamp.

He smiled at her as Emily said, "How can you do a proper inspection without light?"

He stepped closer to Emily, then as he kissed her, he slid his hand to her left breast and caressed it as she put her hand over his.

The inspection then commenced in earnest as they quickly began disrobing each other and used their eyes and fingers to explore for unwanted whalebone or anything else that impeded their need to feel each other's skin.

Kyle may have thought he'd have to be gentle with Emily, but Emily soon let him understand that she wanted much more than simple, light touches and kisses.

Soon, the room was filled with a myriad of sounds of pleasure, questions, answers and more than a few exclamations.

For thirty long, passionate minutes each tried to outdo the other in providing pleasure.

Emily was desperately trying to pull Kyle to her, but Kyle used every bit of patience to keep driving her into higher fits of frenzied pleasure.

Emily was worried she'd pass out as she writhed on the bed like a snake, and even pushed Kyle onto his back to be the one to end this.

She was in complete ecstasy when he finally answered her demands as well as his own and they reached the ultimate level of pleasure before they collapsed to the bed bathed in sweat and breathing heavily.

Emily then rolled halfway on top of Kyle, kissed him and then rested her head on his heaving chest as she said hoarsely, "I needed that, Kyle. I needed you."

Kyle slid his fingers across her damp curves and said, "I can't believe how exciting you are, Emily. You know how much I love you, but this was beyond those dreams I had of you, and I thought they were a bit too much."

"Well, my fantasies are surpassed as well. I guess you didn't find any corsets anywhere, either?"

Kyle laughed lightly, then after he pulled her close and kissed her again, slid his hand across her side, then cupped her left breast in his hand as he said, "I haven't finished my inspection yet, ma'am."

Emily had been so satisfied just moments before, she was a bit surprised when she felt his fingers begin to excite her again and whispered, "So soon? Can you really do it again?"

"Again," he replied, then quickly realized that it wasn't just a simple inspection.

———

When they joined Charles and Abigail the next morning, they were both exhausted physically, having only slept for an hour and a half, but the exultation they both felt made up for the lack of sleep.

At breakfast, Abigail took one look at Emily's radiant face and was as happy as a mother could be for her daughter. After all that time with that poor excuse for a man, she'd finally spent her night with a real man, and she could see how happy Kyle made her daughter.

"Sleep well, Emily?" she asked with a wry smile.

"Very well, Mother," Emily replied and wiggled her eyebrows.

Kyle just looked at Charles and shrugged his shoulders sheepishly.

Charles wanted to laugh badly, but managed to hold it in.

After they ate what should be their last non-breakfast breakfast, they were preparing to start the long list of things to do that day when the morning was interrupted by the chimes from the fancy doorbell.

Charles stood and said, "I imagine that will be the police."

He waved everyone else down and went to answer the door. Kyle understood that this was Charles' forte to handle civilized crises.

When he answered the door, Charles was surprised to see it was the police chief himself.

"Good morning, Chief Plummer. What can I do for you?"

The chief was surprised to see Charles Burleigh, thinking that he was still in Dakota Territory, but this made his job easier.

"May I come in, Mister Burleigh?"

"Certainly. My wife and I just returned last night and are a bit disorganized, so you'll have to excuse us."

"Of course. Is Mrs. Falstaff in?"

"Yes, she's with my wife in the kitchen. Did you want to see her?"

"Yes, I believe you and your wife should be here as well," he said with an uncomfortable grimace.

"Abigail, can you and Emily come in please?" he asked loudly.

Emily looked at Kyle and smiled, then rose from the table and after taking her mother's arm, walked with her down the hallway to the parlor.

Chief Plummer smiled at Emily as the women entered.

Charles said, "Abigail, will you and Emily take a seat?"

As they sat down, the chief remained standing, wringing his hands nervously.

"Mrs. Falstaff, I'm afraid I have some bad news. Your husband, Edmund, was murdered last night. The murderer is also dead, so there will be no investigation or trial. I'm sorry to have to be the bearer of bad news."

Emily was going to play the shocked wife but decided it served no purpose.

"Thank you for your concern, Chief Plummer, but it is no great loss to me. My husband, in addition to being inattentive and vicious to me, was known to be a regular client of the houses of prostitution in the colored section. I know this may sound shocking to you, but I'm only telling you this to relieve you of any anxiety you may have in trying to protect me from the news that he was probably murdered in one of those houses. He was probably abusing one of the women and paid the price."

Chief Plummer was stunned, but appreciative at the same time as he replied, "Thank you for being so forthcoming, Mrs. Falstaff. That does give me a measure of relief. I didn't know how to politely answer any questions about his demise. He was a famous man, though. All of those brave things he did."

Emily avoided sounding nasty as she replied, "He did none of them, Chief Plummer. The man who did all of those and more was Kyle MacKenzie, not my husband. He saved all of us several times and just recently saved the entire garrison at Fort Sully. That novel that had made my husband famous was entirely without merit. My father is going to provide legal assistance to Mister MacKenzie in his libel lawsuit against the publisher. And one more thing, Chief Plummer, I am going to marry Mister MacKenzie. He is the most remarkable man I have ever met, and that includes my father who is an extraordinary man himself."

It was a lot of information for the chief to digest, so there was a long pause before he finally said, "That is an impressive list of extraordinary skill and bravery. I'd like to meet Mister MacKenzie one of these days. Well, this was better than I expected, so once again, thank you for your candor, Mrs. Falstaff. I wish more people were like you as it would make our job much easier."

They all stood and as the chief prepared to leave, Charles asked, "Chief, could you have the coroner send me a copy of the death certificate, please?"

"Oh. Of course," he replied as he smiled, "I didn't have as easy a time at the Falstaffs."

"How are Martin and Gertrude?"

"They were very upset. They had actually read that novel and told me that they knew he always had it in him."

"Well, we'll let them enjoy their moment. I assume that they'll take the body and have it buried in their family cemetery?"

"Yes, that was my impression."

"Well, thank you, Chief Plummer. I appreciate your concern."

Charles shook the Chief's hand before he left the house, still trying to understand all that Emily had told him.

After he heard the door close Kyle walked into the parlor, having heard his almost wife's statements to the police chief and it was one more facet of the extraordinary woman he was about to marry.

————

The next few days were hectic as they had to fill the pantry, cold room and larder, so they visited a grocery store and had a large order of food delivered to the house.

Charles sent the letter to the Secretary of War and Kyle met with Charles' attorney who was confident in Kyle's case and would notify the publisher of the initiation of the libel lawsuit.

Through it all, Emily and Kyle enjoyed as much time together as possible. Instead of tiring of each other's company after a while, just the opposite was true. Each would feel incomplete in those rare times when they were apart and as they continued to explore each other's character, they discovered the other's mischievous side and other more hidden character traits. With each discovery, they found that their added knowledge just enhanced their deep love for each other.

During those hectic days the more serious topics were discussed as necessary. The first was the money. Kyle told her that her money wasn't important and only she mattered, but she pointed out that the money would belong to both of them anyway. In the end, Kyle decided that as long as he didn't pay attention to it and let Emily handle the money, then he could live with it.

The second was a more family-based issue. Where would they live?

Neither Kyle nor Emily wanted to live far from Charles and Abigail, yet in a surprise for Emily, Charles and Abigail were no longer keen on staying in the big estate and living in St. Louis. After that stunning announcement, there was a lengthy discussion. Kyle kept his input at a minimum as he wanted to see what Emily wanted before he said anything.

It was Emily who came up with the solution when they settled on Omaha. They liked the city, and with the Union Pacific using it as a starting point for the new transcontinental railroad, it was going to grow rapidly.

The final solution about the exact location, which met with Kyle's approval, was to buy a good amount of land west of the city and build two houses. Charles would have a telegraph installed, so he could keep abreast of his business at home and would still have close access to a city with almost all of the amenities of St. Louis. He'd also add a new office building and move some staff to Omaha to take advantage of the Union Pacific's push west.

Everything was almost settled for the big move. Kyle and Emily would be married before they left, and Kyle only wished that his parents could be there for the wedding. It wasn't going to be a big affair, but it would be a church wedding, held in St. Cecilia's Catholic Church, the Jesuits and the nuns ensuring that choice.

The wedding would be held the following Saturday and all of the paperwork and requirements of the church were done. Emily had her simple, yet very attractive light blue silk dress chosen that included a veil because of the church. They had picked out their wedding rings, and Kyle had bought his first suit. Emily had commented that buckskins probably wouldn't work at a St. Louis church for a wedding.

Three days later after the wedding, they'd board a train for Omaha, the estate would be sold, and all the furnishings replaced. All that they would take with them would be clothing. They would have some of Burleigh Shipping's workers pack and ship what they would move and then store it in a warehouse in Omaha until the houses were built.

Friday morning, the day before the wedding, started normally with a good breakfast prepared by Abigail and Emily, who thoroughly enjoyed cooking together, which surprised them both. Emily was so absolutely happy with her life that it was infectious. The mood in the Burleigh home was vibrant with pure joy and anticipation and they all believed that nothing could ruin the day.

Around nine o'clock, they were all in the parlor just telling stories when the doorbell rang.

"I'll get it," said Emily as she popped up out of her chair.

Emily opened the door with a big smile on her face, but it changed to disbelief when she saw the face before her. She was stunned. *How could this be? Who did this?*

Staring at Emily were two bright green eyes that were enhanced by the most beautiful face she had ever seen. She was without a shred of doubt, Kyle's mother. She assumed that the smiling face next to her was his father.

"Emily, who is it?" asked Abigail.

"Oh. I'm sorry, Mister and Mrs. MacKenzie, won't you come in, please."

"You must be Emily," said Mrs. MacKenzie, adding a smile to the stunning effect.

Kyle heard the voice, bolted out of his chair and raced to the door.

"Mother! Father! *How did you get here?*"

They stepped into the room as Emily closed the door.

Kyle had always described his mother as the most beautiful woman he had ever seen and the Burleighs had always assumed his eyes were blinded by maternal love. But when they saw her, even in her forties, they knew he hadn't exaggerated one bit. She was spectacular. And the eyes! They were so much like Kyle's that there was no doubting the familial relationship.

Kyle's father replied, "Mister Burleigh had us tracked down and arranged for transportation. He said you were going to get married, and we couldn't miss it, now could we?"

He gave his father a giant hug and then his mother a softer hug and a kiss before turning to the Burleighs.

"Charles, Abigail, and Emily, I'd like you to meet my parents, this is my father, Kirk MacKenzie, and my mother, who now goes by the name of Bonnie MacKenzie. She didn't so much choose the name, it just attached itself to her when my father kept referring to her as his bonnie lass."

Then he looked at his parents and said, "Mother and Father, this is Charles and Abigail Burleigh and their daughter Emily, who will become your daughter on Saturday."

Bonnie stepped over to Emily and smiled at her before taking her in her arms and saying softly, "I've always wanted a daughter, Emily, and from what Kyle wrote about you, you are all any mother could hope for in a daughter."

Charles shook Kirk's hand as Abigail endured a bear hug from Kirk. Abigail hugged Bonnie and Kirk unleashed another bear hug on Emily.

"Now, son, what's all this nonsense we hear about. We tell people that you're our son and they start talking about you as if you were a coward."

"I'll explain, Father. It's just some silly novel that used my name."

Charles said, "Don't worry, Mister MacKenzie, we're going to sue them out of business. I also have contacts in many newspapers and we're going to have them run stories setting the record straight."

"Son, is it true you've given up scouting?"

"Yes, Father. There seems to be no end to it. I just want to live in peace with Emily now."

"That's good, Kyle. We had trouble sleeping sometimes when we heard some of the stories."

"Father, you and mother must be tired from your trip. Come and sit down and we'll talk."

"Where should we put our travel bags?"

"I'll put them in your room, Father."

"Thank you, son. It's not too close to yours, is it? I'd like to get some sleep tonight."

Everyone laughed except Emily, who turned a bright scarlet.

They all sat in the parlor for almost two hours while Kyle filled them in on what had happened and what was going to happen. When he told them of their plans to live in Omaha, his mother glanced at her husband, then looked back at her son.

"Kyle, would you mind if we joined you? We were going to sell the ranch and move away from the coming war with the tribes but didn't know where we should go."

Kyle smiled and replied, "Mother, I would be very pleased to have you and father live with us."

The decision made, all that remained was to have some lunch, so Bonnie joined Emily and Abigail in the kitchen.

With the ladies absent, Kyle spent some time filling in the gorier details of the events that led to tomorrow's happy event while Charles listened in awe of the details he hadn't heard before.

The two families spent the rest of the day getting better acquainted.

That night, as Emily lay tucked in close to Kyle, their skin still damp, she said, "Kyle, you always said how beautiful your mother was, and I thought you were just being a good son, but she's astonishing. She makes me feel almost homely."

Kyle pulled her in closer and said, "Emily, you know that's not even close to being true. The ironic thing about her beauty is that it was her beauty as much as those intense green eyes that marked her as almost an outcast among her people. If she had been average looking or just plain pretty, some might have overlooked the green eyes. But when she was very young and evidently strikingly beautiful, the rumor started that she had struck a deal with the Evil Spirit that he would make her perfect but marked her with his own green eyes. The rumor persisted and everyone, even her parents, feared her.

"To me, what was even more extraordinary was that despite her appearance and being shunned, she turned into one of the most wonderful human beings I've ever met. Until I met you, Emily. I won't tell you that you're as beautiful as my mother as I've never met another woman who was. But you're one of the prettiest women I've ever seen and you're just as beautiful as my mother in your soul, which counts more."

Emily sighed and slid closer to Kyle and kissed him. She couldn't imagine being happier, until....

———

Then came the wedding day. It was scheduled for ten o'clock, so there was no need to rush. It wasn't going to be big affair, unlike Emily's previous wedding. Emily had commented on the difference, a big wedding with a horrible marriage and a small wedding with a perfect marriage.

The Burleighs and the MacKenzies arrived at St. Cecilia's at 9:30 and an hour later, Kyle and Emily MacKenzie emerged with their two sets of parents wearing wedding bands and the completed marriage certificate in Kyle's pocket.

They returned to the Burleigh estate and began preparing for the move. Everything seemed so perfect, so wonderful, it appeared that nothing could go wrong, but that changed on the day before they were to board the train for Omaha.

———

Kyle was with Emily on the front porch, sitting on a double rocker after all the work for the move had been completed. She had Kyle added to her bank account, they had registered the marriage at the courthouse, and everyone was excited about the move as plans were already being made for each of their new houses in Omaha. Each home would reflect the desires of those who would live there, the women's desires taking precedence, naturally.

Kyle and Emily were rocking and discussing that very topic when a carriage turned into the estate.

Emily recognized it immediately and exclaimed, "Kyle, that's the Falstaffs!"

They stood, and Kyle quickly said, "Go inside, Emily. I'll handle this. I'm sure they want to see me."

"I'll stay."

"No, Emily. Go inside. Please."

Emily decided to go and tell her father, so she left.

Kyle stepped down and awaited the carriage, and after it pulled up an older, rounder version of Edmund Falstaff stepped out. He was carrying a single-shot dueling pistol, but it wasn't cocked.

"You! You're that bastard that caused all this! You're Kyle MacKenzie, aren't you."

"I am. And I assume you are Edmund Falstaff's father."

"I am and proud of it. You destroyed him. Telling lies about him and now taking his wife. That was what this was all about, wasn't it? You wanted his wife."

"Honestly, I have to admit that I wanted his wife very soon after meeting her, but I never did anything about it. I never even called her Emily until she was a widow. But, Mister Falstaff, I will tell you this, if she had been married to a man who I could respect in the least, I would still be out in the plains of the Dakota Territory. But your son, Mister Falstaff, earned no respect from me."

"You were just jealous. That's all. He did all those great things and you are nothing but a coward."

Kyle tilted his head slightly as he asked, "Do you honestly believe that, Mister Falstaff? You knew your son better than most. Do you truly believe in the depths of your soul that your son fought off Santee Sioux warriors or killed the miscreant guides who were going to kill the Burleighs?"

Mister Falstaff paused as Kyle heard the front door open behind him but didn't turn to look.

"It doesn't matter. You caused his death with your lies."

"Did Chief Plummer tell you how or where he died?"

"He said he had been murdered and the murderer had been killed. I initially thought it was you who had been killed until I heard about the wedding. Now I'm here to bring justice for Edmund."

"Mister Falstaff, your son died in Mary's Parlor, a brothel of colored women that he frequented. He was killed by a young woman name Marie Martin. She was the daughter of one of those guides that were planning on robbing and murdering the Burleighs and your son.

"She believed the tales in that novel, just as you did. If your son hadn't taken credit for all that had happened, he'd still be alive. But he didn't kill her father Louis Martin, I did. She should have tried to kill me, Mister Falstaff, to soothe her need for vengeance. It was his own self-importance that spelled his demise, not me."

It was too much information for Mister Falstaff to absorb. *His son was killed in a whorehouse by a colored woman? He had been engaged in fornication with a member of an inferior race?* He knew then that Kyle MacKenzie was lying. No Falstaff would ever do such a thing. He quickly cocked the hammer and was bringing the pistol upwards with Kyle standing four feet away.

Just before he brought the pistol to bear, Kyle threw up his arms and shrieked his war cry while still staring at Mister Falstaff, his flaring green eyes boring into his soul. Mister Falstaff jerked back, causing the pistol to discharge, blasting a crater of dirt between Kyle's feet.

Kyle took one long step forward and took the pistol from Mister Falstaff.

"Mister Falstaff, I never lie. What I told you was the truth. Go and talk to Chief Plummer. Tell him you want to know the truth about your son's death. You need to know how he died."

Mister Falstaff was still shaken. He had come to kill Kyle MacKenzie and instead, his whole world had come crashing down around him. His only son, who had married into money and saved the family's fortune had now caused the very pillars of the family's monument to turn to dust. He knew that sooner or later the truth of Edmund's escapades and death would escape. The vaunted name of Falstaff would be reviled almost as much as the name of John Wilkes Booth.

He turned in a daze and climbed back into his carriage. The driver snapped the reins, turned the carriage around and slowly left the grounds.

Kyle exhaled and turned to find everyone standing on the porch. Emily was holding one of his pistols in her hand.

He walked up the steps onto the porch and smiled at Emily as she handed him his gun.

"I didn't know how to shoot it. I pulled the trigger, but it didn't work."

"I'm glad you didn't, Emily. You probably would have shot me."

They returned to the house and that night, as the newer Mr. and Mrs. MacKenzie lay in bed, Emily asked, "Kyle, when we get to Omaha and move into our house and you have to work in the city, do you think that you can ever be content? You've spent so much of your life alone and in out in the wilderness."

He kissed her and replied, "In my entire life before we've been together, I've only been truly content once before. That was years ago when I was with Snow Cloud in our lodge in her village. It's not where I am, or what I'm doing that makes me happy and content, Emily. It's when I can share my life and my love with one who I treasure."

Emily sighed and whispered, "I know that I am happy and content because I treasure you and one day, I will give you a gift that we both will treasure."

Kyle kissed her again, then played the 'what if' game in his mind when he looked back at the almost impossible sequence of events that had brought them together, beginning with a thick water-logged cottonwood trunk floated free in the Missouri River.

EPILOGUE

A week later, they were all ensconced in the Herndon House in Omaha and had each bought a twenty-acre parcel northwest of Omaha, just on the outer edge of the city limits and construction was already underway. Neptune and his fellow Kyle horses were all in a Burleigh shipping stock area and being treated like royalty by the handlers.

The stories of Kyle's true adventures had been published in the St. Louis, Kansas City and Omaha newspapers after review by Charles. Once they had been published there, the stories had been picked up by almost every major newspaper in the East, who were tired of war stories now that the war was finally officially over. The added Falstaff family scandal only added more spice to the stories and required extra printings in most markets.

When the houses were completed in mid-August, it took another week for all the furniture and accessories to be moved in and set up. Burleigh Shipping had just purchased an empty office building and the telegraph line had been run to Charles' house.

On August 23rd, Kyle and Emily were busy in their house still doing all those little things that needed attention. Naturally, as newlyweds, there were frequent interruptions, but this interruption was different.

The doorbell rang during the mid-morning and Kyle was the first to the door, swung it wide and smiled.

"Hello, Kyle."

"Hello, Colonel, Mrs. Carpenter. Come in, please."

They entered the house and Emily had to step down from her short stepladder to greet the guests.

"Colonel, Mrs. Carpenter, I'd like you to meet my wife, Emily."

Colonel Carpenter smiled and said, "So, you're the Emily that had him in a daze, and I can understand why. Emily, this is my wife, Madeline."

Emily and Madeline shook hands as Kyle looked at his old commander and said, "Colonel, I can tell that you're doing better now than the last time I saw you. You're even wearing eagles now."

"Someone brought my case to the attention of the Secretary of War, Mister Stanton and that had a bit of an impact on the investigation. Who did that, anyway?"

"That was Emily's father. So, are you just passing through?"

"Remind me to thank your father, Emily. I heard that he also tracked down the foreman in his shipping company in St. Louis that was managing the gunrunning operation. He's not going to managing anything anymore, except trying to manage his cellmates so they don't become too friendly. As to your question about passing through, the answer is no. We're staying because I'm in command of Fort Omaha now."

"Now that's good news," Kyle said as he led them into the parlor where everyone took seats.

Kyle then said, "Fort Omaha is where the whole adventure started for me. I picked up those wagon tracks leaving Fort

Omaha. If I hadn't come here first before going to Fort Sully, I never would have met Emily. It's strange that so many changes in our lives come about from one quick decision. I was debating about going straight through to Fort Sully, but then decided I'd swing down to Fort Omaha to resupply and get caught up on information."

They talked for another hour, had lunch, and then Colonel and Mrs. Carpenter had to return to finish arranging their own new quarters on the post.

Another week passed before the next significant event when Kyle's lawsuit, which had been going back and forth between the Burleigh attorneys and those of the publishing firm, was settled.

Kyle originally had asked how much it would take to put them out of business, but eventually decided it wasn't their fault, at least not entirely. They settled for a lump sum payment of twenty-five thousand dollars, almost a full year's profits for the company. Kyle felt better because with his previous bank balance and the cash he had deposited, the amount of money that he had put into the family account was almost as much as his wife's, or at least it was close enough to make him feel less guilty.

Kyle kept all his weapons including Night Bear's knife in a room attached to his office and worked with Charles in operating the shipping company, becoming indispensable.

On the twelfth of September, near Fort Pierre, Sarah Jameson gave birth to a healthy, brown-eyed baby boy who was christened Kyle MacKenzie Jameson.

Just ten days later, Cal Coleridge met his demise, ironically, in Abilene, Kansas, when Abilene Jones was interviewing Two-Gun Larson. Two-Gun was displeased with something that

Coleridge had written, and Coleridge had then compounded his error by calling Two-Gun an ignorant buffoon. Two-Gun didn't know what a buffoon was, but he took offense and one of Two-Gun's guns made an effective, but loud, counterpoint. When Coleridge was buried, the stone carver was unsure of whether to carve Cal Coleridge or Abilene Jones on the tombstone, so he thought he'd save himself some time in his labors, so Cal Coleridge's grave was marked with a headstone reading Cal Jones.

At the end of the month, Kyle and Emily decided to take a carriage ride out to Desoto to see site of *The Bertrand's* sinking, the instigating event for their current state of marital bliss. She had told Kyle the night before that she was pregnant, which had prompted the visit. The wonderful news made the couple even more joyous as they drove out of town, despite their almost daily belief that they couldn't possibly be any happier.

It was a three-hour ride and they arrived at the site of the sinking before noon and had packed a picnic basket, so there was no rush to return.

The area around the boat was still tramped down from scavenger hunters, and the boat was stripped of anything remotely valuable. Of course, most of the cargo was still underwater buried under a lot of silt from the ever-moving Missouri River.

Kyle stepped out of the carriage, then assisted his now-pregnant wife from the conveyance before they strolled to the riverbank.

"There's not much left. Is there, Kyle?" Emily asked as she stared at the small amount of the grand riverboat that remained above the water.

"No, Emily, other than the smokestacks, just the pilot house and bridge are left above water now. It's going to its grave slowly now."

"I recall the day it sank. We were all standing right about here when mother swore that she'd never get on one of those deathtraps ever again. It was her fear of water that had made father rent that wagon to go to Yankton."

"We owe a lot to *The Bertrand*, Emily."

"I guess you could look at it that way, I suppose."

Kyle moved behind Emily, then put arms around his wife and slid his right hand over her abdomen.

"Emily, if we have a son, I have a preference for his name and would like your opinion."

Emily thought about it as she stared at the small structures of the riverboat that were still above the flowing brown water. She supposed she could get used to Bert, for short, *but Bertrand MacKenzie?*

But Emily knew that she couldn't deny him anything, so she said, "I have no objections, Kyle. If you want to call him Bertrand, I can live with it."

Kyle laughed and replied, "Are you serious? Bertrand? I was thinking about Kirk Charles MacKenzie."

She laughed, then turned around in his arms, kissed him and looked into the amazing green eyes of her husband, Kyle. He may be Mister MacKenzie to many people, but she would never call him by any other name except Kyle for the rest of her life.

———

Author's Note

The river steamboat *Bertrand* sank at the Desoto Bend about twenty-five miles north of Omaha, Nebraska on April 1st, 1865. She was bound for Fort Benton, Montana. All her passengers and crew safely made it to shore. Some were picked up by the *General Grant* and brought to their destinations. The *General Grant*'s pilot and some crewmembers were attacked by the Santee Sioux, killing three. Ironically, *The General Grant* sank almost a year later when it struck ice on March 18, 1866 near Bellevue, Nebraska, where this book was written.

After the Missouri River changed channels, *The Bertrand* was covered in mud and silt and relegated to history for almost exactly a century when treasure hunters found the wreck. The almost 300,000 artifacts recovered from the riverboat represent the largest single collection of Civil War articles ever recovered in one location and are stored in a museum at the Desoto National Wildlife Refuge.

1	Rock Creek	12/26/2016
2	North of Denton	01/02/2017
3	Fort Selden	01/07/2017
4	Scotts Bluff	01/14/2017
5	South of Denver	01/22/2017
6	Miles City	01/28/2017
7	Hopewell	02/04/2017
8	Nueva Luz	02/12/2017
9	The Witch of Dakota	02/19/2017
10	Baker City	03/13/2017
11	The Gun Smith	03/21/2017
12	Gus	03/24/2017
13	Wilmore	04/06/2017
14	Mister Thor	04/20/2017
15	Nora	04/26/2017
16	Max	05/09/2017
17	Hunting Pearl	05/14/2017
18	Bessie	05/25/2017
19	The Last Four	05/29/2017
20	Zack	06/12/2017
21	Finding Bucky	06/21/2017
22	The Debt	06/30/2017
23	The Scalawags	07/11/2017
24	The Stampede	07/20/2017
25	The Wake of the Bertrand	07/31/2017
26	Cole	08/09/2017
27	Luke	09/05/2017
28	The Eclipse	09/21/2017
29	A.J. Smith	10/03/2017
30	Slow John	11/05/2017
31	The Second Star	11/15/2017
32	Tate	12/03/2017
33	Virgil's Herd	12/14/2017
34	Marsh's Valley	01/01/2018

35	Alex Paine	01/18/2018
36	Ben Gray	02/05/2018
37	War Adams	03/05/2018
38	Mac's Cabin	03/21/2018
39	Will Scott	04/13/2018
40	Sheriff Joe	04/22/2018
41	Chance	05/17/2018
42	Doc Holt	06/17/2018
43	Ted Shepard	07/13/2018
44	Haven	07/30/2018
45	Sam's County	08/15/2018
46	Matt Dunne	09/10/2018
47	Conn Jackson	10/05/2018
48	Gabe Owens	10/27/2018
49	Abandoned	11/19/2018
50	Retribution	12/21/2018
51	Inevitable	02/04/2019
52	Scandal in Topeka	03/18/2019
53	Return to Hardeman County	04/10/2019
54	Deception	06/02/2019
55	The Silver Widows	06/27/2019
56	Hitch	08/21/2019
57	Dylan's Journey	09/10/2019
58	Bryn's War	11/06/2019
59	Huw's Legacy	11/30/2019
60	Lynn's Search	12/22/2019
61	Bethan's Choice	02/10/2020
62	Rhody Jones	03/11/2020

Made in the USA
Columbia, SC
10 April 2020